SIEVE AND LET DIE

SIEVE AND LET DIE

VICTORIA HAMILTON

THORNDIKE PRESS
A part of Gale, a Cengage Company

Copyright © 2023 by Donna Lea Simpson.
A Vintage Kitchen Mystery.
Thorndike Press, a part of Gale, a Cengage Company.

LIBRARY OF CONGRESS CIP DATA ON FILE.
CATALOGUING IN PUBLICATION FOR THIS BOOK
IS AVAILABLE FROM THE LIBRARY OF CONGRESS.

ISBN-13: 979-8-88579-922-5 (softcover alk. paper)

Published in 2024 by arrangement with Beyond the Page Publishing, LLC.

CAST OF CHARACTERS

IN THE VINTAGE KITCHEN
MYSTERY SERIES

Jaymie Leighton Müller: wife, stepmom and collector of all things vintage kitchen-y!

Jakob Müller: her husband, dad to Jocie, Christmas tree farmer and junk store owner

Jocie Müller: *little* little person (as she says!) and happy daughter to Jakob and Jaymie

Becca Brevard: Jaymie's bossy older sister and co-owner of QFA (Queensville Fine Antiques)

Valetta Nibley: pharmacist and lifelong friend to Jaymie and Becca

Brock Nibley: Valetta's older brother

Mrs. Martha Stubbs: Jaymie's elderly friend and confidante

Heidi Lockland: Jaymie's friend

Bernie Jenkins: Jaymie's friend and a police officer

Detective Angela Vestry: Queensville Township Police Department detective

Brouwer Family: Lise and Arend, son Bram,

5

and his son Luuk. Own the land opposite the cabin

Hoppy: Jaymie's Yorkie-Poo

Lilibet: Jocie's tabby

CAST OF CHARACTERS

IN *SIEVE AND LET DIE*

Mandy de Boer: Widow of Chad Manor of Manor Homes, which she now co-owns

Candy Vasiliev: Her sister

Hendrik "Henry" de Boer: Mandy and Candy's father

Hien Sang "Ti" (pronounced "tea") Pham: Mandy's best friend and director of the food bank

Greg Vasiliev: Candy's ex-husband and high school friend of Val's

Trina Manor: Mandy's daughter

Randall Kallis: Co-owner and CFO of Manor Homes

Huynh "Win" and Helen Pham: local contractor and his pharmacist wife

Dina and Connor Ward: Manor Homes homeowners not happy with their purchase

Olivier Ricci: Receptionist at Manor Homes

Shannon Manor-Billings: Mandy de Boer's sister-in-law, sister to the late Chad Manor

7

Taylor Bellwood: waitstaff at the Queens-ville Inn and college student

ONE

Does everyone have a favorite time of day, a favorite day of the week? Jaymie did, and this was it, Sunday, this exact moment when Jocie was upstairs doing her homework and she and Jakob prepared dinner. She stared out the kitchen window. The October sun was already descending behind the trees. Long shadows stretched across the gravel road in front of their cabin as wind skittered golden leaves into piles. Jakob's chili bubbled in a big pot on the stovetop. She would make biscuits flavored with chili powder to echo her husband's dish.

She got out the ingredients and lined them up on the counter as Jocie clattered down the stairs, homework done, and joined them, dragging her stool over beside Jaymie and hopping up on it so she could help. Though ten years old, she was a *little* little person, as she said. "Teach me how to make biscuits?" she asked.

"Certainly, my little chickadee," Jaymie said, smiling fondly down at the chubby-cheeked blonde girl. "First, hand me that sieve," she said, pointing to a fine mesh tool hanging from a hook on the wall.

Jocie hopped down, retrieved it, and hopped back up. They proceeded.

"Why are you putting the flour through that?" Jocie asked, leaning against Jaymie.

"A sieve has many purposes." With her free hand Jaymie rubbed Jocie's shoulder, enjoying the warmth of her small body leaning into her. "You can use it to drain or rinse things, like vegetables. In this case sifting flour through the sieve breaks up clumps and helps blend the flour and the baking powder and salt, introducing air into the flour, making for lighter biscuits."

They proceeded until they had dough, which Jocie rolled out, following instructions in using an acacia wood French rolling pin, a long stick tapered at both ends.

"When is a sieve not a sieve?" Jocie said, examining her work and sneaking a peek at Jaymie.

"I don't know, when *is* a sieve not a sieve?" Jaymie asked, exchanging a glance with Jakob, who was stirring and turning down the heat under his chili. This explained why Jocie had been quiet. She'd been thinking up a joke, her new pastime.

"When it's a riddle!" she said, and laughed until she doubled over.

"I don't get it," Jaymie said.

Jocie straightened, disappointment on her round face. She rested the rolling pin on her shoulder like a baseball bat. "When it's a *riddle,*" she repeated slowly, for the dense adults.

"I still don't get it."

"I don't get it either, honey," Jakob said.

Jocie sighed and rolled her eyes. Since her tenth birthday, the eye roll was becoming a regular feature. "At the FFA meeting last month we were studying tools used in the spring in seed planting," she explained. She had started going to Future Farmers of America meetings with her cousins. "A riddle is a big sieve used to separate soil into finer clumps so the seeds can get a good start."

Jaymie burst into laughter, as did Jakob. "Has to be the best joke I needed explained to me," she said. "Which leads me to more information. There are many kinds of sieves, and they have different names. There are strainers, colanders, and sifters."

Grabbing her tablet, Jocie leaned on the counter and tapped in a search. "And a *chinois,*" she said, "is a French word meaning

11

Chinese, describing a conical sieve used to strain custards and sauces. And a *zaru,* which is a bamboo draining basket."

Eyes wide, Jaymie exchanged a look with her husband. Learning cooking facts from a ten-year-old?

"Don't look at me," he said with a chuckle. "She's your daughter."

She laughed out loud, getting his allusion. Jocie had become as addicted to research and learning as Jaymie was. She may not be Jaymie's biological daughter, but she was absorbing her influence, hopefully only in good ways.

Jaymie took up her cell phone, found a certain song on a seventies playlist, and, using her spatula as a microphone, struck a pose and sang, when they got to the chorus, "Sieve and let die!" to Paul McCartney and Wings' Bond theme.

Jocie dissolved in giggles. Sunday silliness was a tradition, too.

Jaymie scanned the gathering along the road on Monday, faces golden in the slanting rays of the sun. They had come together to plan the public nature trail through the woods across from the Müllers' cabin to honor Alicia Vance, whose life had ended tragically weeks before in this forest she had liked to roam. Bram Brouwer had suggested to Jaymie the public would be more invested if they had a say in how the trails wended their way through.

Gathered were Alicia's sister Erin, her mother Kim and her daughter Mia, as well as a dozen or more other people. They had gotten a good turnout. Walking Together would, she hoped, bring people of diverse backgrounds together to walk for fitness and nature study, art, photography and botany.

Jocie stood, arms linked, with Mia, Alicia's daughter, two tiny girls solemnly separate from the adults. Jaymie had worried it might be too much for Mia, but Kim, her grandmother, said the girl wanted to be a part of it.

A car pulled into the Müller driveway across the road. Becca, Jaymie's sister, climbed out of the driver's seat and walked toward them, joined by her husband, Kevin, who carried a walking stick and had a fancy camera slung around his neck. They crossed the road, Becca zipping her cable-knit cardigan.

"Glad you could make it!" Jaymie said with a smile.

"Where's Jakob?" Kevin asked.

"Gus is moving in a few days and needed a hand with some stuff." Gus was Jakob's business partner in the junk store, The Junk Stops Here.

One of the next tasks was to install a culvert in the roadside gully, then create a footpath over it to make access to the woodland trail easier. The son of the land owners would work on that alone before the ground froze in winter. Today the trail volunteers clambered down into the roadside gully, up the other side, and pushed open the basic gate Bram had installed in the fence for roadside egress. Bram Brouwer and his son, Luuk, a school friend of the girls', knew the woods intimately. Luuk, a sturdy quiet lad, would lead Jocie and Mia, while Jaymie, who also knew the woods from her own walks with Hoppy and Jocie, divided the others into teams and gave each leader a hammer and a bundle of florescent yellow-tipped sticks from the stash Bram had left by the fence.

Each team was to find a way — the path of least resistance, Jaymie told them, but not a straight line — through the woods to the center, which had been boldly marked and would someday have a clearing and a memorial bench for walkers to enjoy. Along the way they were to pound the stakes into the damp ground so Bram could begin the arduous task of clearing paths for the Alicia

Vance Memorial Trail.

Jaymie had originally placed Becca on a team with her husband but her big sister, bossy by nature, had stoutly insisted on joining Jaymie's group with Valetta. Kim and Erin wanted to join Mia and Jocie. It ended up that everyone joined the team they preferred. Jaymie, *not* bossy by nature like Becca, shrugged as Kevin joined his wife. *Organized chaos, here we come,* she thought.

Bram, as the most knowledgeable, would be the ultimate arbiter of the path directions, but it was a start. He walked the teams to different points on the perimeter of the woods.

Jaymie had insisted on starting at the edge of the forest facing their cabin. She knew how the trail should go from there and wanted control of the direction it took to the heart of the woods. Okay, so she *was* a little bossy by nature.

Val, who had bit her lip to keep from laughing as Jaymie and Becca argued over the direction they'd take, wielded the hammer and pounded the first stake exactly where Jaymie wanted it, against Becca's "advice." Gradually Becca stopped worrying about the placement of the stakes and ambled beside them chatting. Kevin wandered off with his camera to photograph birds in the interesting shadowy light of the dying day as they scolded and flitted from tree to tree.

"Val, you'll never guess who came into the antique store the other day," Becca said, pulling up her cardigan collar against the damp chilly air.

"Mick Jagger," Val said, pounding a neon stake in place. "Jon Bon Jovi."

"Bruno Mars," Jaymie said, giggling, with a sly glance at Val, then added, "Queen Latifah!"

Becca sighed in exasperation. "Don't be idiots." She paused, then said dramatically, "Mandy de Boer!"

"Who is that?" Jaymie asked.

"One of our classmates in high school. She's changed so much I'd hardly recognize her. She looked terrible!"

"Really?" Val said, pausing in pounding in a stake. "She was always so put together. What was wrong?"

"I don't know," Becca said, squinting into the distance. "She looked . . . odd."

"What do you mean, odd?"

"She looked sad. Confused. I don't know how to explain it."

Val leaned on the mallet handle and frowned. "What did she say?"

"Not much, really."

They were coming close to where Alicia's body had been found. This was challenging, and Jaymie's eyes prickled, tears welling. She kicked aside a stick, indicated another spot, and Val took up her mallet, pounding in another stake. They could hear voices through the woods. Someone was singing, and another was laughing. She smiled past tears.

Jaymie led them onward. She pointed to another spot, and Val placed a stake.

"I've seen Mandy off and on over the years and she seemed just fine," Val said. "I worked with her on a committee for the food bank with a mutual friend a while back, but I haven't seen her for months."

"She's gained a lot of weight. Her sister Candy is selling this weight-loss shake crap. *The best salesperson in the region,* Mandy said, as if I'd care. She had the nerve to offer me a pamphlet and a discount coupon." Becca's pudginess was a sore spot with her.

"Mandy and *Candy*?" Jaymie asked.

"Back in the day it was cute to name twins or sisters rhyming names. Before individuality became the buzzword," Val said with a wry smile, but then turned to Becca and doggedly pursued the topic. "You said she seemed odd. What did you mean? Where

17

did you see her?"

"She came into QFA," she said, naming her and her husband's store, Queensville Fine Antiques, "with an iridescent glass vase she thought might be Tiffany Studios. She wanted to sell it to us, but I had to tell her the truth. It was a copy from the eighties, and we weren't interested. She had been had by some dealer who sold it to her as the real thing."

"She's suddenly interested in antiques?"

"C'mon, walk and talk, people. Let's get the last stakes in," Jaymie urged. "Right there."

"She looked over Kevin's Bakelite radios and asked a few questions about them," Becca said as Val pounded. "Then said something about vintage homes."

"You remember she married Chad Manor? His family was Manor Construction? He died a few years back and she took over as president," Val said as Jaymie held a stake for her to hammer.

"I've heard of Manor Homes," Jaymie interjected. "They've built developments on the perimeter of Wolverhampton."

"Brock told me Manor Homes is developing a subdivision called Vintage Manor Estates based on mid-century plans," Val said, striking a hard blow to the marker.

18

Brock, Val's older brother, was a real estate agent.

"Maybe that's why Mandy's suddenly interested in vintage stuff," Jaymie said.

"Staging for new homes? Maybe," Becca said, shoving her hands in her pockets and shivering. It was getting chilly and would only get more so as the sun dipped. "I thought she moved away."

"Only for college. After she and Chad married, they bought an older home in Wolverhampton. She's best buddies with a friend of mine, Ti Pham, who runs the food bank, so we've worked together before on food drives," Val said, pushing her glasses up on her nose. "I don't think I get, though, why you said Mandy seemed odd."

"There was something off about her, like she wasn't all there. You know what she was like in school — Miss Popularity, everyone's friend, voted best smile, best pom-pom squad leader, best everything. That girl seems completely gone. It was troubling."

Val shook her head. "I don't know what to say. Maybe she has a lot on her mind, or maybe she was having a bad day."

"It felt like more than that," Becca mused.

In the center of the woods the group gathered. Jaymie peered through the shadowy gloom at the weary faces and smiled.

"Thank you all for taking part today. Bram, how did we do?"

A big stocky fellow with dark hair, he pulled his son to his side and smiled around the group. "Everyone did real good. Especially the kids. Jocie, Mia, Luuk, you all did super good and we appreciate it. Tomorrow I'm gonna start on the far side with the skid-steer to clear some of the bigger shrubs and bushes. I'll make rough trails and come through with the stump grinder, then we can clean them up by hand and groom 'em with mulch, to start. This was a solid beginning! We should be able to have it open for next spring."

Alicia's mom and sister, Kim and Erin, clapped, their eyes glittering with tears. Their loss was so fresh this must have been difficult for them, but they took part for Mia, for healing.

There were hugs all around as the gathering broke up, and they dispersed. Jaymie and Jocie entered the cabin, greeted by Hoppy and Lilibet, who were eager to sniff them all over to see where they had been and what they had been doing and who they had been with. Jocie played with the animals while Jaymie started dinner.

It had gone so very well, but the sadness that saturated her during the walk bled over into Becca's concern for their old friend. People changed as they got older, she supposed. Folks, her grandma said, could become careworn. Did that describe Mandy de Boer?

She shrugged it off as Jakob arrived home and they sat down to dinner, chatting quietly about the trail marking.

TWO

"What did you think about what Becca said concerning your school friend, Mandy?" Jaymie asked as she pounded nails. She was at Valetta's Tuesday morning, helping her build (from a kit) a catio for Denver, once Jaymie's crabby tabby but now Valetta's pampered feline fella. The multilevel deluxe catio would replace the rudimentary one a local handyman, Bill Waterman, built on her back porch.

"I don't know what to think. Without seeing Mandy myself I can't say. It's odd, for sure."

October is finicky in Michigan; there had been some cold days already, but today the sun was out and it was warm and lovely in Val's backyard. Val had taken the day off from the pharmacy to finish the project. She pushed her glasses up her sweaty nose — she was going through "the change," as she called it, and frequently felt like a furnace

— and tucked her own hammer in her tool belt.

"What was her sister, Candy, like?" Jaymie often asked questions like this, trying to get a feel for what life was like for her sister and friend in a time she was too young to remember.

"Candy? Just a normal teen, I guess."

"Did Candy marry? You said Mandy married Chad Manor, of Manor Homes."

"Chad and Mandy married after college. Candy married practically out of high school."

"Who did she marry? Anyone you knew?"

"Greg Vasiliev, who was in Candy's grade, one higher than Becca and me."

There was, in Val's voice, an oddly warm tone. "You liked him," Jaymie said, straightening and swiping her bangs out of her eyes. "Did you have a crush on him?"

"We were kids."

"That didn't answer the question."

"That's all the answer you'll get," Val said tartly.

"What was he like?"

"Too nice for Candy de Boer."

"Are they still together?" Jaymie asked.

"Nope. Divorced many years back."

"How do you know?"

Val slid a glance sideways. "He friended

me on social media a while ago."

"He *friended* you? Then what happened?"

"We've gone out for coffee a few times. That's all."

"That's *all*?" Jaymie screeched. Hoppy yapped, trotted toward them and stopped, head cocked to one side. "What do you mean, *that's all*? That's big."

"Why is it big?"

"Well, you know, you don't date very often. And not in the last few years." Val's steely gaze warned her she was muffing it. "So, it's big," she finished.

"We've been out for coffee. That's *all,*" Val said, firmly shutting the door on further chatter. She stood back and eyed the catio, the frame of which was now built. "How about we break for lunch?"

Jaymie got the hint; subject closed. "I'd love some."

After lunch they got back to work attaching the wire mesh on the frame while Hoppy wobbled happily around Val's fenced yard enjoying the freedom he could not experience at the cabin, with coyotes afoot and no fenced boundaries from the gravel road. Together they moved the catio to the concrete foundation (already poured and cured) along the side of the house and attached it with lag bolts to the clapboard siding around the window in Val's spare bedroom — *Denver's Domain,* as it was designated on the custom nameplate on the door. She could easily open his window and let him go in and out of his catio as he desired.

Standing back, they admired their work. "You are the best person to work with," Val said, slinging her arm over Jaymie's shoulders.

"Thanks! You mean you wouldn't have preferred Becca?"

Val snorted in laughter. Becca was a control freak and did not work well with others. Her marriage survived because her unflappable English hubby let her talk, then did his own thing. Jaymie admired his calm resolve because Becca drove her crazy.

They went inside and held a little ceremony for Denver in his room, opening the catio door for him with a "ta-da" flourish. He took one look at it, turned his back, and went off to sleep under a bed. "Maybe he'll like it better tomorrow," Val said, and the two women laughed and retreated to the living room. The day was getting chilly despite the sunshine slanting obliquely in the front window, casting long shadows outside. They shared a pot of tea, lovely black orange pekoe brewed in a gorgeous vintage Fitz and Floyd pumpkin-shaped teapot. Val had made a tray with a fall tea towel, the teapot and matching pumpkin cream and sugar, along with some pumpkin cookies on a pumpkin plate.

Jaymie exclaimed over the presentation, then said, "I'm surprised you're not serving pumpkin spice tea!"

"Blech! Loathe the whole pumpkin-spice flavoring thing. But I found the pumpkin teapot at an estate sale, and the rest I gathered from here and there, there being Thrifty Dan's in Wolverhampton more often than not. He calls me whenever he has something he thinks I'll want. He's like a dealer feeding my habit!" She pushed her glasses up her nose, glancing around her kitsch-cluttered living room with a grimace. Shelves laden with knickknacks lined the walls. "If I buy any more junk I'll run out of space to live."

"Don't let Becca see this living room or she'll start a decluttering campaign."

"Too late. She and Kevin came over for lunch this past weekend and it began. She kindly offered to 'help' me sort out my stuff and get rid of it."

Jaymie laughed. "She means well."

They both dissolved into gales of laughter. *She means well* was a constant phrase when

26

speaking of Becca. Jaymie's cell phone pinged and she checked it. "Becca must know we're talking about her." She answered the phone with *"Were your ears burning?"* but then listened. When she hung up she frowned. "Becca says Mandy de Boer came into the store again. This time she was asking pointed questions about *you.*"

"Like what?" Val said, alarmed.

"She asked if it was true that you'd bought a house, and were you still working at the Emporium pharmacy, and did you have a husband."

"Nosy parker," Val said. "She could have asked Ti if it was important to her. She knows we're friends."

"Do you think she caught wind of you dating her sister's ex?"

"Greg and I are not dating. We're friends," Val said.

"Okay, do you think she found out you're friends with her sister's ex?"

"Why would she care?"

"I don't know." She let it drop and they finished their tea. "I guess I'd better get going. Hoppy," she called. "Let's go, buddy!" He wobbled into the living room from Denver's room, where he had been under the bed getting reacquainted with his former nemesis, and stood still while Jaymie clipped his leash to his collar.

"Take some of the pumpkin cookies back for Jakob and Jocie," Val said, retrieving a baggie from the kitchen and sliding the rest of the treats into it.

Val accompanied them outside and down to the driveway. Jaymie opened the SUV and helped Hoppy into it, then tossed her purse on the passenger seat and the cookies into the purse.

"I'll tell you how much they liked them when I see you tomorrow," Jaymie said. She was working at Becca and Kevin's shop the next day so Georgina, Kevin's sister and manager of the store, and Becca and Kevin could go to brunch at the Queensville Inn. Val would close the pharmacy and bring lunch for both of them to QFA. They stood for a few minutes more, chatting, then hugged. Jaymie climbed into the driver's seat and buckled up as Val came to the car window to say goodbye.

On the street a maroon SUV cruised by. Both women looked — as one does when a car drives by slowly — and Val stiffened, staring at the driver, a woman who stared at them both.

"Who is that?" Jaymie asked.

"I'd swear it was Mandy de Boer; same flaming red hair." She began to walk down

28

the drive toward the slow vehicle, but the driver gunned the motor, the tires screeching on the pavement as she sped away.

Val, looking troubled, said goodbye to Jaymie and climbed the steps to her veranda, where she waved before returning inside.

Wednesday, hump day, Jaymie thought with an internal groan, listening for the third time to Georgina going through the new antiques in the front room of the antique store.

The older woman glared at Jaymie sternly and said, an accusing tone threaded through her polished English voice, "You're not listening, child."

"But I am, Georgina," she said pointedly, to counteract the "child" reference. So what if Georgina was twice her age? It didn't give her the right to treat her like a sulky teenager, Jaymie thought, then realized that notion was worthy of a sulky teenager.

"Then tell me what I said." Georgina folded her sweater-clad arms over her flat bosom.

Jaymie held back a sigh and recited what Georgina had told her.

The woman squinted. "You didn't remember that the hallmarks on the silver candelabra indicate a late Georgian-era piece. Very important."

"You said they were *possibly* late Georgian; not quite the same thing."

"Do not be snippy with me, young la—"

"Georgie, come on now, let's get going," Kevin Brevard, her brother and Becca's husband, said to his older sister. "I'm sure Jaymie has it all memorized."

"I doubt it," she remarked crisply, looping her silk scarf around her neck and retrieving her oatmeal Harris tweed jacket from the employees' lounge, a small room off the main sales area. She was one of those timeless Englishwomen: thin, upright, her short hair carefully curled and sprayed with Aqua Net to within an inch of its life. She always, even after a gin and tonic bender, appeared put together. "Excuse me for a moment," she said to her brother. "I need to powder my nose." Code for peeing. She only ever obliquely referred to bodily functions. "Jaymie, here's a dustcloth," she said, tossing her a microfiber cloth. "There is always dust in an antique shop!"

As she slipped from the room to the back employees' area Becca, buttoning her navy blue cardigan against the cool autumnal weather, joined Jaymie looking out the front window. "Val called me last night. I guess you two saw Mandy de Boer yesterday?"

"She thinks it was her driving past the house real slow. Why would Mandy be cruising by? Was she spying on Val?"

"Don't know." Becca hefted her purse up on her shoulder and perched on a bench beneath the window as Jaymie got busy with the dust cloth on a hallmarked silver tea set. "Funny how you can not think about or see a person for ages and then suddenly their name is everywhere. Dee said I should know all about Mandy." Dee Stubbs was an old friend of Val and Becca's and attended high school with them.

"Why?"

"Dee writes the high school alumni newsletter. She's mentioned Mandy many times, she says. I don't read it, to be honest."

"Becca!"

"I get busy and forget about it. Then I feel guilty for not reading it, which makes me stubborn. Dee tells me she went to Mandy's wedding many years ago."

"To Chad Manor, of Manor Homes."

"Back then it was Manor Construction. Dee says they got rich building crappy homes that are now falling apart."

How could they last if they built crappy homes? "I think I've seen the company name in the *Howler* lately," Jaymie said of the *Wolverhampton Weekly Howler,* the

31

newspaper for which she wrote her "Vintage Eats" column. "Something about a lawsuit, or . . . oh! Homeowners talking about launching a class action suit."

"Wow, how bad do the homes have to be to inspire a class action suit?" Becca said.

"Why would Mandy be stalking Val?" Jaymie mused. She took her cloth to a row of vintage Bakelite radios, carefully wiping specks of dust from tuning knobs.

"Maybe she's curious about her."

Or maybe Mandy had heard Val was seeing Greg, her sister's ex-husband, Jaymie thought but didn't say. "They share a friend, from what Val said."

"Ti Pham, I think that's the name. Maybe Mandy feels Val is threatening their friendship." Becca hadn't said Greg Vasiliev's name, so maybe she didn't know Val was seeing him.

"I guess it's possible." Becca frowned. "Anyway, yesterday a couple of weird things happened. First, the Queensville Pharmacy received a prescription for Mandy."

Jaymie turned and stared at her sister. "Seriously? Why would it come to Val's pharmacy? Wouldn't it go to a drugstore in Wolverhampton?"

"I know, right? It's odd. It came in yesterday, but of course Val was off."

32

"Building a catio with me! I wonder if Denver likes it yet?"

"Anyway, the prescription was filled by Helen. You know, Helen Pham, the new pharmacist working for Val? She's married to Ti Pham's brother. I guess Helen called the doctor's office to confirm, since they hadn't handled prescriptions for Mandy before, but the change in pharmacies is on the level, by request of the patient. So, she filled it."

"I can't believe Val told you all that," Jaymie said, staring at her sister. "She *never* talks about her clients."

Becca squirmed. "I, uh, didn't get it from Val, it was from an acquaintance of Dee's, the receptionist in Mandy's doctor's office. I called Dee to talk to her about the auction we're all going to tomorrow evening, but she can't come. Anyway, the receptionist told Dee, and Dee told me."

That was quick, Jaymie thought. The Queensville/Wolverhampton gossip pipeline was a mighty transit route, no tidbit too small or uninteresting to pass on. It was probably just as well Becca didn't seem to know Val was seeing her high school crush, or it would be common knowledge. Val was famously discreet about her private life, which she liked *private.*

"Anyway, Mandy's sister Candy came into the Emporium this morning and accused Val of stalking Mandy on social media."

"*Candy* did? That's crazy!" Or maybe not, if she knew about Val seeing Greg.

Georgina returned from the restroom and she and Kevin rejoined them. They headed to the Queensville Inn for their brunch, which, in the older woman's case would mean several more gin and tonics than would allow her to work the rest of the day. Kevin whispered to Jaymie that Becca would be back at some point in the afternoon to watch the store for the rest of the day, while he made sure his sister got back to her apartment in the back of the store for "a rest."

Jaymie finished dusting and took out her laptop. She got quite a bit of work done between serving customers, who were largely repeat clients coming in to pick up items they had already paid for. Time sped by. Niggling in the back of Jaymie's mind, though, was the question of why Candy would accuse Val of such a ludicrous thing as stalking anyone online. Val was going to bring over lunch at one, so they could talk about it then.

One p.m. came and went. Then one thirty. Jaymie tried calling the pharmacy line, but it was busy. She texted Val but got no response. Finally, she went out to the porch and looked toward the Emporium, wondering if Val had a sudden surge of business, but there was only one vehicle parked in front of the building.

A maroon SUV.

Jaymie put the *Back Soon* sign in the window, grabbed her cardigan and locked up. She hustled down the street and trotted up the steps of the Emporium.

She glanced at Gracey Klausner, who was at the cash register at the front of the Emporium. The young woman grimaced and glanced toward the back, motioning with her head to the pharmacy. The sound of raised voices drifted forward. Jaymie threaded her way through the canned goods aisle to the pharmacy counter, where several customers waited, scripts in hand, eyes wide, as a beleaguered Val, within her pharmacy booth behind the glass divider, listened to a plump red-faced woman — tousled ginger hair matted, clothes rumpled, wearing a heavy rust-colored cable-knit cardigan with a fur collar — who screamed at her.

She was in the middle of a stream of invective. ". . . to use your trusted position as a pharmacist to poison me is —"

"Wait a minute!" Val said, putting up one hand in a *stop* motion. "Mandy, you're the one who requested the change, so —"

"I never changed my prescription!"

"I didn't change your prescription delivery," Val repeated firmly. "Either you or your doctor had to have. And I didn't fill your prescription, my colleague did yesterday. You *know* that, since you were the one who picked it up, and you know Helen Pham; she's Ti's sister-in-law. She called and checked with your doctor's office, but they said it was by request of the client. Though I trust her completely, I'll still check the script for you and —"

"You think I'd trust *you*? Why would I . . ." Mandy de Boer paused, looked confused for a moment, shook her head, pushed her shaggy hair back, cussed colorfully, looked around at the other customers, then said to Val, "I demand an admission and an apology right here and now, you conniving witch!"

Val said, "Mandy, *please* calm down. I don't know what you're talking about."

The woman frowned and pushed her hair back again. "I don't feel well. It's got to be what you gave me!"

"But I didn't give you anything!"

Jaymie had never seen Val so agitated. Trip

36

Findley, Jaymie's Queensville across-the-back-lane neighbor, and a couple of other locals were avidly watching the exchange, heads swiveling like it was a tennis match. Jaymie met Val's eye. "Val, I know darn well there *is* no mistake, but for this lady's sake, maybe you'd better close for an hour while you call her physician to confirm the prescription and recheck your records?"

Stiffly, Val said, "I've already called Ms. de Boer's doctor, as Helen did yesterday before filling the prescription, and I'm awaiting a callback." Val turned to the other customers. "Folks, if you leave your prescriptions with me, I can fill them and have them delivered to your home. Or I'll call and see if you want to pick them up."

"I'll come back later, Val," Trip said. "I can see you got your hands full, but I know you didn't make no mistake. You've got my prescriptions, so I'll be back! No hair off my chin." He turned and strolled away, but the other two customers shook their heads and held on to their prescriptions.

"I must go to Wolverhampton anyway, to the Walgreens. I'll get my prescription there this time," a well-dressed seventyish woman said. "No offense, Valetta."

"None taken," Val said, gritting her teeth as the woman walked away, followed by the other customer. "Have the pharmacy there call me to transfer the script." She took a deep breath and turned to the flame-haired irritated woman. "Mandy, your doctor's office should get back to me any moment. I can also call Helen, if you like."

"As if I'd trust you!" Mandy said. "You've been stalking me online for a month now, Val."

"Stalking you?" Jaymie yelped. "Why would Val —"

Val put her hand up in a *stop* motion again. "Mandy, I'm worried for you," Val said. "Are you okay? Can I call someone else for you? Maybe your sister?"

Mandy touched her head and rubbed, frowning. She was plump, as Becca had said, with frazzled red hair coming out salt and pepper, graying at the roots. Her complexion was sallow, there were deep circles under her eyes, and she looked older than her years, like time and trouble had worn her down. But with her hands on her hips, her fur-collared cardigan rucked up, she appeared, as Mrs. Stubbs would say, as if her dander was up, her cheeks marked by red rashy-looking spots of high color. She glared at Jaymie. "Who are you, anyway?"

"This is Becca Leighton's little sister, Jaymie," Val said. Her phone rang and she turned away as she held the pharmacy landline phone up to her ear. She spoke to someone on the other end.

"Becca moved away," Mandy said, distracted and puzzled.

"But she's back." Jaymie stared at her. "You know that already, because you were in her store the other day, Queensville Fine Antiques, talking to her. You tried to sell her a fake Tiffany lamp and looked at some Bakelite radios."

"Oh, sure. I guess I forgot." She fell silent, swaying on her feet.

"Are you okay?" Jaymie asked, becoming concerned.

Val turned and said, "Mandy, your doctor is on the line. You can talk to him right now if you want. I'll pass you the phone. He said the prescription is the right medication and the right dose. If you have concerns about what Helen dispensed for you, you're to take it in to him and he can have a look at it. You can either speak to him or go and see him now."

The woman shook her head, then turned, and without another word unsteadily walked away, down the aisle and out of the store. Jaymie and Val stared after her, then met each other's gaze.

"What the heck was that all about?" Jaymie said.

"Beats me."

They sat on the front step of the Emporium to share lunch. Val poured homemade tomato soup from a thermal bottle into mugs, set it between them on the step, and they split a wax paper–wrapped ham sandwich. A couple of locals strolled by. Val waved, but they didn't wave back.

"Odd," Jaymie said, biting into her sandwich.

The next time it happened, Val called out, "Hey, Alice, everything okay?"

The woman said, "Sure. I'm in a rush." She walked away quickly.

Both Jaymie and Val sat in silence for a few minutes, eating and drinking their soup. Appetite satisfied, Val mused, "Why would Mandy de Boer do that? I don't get it."

"Malpractice suit?"

"It doesn't make any sense. I'm careful, as is Helen," she said about her pharmacist colleague, a woman who had almost thirty years' experience as a pharmacist in Ohio before she moved to Wolverhampton with her husband a few years earlier to "retire."

Jaymie knew the whole story, of course. Val had been looking for a permanent part-time colleague and Helen had become bored with retirement, so after a couple of years subbing at pharmacies in Wolverhampton, she took the part-time position with Val. As her friend's sister-in-law, Val had known her for years, even before she and her husband moved to Michigan when he started a construction company here.

"There is no mistake on our end," Val said. "But this is still not a good feeling. And what she said in front of customers!" She trailed off and shook her head. "It makes me feel ill." She set the last of her sandwich aside and put one hand over her stomach.

"Val, everyone in Queensville and Wolverhampton knows you. You don't make mistakes. And you didn't dispense the meds anyway!"

"I have a bad feeling about this."

"She'll go to her doctor, who will prove you right. It will all be okay."

"I don't know," she said, hugging her cardigan around herself. "People are acting strange."

"Those people were in a hurry. Another day you wouldn't even notice."

Trip Findley strolled toward them. "Good time to get my prescription?" he asked.

"Sure, Trip." She started tidying the thermos and scraps.

41

Jaymie helped, then joked, "I'd better get back to work before I'm fired."

"Hey, did you gals hear?" Trip said, putting one foot up on the bottom step and leaning forward for a good gossip. "You know that nutty gal who was in here earlier? She had a car accident. Ran into a telephone pole out on the highway, then careened further and hit a house porch. Heard it on my scanner and phoned my nephew, who lives along there. He saw it all." His gaze slewed between them, and he nodded, eyes gleaming. "Yup. She ran into the pole and house but said it was 'the other guy's fault,' even though there wasn't no other guy."

Jaymie and Val exchanged a glance.

"She didn't look well," Jaymie said.

"She drove away before the cops could get there. Homeowner is fuming!"

"How did she manage that? Didn't her airbags deploy?"

He shrugged. "Mebbe had them disabled."

"Can you do that?" Jaymie asked.

"Sure," he said. "Some have an on/off switch, or you can take out the fuse."

"I wonder what's going on with her?"

"I don't know, but I'm going to find out," Val said. "See you later, Jaymie." She entered the store with Trip trotting behind.

THREE

Thursday turned out to be one of those mornings when everything went awry. Lilibet threw up her breakfast, Hoppy stepped in it and trailed it about the cabin, Jocie — grossed out — refused to clean it up, and Jaymie had a rare meltdown, after which Jocie hurriedly cleaned the mess and tearfully apologized, which made Jaymie feel worse. However, she summoned her new mom skills and took a deep breath.

Hands splayed out, she gathered her little family in her gaze: Jakob, Jocie, Lilibet, Hoppy. "Everyone, this was a bad start, but let's have a morning reset. We're not going into our day at odds with each other. Deep breaths in aaaaand out." They all stared at her. "Come on, breathe." The two humans obeyed. "Jocie, later we'll talk about why it is your responsibility to clean up after Lilibet and why this won't happen again. Right now, why don't you tell us your plans for the day while we eat breakfast, and we'll all have a good day."

After that everything went a little more smoothly, but it had already set them behind. Jocie missed the bus. Jakob kissed Jaymie goodbye for the day, then drove their daughter to school, after which he had a busy day planned, with deliveries to the junk store and a preholiday meeting with his brothers, partners in the Christmas tree farm.

Other than a text from Val saying the doctor had confirmed to her that Mandy de Boer's prescription — he examined the bottle himself — was perfectly fine, Jaymie didn't hear anything more from her friend. But still, the confrontation from the previous day weighed heavily on her mind. Val was the least paranoid person she knew, and the looks passersby had given them as they walked away the day before *had* been distinctly odd. A pharmacist was dependent on her reputation in a small town like Queensville, so it mattered if Val lost hers.

But she had to let it go, for now. Jaymie settled on the sofa with her laptop and worked on her next "Vintage Eats" column for an hour, then uploaded an entry to her food blog. She was about to shut the laptop down, but yesterday's events still nagged at her. Mandy de Boer had not looked healthy, nor had she seemed completely coherent. The accident she then had and her behavior after, as reported by Trip, were also odd. Curiosity was her besetting sin, Jaymie always said, though her writer friend Melody Heath said without curiosity *she* wouldn't have become a writer. Some background was required. After an hour on the internet, diving into social media, news sources, and local sites, she had discovered a lot.

Mandy de Boer had recently gone back to her maiden name, almost exactly five years after the tragic death of her husband, Chad Manor, in a car crash on the highway late one night. Together they had one daughter, Trina, who was currently following her father's footsteps at university in England, studying for a master's degree in architecture.

There were photos aplenty. Judging solely by them, Mandy was a woman she would want to be friends with. She looked different in the photos, her red hair sleek and coiffed instead of a frizzy mess. She wore stylish outfits, favoring jewel tones. *That* Mandy smiled easily, appearing affectionate with her daughter, a pretty twentyish girl. As recently as that summer she had been waterskiing, dancing in a club, and vacationing in Vail. There was a good-looking fifty-ish man in some photos, dark-haired with silver highlights, trim and fit, with a compelling stare into the camera lens.

There was a more recent photo of Mandy from September, volunteering at the local food bank with two other women, one of whom looked remarkably like her. Jaymie read the caption and discovered the look-alike was Mandy's sister, Candy Vasiliev. Mandy, who had gained weight from the previous photos, had her arm slung affectionately over her sister's shoulders. The other woman was Val and Mandy's mutual friend, Hien Sang "Ti" Pham, co-director of the food bank. In a linked press release Mandy had announced that Manor Homes would partner with the food bank to provide support to low-income families, children in particular, as well as initiating a school lunch program, details to be provided when more were available.

Jaymie next did a quick search of the *Howler* website and found a couple of articles, one from five years back relating the circumstances surrounding Chad Manor's death. Another stated the company was now in the hands of his wife, Mandy. She remembered the car accident, a horrific winter mishap involving his SUV and a snow plow that had led to calls for better plowing practices on Michigan highways. How tragic for the family.

As well, there were various announcements over the years of housing developments, two in Wolverhampton and one northwest of Marine City, with another in the planning stages. Recently, though, there had been a growing list of disgruntled homeowners complaining about cracking foundations, leaky roofs, substandard construction practices and shoddy plumbing fittings. The company was in trouble. Mandy, interrogated by a *Howler* writer, said she was looking into the complaints but offered no further comments.

Maybe that was why the woman appeared stressed. None of what Jaymie discovered explained her recent obsession with Val, though, or her claims that Val was stalking her.

Jaymie frowned down at her laptop and hesitated, fingers over the keyboard. Mandy's stalking accusation was ridiculous. And yet doubt, once sown, was hard to completely overcome. She did a quick search on social media and came up with a profile of someone named *Valeta Nibely.* The profile seemed new, but it used as a profile photo the exterior of the Queensville Emporium and listed the profiled person as a "farmacist." No one who knew Val would think this was her, but at a casual glance . . .

She went back to Mandy de Boer's social media profile and looked at her posts. There were several nasty comments aimed at her by *Valeta Nibely.* She *did* have cause to think Val was stalking her, albeit a reason based on a fake profile. She texted Val a quick note about what she had discovered, and then reported the profile for pretending to be someone she knew. Not that it would do any good; the damage was done.

None of this explained the accusation Mandy had made against Val, that her pharmacy had made a grave error, a more serious charge than social media bullying. Val had often commented that a pharmacist held the lives of her clients in her hands, and she took the responsibility seriously. To make such an accusation, that Val or her colleague had made an error resulting in illness, was outrageous unless one believed it.

What could happen to make Mandy believe it?

Maybe it was the causation/correlation mix-up. If she had started taking a new medication and coincidentally began feeling poorly, she might attribute it to the medication. If she had been reassured the medication could not have that effect, it was not a major leap to believe the pharmacist had made an error.

Would Mandy believe that? Maybe. It was like there were two Mandys, the one who helped the food bank, ran a company, and vacationed in Vail, and another who was paranoid, made wild accusations, and crashed her car. And none of it explained why she had her prescription sent to the Queensville Pharmacy in the first place. It didn't make sense.

There was no solution to the puzzle, and it was time to get moving. She had things to do.

It was a sparkling fall morning, and there was no lovelier place to be than the Queensville Historic Manor. She parked beside the lone car in the parking area — the elderly Cadillac informed her that faithful volunteer Mabel Bloomsbury was there and working — got out of her SUV, and stood for a few minutes, letting the sunshine warm her face, breathing in the crisp fall air, and enjoying the sight of the far edge of woods, clothed in brilliant fall foliage. Long-term plans for the house included period authentic gardens around it, as well as plots turned over to the garden society to make a vegetable garden featuring heritage vegetables and plants.

Maybe an orchard, and a duck pond. Maybe a walking woods to identify wildflowers. But she was getting ahead of herself.

All these hopes and dreams and plans made it a good day to be alive. She thought again with melancholy compassion of Jocie's little friend Mia, who had tragically lost her mother. What could be done to soothe the poor kid? Maybe a fall party, or even a sleepover, with Jocie, Mia, and some of Jocie's other friends, like Noor, Gemma and Peyton. Decision made, she texted Jakob about the timing.

She retrieved a box of Autumn Glory Pyrex from the back of the SUV, hefted it on her hip, climbed the steps to the front porch, entered the historic home and greeted Mabel with a side hug. The older woman was putting the finishing touches on the fall décor in the dining room. Jaymie stared in dismay; it was full-on fall decor in the modern sense, with signs printed with *Fall Y'all* and other folksy sayings, along with multicolored sequinned pumpkins and old pickup trucks on more tiny signs extolling pumpkin spice lattes.

Jaymie set her box of Pyrex down with a clunk on the dining table and said, in as diplomatic a way as possible, "Isn't it a little late for fall décor changes?" She wanted to say that it diminished the elegant display Mabel had already arranged, with chrysanthemums, cranberry glass, and a gorgeous setting of Hall's Autumn Leaf pattern dinnerware.

Mabel gazed at her with a tragic expression. Her bottom lip quivered. "I know," she wailed. "It's too much. Too modern. Too. . . . too *pumpkin-y*! What am I going to do?"

"What do you mean?" It seemed a simple matter; take down the offending décor.

"It's Mrs. Bellwood! She sent her granddaughter, Taylor, to help me with some things. I needed younger knees than mine to climb the footstool and place some of the dishes in the display cabinet," she said, flapping one beringed hand at the cabinet in the corner. It was full of more of the Hall china.

"And?"

"She was so lovely, and so helpful, and asked if she could bring a few fall things to 'brighten the place up,' " she said, doing air quotes.

"And you replied . . . ?"

"I said yes. What else could I say?"

"You could have said thank you very much, but the décor is strictly vintage and antique."

"I didn't know at the time what she was bringing. I thought maybe Mrs. Bellwood had given her a brass urn, or some crystal candle holders. She has such lovely things in her home. I thought that's what Taylor was talking about, something from her grandmother's." In a mournful tone, she added, "She kept saying things like she was all about *PSL life,* and I didn't know what she meant."

Jaymie bit back a laugh. "I think in this context it means Pumpkin Spice Lattes, but I could be wrong. Mabel, you know this isn't right. We're giving people an authentic look at what living in the Victorian era or early twentieth century would have been like." She paused, but then, heaving an inner sigh, said, "Would you like me to handle it?"

"Would you?" she asked, brightening up.

"Anything for you, Mabel. Box this stuff up — I'll empty this one I'm carrying and you can use it — and I'll stick it in my SUV. Taylor has moved into the apartment over the Emporium. I'll take it to her and suggest she use it for her new place."

Jaymie delivered the empty box to Mabel, then continued in the kitchen with the new display, placing the fallish Pyrex on the shelf above the sink. She surveyed the room with satisfaction, the vintage color scheme, the steadily improving décor. Local handyman Bill Waterman had built and mounted on the kitchen walls shadow boxes within which Jaymie hung some of the more valuable and unique vintage whisks, knife sharpeners, slotted spoons and beaters. Later in the fall, toward the holiday season, she was running a school program and needed to get the place perfect.

Jaymie finished her tasks for the day and said goodbye to a grateful Mabel, carrying the box of fall ornaments out and shoving it into the back of her vehicle. She bypassed Queensville, driving straight to Wolverhampton for a meeting with Nan to discuss in more depth her "Vintage Eats" column for the coming holiday season. Nan liked Jaymie to pair her offerings with vendor ads, so turkey, apple, cranberry and sweet potato recipes were discussed.

Finally, Jaymie was ready to go, except for one question. "Nan, my good friend Val Nibley had an unsettling episode with a prominent Wolverhampton woman. I wonder, do you know Mandy de Boer?"

"I don't think I . . . wait, do you mean Mandy Manor? Of Manor Homes?"

"She's gone back to her birth name."

"We've attended the same fundraisers and

parties, and we both belong to the business-women's association."

As briefly as possible, Jaymie explained what had happened, the prescription mix-up, the stalking accusation, the confrontation, and the accident.

"Hmmm. I've heard some things . . ."

"Like?" Jaymie urged when the editor stopped.

"Unsubstantiated rumors." She stopped and stared off into space. "This is interesting, though."

"Interesting how?"

"Interesting considering the class action lawsuit I've heard rumblings of in the business community. Mandy was always level-headed, but lately some folks I know have called her erratic. Leave it with me. I'm intrigued."

"I know the *Howler* has reported on her company's recent problems," Jaymie said, stubbornly probing for more information. "I'm wondering if it's all related."

Nan jumped to her feet, a sign the chat was over. "Like I said, leave it with me."

"Nan, I —"

"Jaymie, I *said,* leave it with me."

"I'm not leaving until you give me *some-*thing. I will not have Val vilified without do-ing everything I can to clear her. Now, what do you have?"

Nan glared up at her, lips compressed into a thin webbed line. "You've come a long way, Jaymie," she finally said. "Look at you, standing your ground, pressing for info. When you first came into my office you were quaking in your boots."

"That was then; this is now."

She tossed her hair, then sat back down and tapped at her computer. "There are many moving parts to this. Off the record . . . and I mean it. You didn't hear this from me," she said, glaring up at Jaymie. "A few years back there was a rumor floating around in certain circles that Mandy had an affair with a fellow in the company. When her husband died he became a partner in the firm."

"That would be Randall Kallis?"

Nan snorted. "I've heard a lot about him. He's a hit-it-and-quit-it type. There is no woman in Wolverhampton he hasn't dated or tried to date."

"Interesting. Anything else?"

Nan moved her mouse and clicked, bringing up another document. She scanned it for something, then said, "Here it is. We've got a reporter moving on this issue. The problems with the Manor Houses homes go beyond simple fixes; there are cracking foundations, groundwater leaking in, plumbing done wrong. That's bad, and I know from experience." She looked up from the monitor. "Maybe the stress is affecting her stability."

Jaymie frowned. Even fully stressed, people didn't change so quickly. There had to be more.

The editor jumped back up from her desk, put one hand on Jaymie's shoulder and turned her, giving her a little push. "Now, go. Go home and write."

Moments later Jaymie was outside, buttoning her heavy cardigan against the chilly wind that had come up, as it will in October in Michigan. Despite Nan's admonition to go home and write, she had an hour or so to kill; what should she do? Val's mention of Thrifty Dan's store had reminded her how many great bargains she had found there. She headed down the Wolverhampton main street.

"Jaymie!" Dan cried as she entered. He came around the sales desk and folded her in a hearty hug. He was a big guy, and hugged hard. "Just the gal I've been waiting to see. I've got some stuff you might want."

He retrieved a battered box overflowing with dusty junk. She sorted through the box, setting aside those few things she did want and piling the rest back in the box. "I'll take these," she said, pointing to the assorted kitchen tools, along with a couple of books for Jocie. "But I have no use for the rest. I'll look around and see if there is anything else I can take away with me."

She shopped for a half hour and found a few items. When she came back to the register, she said, "Thin pickings on kitchen stuff right now. Keep an eye out especially for vintage or unusual sieves. I'm putting together a collection."

His eyes widened. "Oh, gosh, I wish I knew that this morning."

"Why?"

"Mandy de Boer was in and bought a bunch of kitchen items, including three vintage copper sieves; said she was going to punch bigger holes in them for electrical fixtures and turn them into kitchen lighting."

"I hate it when people take usable vintage items and destroy their value."

"You must hate reno shows then," he said with a laugh. "Next time I see some home stager painting an antique English rolltop desk black, I'll think of you."

"How weird that Mandy, who I had never met before yesterday, now comes up in every conversation I'm having. Did you hear

57

what she did to Val Nibley?" She filled Dan in.

He leaned forward, his elbows on his glass counter, and oohed and aahed in the right spots. "So bizarre! I heard from a friend of a friend that she had a little accident the day you're talking about —"

"She did! I heard about it too. Ran off the road into an electric pole and a house then took off."

"— but when someone in here asked her about it, get this: she denied it ever happened!"

"But it *did* happen. Maybe she meant it didn't happen like people are saying?"

"No, girl, nuh-uh. She flat out denied it happened."

"Troubling." She needed to tell Val about this. She paid, shoved the box into the back of the SUV, then sat for a moment fretting at the problem. It was puzzling, and she couldn't let a puzzle rest until it was solved. She texted Val with what she had heard. *What's going on with Mandy?* she finished.

FOUR

Jaymie, Val, and Becca were attending a large auction that night, and met outside the building, a long former industrial warehouse. Becca, who was eager to preview some mid-mod china and teak furniture, surged in ahead of them. Val lingered behind and grabbed Jaymie's sleeve. "I called Dan and he confirmed what he told you," she said.

"You didn't believe me?"

"Of course I believed you, but I like it from the horse's mouth. It's concerning." She pushed her glasses up on her nose and folded her arms over her chest, clad in the hand-knit sweater Jaymie had commissioned for her two Christmases ago.

They entered the huge auction facility. Jaymie happily breathed in the scent she thought of as Eau de Old Stuff, a mixture of dust, mold, ancient wood, and some unknowable fragrance she smelled in old buildings and junk stores. Heaven. The auction was half furniture and half box lots. Becca was interested in the furniture — teak sideboards and dining sets lined up along the walls — for her store. Tables stretched the length of the center of the old warehouse floor, piled high with boxes of small appliances, books, knickknacks (Val was in heaven), china (likewise Becca), and vintage mixed lots of kitchen utensils (likewise Jaymie). They all went their separate ways, writing down the numbers of lots they were interested in.

Becca found Jaymie and muttered, "Lookit who's here!" She nodded down the row. It was Mandy de Boer with a woman who must have been her sister Candy. Mandy was wearing the same outerwear as the day before, a heavy cardigan with a fur collar, and as before her hair was a wild tangle of faux ginger curls. "She looks like she's been dragged through a bush backward, as Grandma says. And *bruised.* Her face is black and blue."

"She was in an accident. Didn't you hear?" Jaymie glanced Mandy's way and was stunned by the greenish-purple patches on the woman's cheek. The accident must have been worse than Trip Findley indicated, even though she drove away from it.

"Candy, on the other hand, looks relaxed and tanned," Becca said. "How is anyone in Michigan tanned in October?"

"There's Val," Jaymie said. She found their friend and whispered the news. Val's first instinct was to check on Mandy herself, to see if she was okay, but Jaymie talked her out of it by saying the woman had her sister with her and was at a public auction. She must be all right. They found seats. Jaymie sat between Becca and Val. Mandy and Candy took seats almost exactly in front of them, without seeming aware.

"I'm tired," Mandy muttered. "I don't know why we came tonight."

"I wanted you to stay home and rest but you said you needed more vintage stuff for the Vintage Manor Estates," Candy replied.

"I guess I did." Mandy yawned. "It's easy for you. You're all rested up after vacation. Where'd you go, Mexico again?"

"That explains the tan," Becca whispered, leaning into Jaymie.

"*Not* Mexico," Candy said. "I went to Colorado for early skiing."

"Who goes skiing in October?" Becca hissed.

Jaymie whispered to Val that the lot she wanted had in it the most beautiful antique brass sieve she had ever seen. It would become the centerpiece of her whole sieve collection in the Queensville Historic Manor collection. "The patina on it!" She sighed, in the ecstasy only a lover of antiques could feel. "It is spectacular. I hope it doesn't go over my budget."

The auction commenced. Mandy wanted the same items as Becca. She bid on the teak sideboard and dining sets, as well as a mid-century modern buffet with matching china cabinet. Becca's smile turned into a scowl as Mandy bid wildly and won set after set. Finally, after losing a box of Atomic patterned mid-century modern dinnerware that Mandy overbid on, she admitted defeat.

"*Some* people are willing to overpay horribly for stuff, apparently," she said loudly.

Candy Vasiliev turned in her seat and spotted Becca. "Oh, hi, Becs. Haven't seen you for a while. How's it going?" She drained her plastic shaker bottle, labeled *Keto Kolonics,* noisily sucking on a straw.

The auction was moving along apace as Candy and Becca chatted briefly. Jaymie's lot came up and she raised her paddle. Mandy raised hers. Jaymie bid higher, as did Mandy. It swiftly went higher than Jaymie was willing to pay; the box of copper and brass sieves went to Mandy.

"More light fixtures for the Vintage Manor

Estates!" she crowed as she high-fived her sister. "Homes like your grandparents built!"

"Oh, Lord, please say she's not going to destroy all those beautiful sieves by drilling holes into them and making them into light fixtures!" Jaymie muttered to Becca.

"She doesn't care about vintage. All she cares about is making money," Becca grumbled, still stung by losing out on the furniture she had hoped to sell for a nice profit in the store.

"If you buy a Manor Home, you can be guaranteed one thing: it'll fall apart and leak like one of those sieves!" a white-haired man said, his tone loud and sour.

The hum of conversation quieted and those seated nearby whirled to look at him and his companion, a slim gray-haired woman who looked like she wanted to sink through the floor.

"Connor Ward, I *told* you we'll take care of your house," Mandy said, jabbing her finger in the air at the man. "If you'd let our crew in to fix —"

"Like I'd trust your workmen to hammer a nail in a wall!" he jeered, his narrow face darkening to magenta, the color suffusing his cheeks and neck in blotches. "We sunk our retirement into a leaky lemon, and now we'll be lucky if we can unload it for less than we paid two years ago."

"Connor, take it easy," Becca said. "Wait for the courts to sort it out."

"Who is that?" Jaymie muttered to Val, but her friend didn't answer, riveted by the conversation in front of her.

Mandy stood and glared at the man, then turned to Jaymie's sister. "Are you taking Connor Ward's side?"

"The Wards are customers of mine," Becca replied. "Mandy, I'm not trying to be mean, but I know for a fact that Dina and Connor had to sell me her mother's china and a few other nice items to pay for repairs to the sinkhole you sold them." She looked around for the couple, but they were on their way to the door, the woman tugging her reluctant, muttering husband after her. "They've told me all about it — water seeping into the basement, roof leaking, soffits falling apart, drainage issues and cracking foundation. Plumbing that rattles and sparking electrical outlets."

Tears filling her eyes, Mandy whirled toward Val, who flinched when she fully witnessed the extent of the woman's bruising. "Valetta Nibley, *you're* the one turning people against me."

"That's not true, Mandy," Val said. "I

64

haven't done a thing."

"I've got proof. Nasty messages, horrible gossip and now poison pills!"

Val shook her head, perplexed. "You know that's not true."

"Mandy, leave Val alone," Becca said. "She has nothing to do with this."

"Hi, remember me?" Jaymie said. "Becca's sister? Val is telling the truth, Mandy. We checked it out online. Someone is *pretending* to be Val. *That's* who's harassing you."

Candy stared at her and frowned. "That's ridiculous," she said. "Why would anyone do that to my sister?"

"Why would Val harass her?" Jaymie countered. "That doesn't make sense either."

Grudgingly, Candy nodded.

"But you've been telling people I had a car accident," Mandy sobbed, pointing at Val. "And you said that I'm an addict, or something horrible like that!"

"You *did* have a car accident," Val said. "I'm not the one who said it, others told me. But an addict? I never said that to anyone, Mandy. It never even crossed my mind, I promise. It's crazy to say —"

"See? She's calling me crazy!" Mandy said, now weeping, distraught, her bruised face wet with tears. "You'd think a pharmacist would have morals, better than to gossip about their clients and then send them home with the wrong drug. You could have killed me!"

Valetta's face pinkened. "Mandy, please listen to me. Neither Helen nor I gave you the wrong medication. You can't go around saying that to people."

This was a losing argument and gathering more attention than necessary. "Val, let it go," Jaymie urged. She had been watching Mandy de Boer; the woman's eyes were wild, and she looked scared. Confused, yes, but frightened, too. It was heartrending.

"I can't let it go," Val said. "Mandy, believe me, I have never made a mistake in my whole career."

"I'll report you, that's what I'll do!" Mandy said. "I'll make sure your license is taken away. I'll make sure you'll never give out drugs again!"

Jaymie clamped her fingers around Val's arm. "Let's get out of here," she muttered.

Candy tugged at her sister's arm. "Come on, Mandy, calm down, will you? Please?" She glanced at Val in alarm, then back to her sister. "What's wrong with you? You're getting hysterical." She looked toward Becca, who was staring in confusion, her gaze swiveling between the bruised woman and Val. "Becs, *please,* can't you do some-thing?"

"Like what?" Becca said.

"Get Val out of here. It's her presence that's upsetting Mandy. Can't you see that?"

"Let's get out of here, guys." Val shoul-dered her purse and stumbled along the row of chairs, stepping on toes.

Jaymie and Becca followed, joining Val out in the parking lot. Jaymie threw her arms around her trembling friend. "Are you okay, Val?"

The woman nodded and sniffed back tears.

"Only a few people heard her," Becca said, looking back at the auction house with a puzzled frown. "It'll blow over by morn-ing."

FIVE

The next day as she ate lunch in front of her laptop, Jaymie called Val. They talked about the previous evening for a few minutes, and then Jaymie said, "I don't get what is going on. She can't really believe that you're behind some scheme to drug her. Can she?"

"I don't know," Val said. "I've been worrying about it all night and I can't figure her out."

"You said Greg Vasiliev was married to Candy once. Maybe he'd have a handle on Mandy's behavior."

"Good idea. Call you back in a minute." When she did, she said, "Candy called Greg this morning. She's really worried about her sister and is trying to get her to see her doctor. Maybe she hasn't been taking her medications or something. I don't know what else to think. I'm worried. She wasn't like this in high school."

"Candy did look pretty upset," Jaymie mused. "She kept trying to get her sister to stop. Mandy was so bruised. It was shocking." She paused, then asked, "Val, what are your options if she keeps telling people you gave her the wrong drugs?"

"I could take legal action, I suppose. My job and this community are my life. Accusing me of a dispensing error is serious business. I won't stand for it."

"How long will you wait to see if she backs off?"

"I don't know. A few days. A week. It's shaken me, I will say that. I just don't understand any of it. We were friends, once. I don't know what happened, but something did, and she stopped talking to me." She shrugged. "Just one of those things. She was popular. I wasn't. I thought that's what it was, so I let it go."

"What's the next step?"

"It depends. If she makes an official complaint, I can at least answer that."

"You did everything right."

"And it's all on record. It wasn't me who dispensed the medication, it was Helen. I don't know how Mandy can accuse me. Helen called to make sure the prescription coming to us wasn't a mistake before dispensing it. When Mandy complained, I checked the prescription. I had her *doctor* check the prescription. I advised her to take the bottle of pills to her doctor. I made sure it was right." She took a deep breath. Reviewing the steps she had taken calmed her.

"I looked into her socials, and she's been even keel for years now," Jaymie agreed.

"We have a mutual friend, Ti Pham. Knowing Ti, I can't imagine she'd be friends with Mandy unless she was a rational woman."

"You mentioned her, someone you work with when you volunteer for the food bank. And she's related to Helen?"

"Her sister-in-law. I've actually known Ti longer. That's how I met Helen. I called Ti this morning and she's worried about Mandy too. What has changed? Why is she behaving like this?"

"The car accident?" Jaymie hazarded the guess.

"You saw her in my pharmacy. She was acting out *before* the car accident. It feels like some elaborate setup."

"What do you mean?" Jaymie asked.

"I don't exactly *know* what I mean. But why did she have this particular prescription sent to me to fill? She's never dealt with us before, why now? And then to accuse me

70

of making a mistake when it was Helen she dealt with? I don't understand and I don't know what to do."

"But you can't let this go, Val."

"Agreed. But I'm going to wait and see. I don't want to jump the gun."

Jaymie worked on her laptop in front of a fire in the fieldstone fireplace as Jakob did the dinner dishes and Jocie helped. Over dinner they had discussed a Halloween sleepover with her friends. Jocie was madly excited, planning the "menu," as she called it, for foods she could make herself, like rice cereal treats and cookies. It would be a sugar rush occasion, with hopped-up ten-year-olds in sleeping bags in front of the fire, probably not sleeping a wink. Jaymie sighed, thinking of it, but looked forward to it, too.

She received a call from Heidi, whose best friend was Bernie, who had just received a promotion in the QPD.

"I heard about what went down at the auction last night," Heidi said. "Between Val and Mandy de Boer. And guess what?"

"I can't guess," Jaymie replied. Jocie wound her arms around Jaymie's neck, whispered *thank you* for the sleepover to come, kissed her good night, and headed

71

upstairs. Jakob turned off the kitchen lights and sat down beside her on the sofa.

"Don't tell anyone I told you, but I heard this straight from Bernie. That Mandy woman is being investigated!"

"Investigated? By the *police*? For what?"

"The accident she was in. It was a single-car accident, but still, there was property damage and she drove away from the scene. I guess they tried to find her at home, but she wasn't there. By the time they caught up with her it was the next day, so there was no way to judge her impairment. It's up in the air whether charges will be laid, but the property owners might sue, or whatever."

Jaymie called Val and passed on what Heidi had said. Val expressed concern for Mandy; despite what had happened, she did want the best for her former friend.

"What is that noise?" Jaymie asked her friend, hearing voices and the clink of silverware on china.

"I'm at Ambrosia, for a dinner," Val said.

"Ambrosia? Who with?"

"Greg called and invited me. He said I needed cheering up." Her voice had a smile in it. "He's waving right now and saying he hopes to meet you someday."

"I hope I do meet him," Jaymie said, and

hung up smiling, happy her friend had made a life beyond her family and work.

Jaymie leaned on Jakob, laying her head on his shoulder.

"What's up?" he murmured. "You okay?"

"I am now." She told him about her call to Val. "It was so nice to hear her out to dinner, at a nice restaurant, with someone she likes. She deserves everything good." She paused. "I can't help but worry. I hate that Mandy de Boer is telling people lies about Val."

"It's rotten for it to happen to such a good person."

"And maybe some people *will* believe it. That's what I'm afraid of." Together they did the tidying necessary to keep the house from falling to wrack and ruin, but as she was putting the broom away her phone buzzed. "It's Val," she said, picking it up. "Hey, what's up?"

"I just got home and the catio was vandalized. Denver is *gone*!" she sobbed. "He's gone, and I can't find him and he'll be scared and it's cold! What am I going to do?"

Twenty minutes later Jaymie, Jakob, Jocie (in her PJs, but with a parka on over them, and warm boots on her feet), and Brock were at Val's home surveying the damage as she paced outside of the house, calling to Denver. Jakob flashed the beam of his flashlight over the structure they had just finished. The wire mesh had been slit and torn. Denver was gone, but the catio wasn't damaged irreparably. Jakob could easily fix it. It was unclear whether the cat had been taken or escaped after the vandalism.

"I shouldn't have left the catio open to him while I was out. What an idiot I am!" she cried. "Den-ver! Come on, baby, come home!"

"It's okay, Val," Jaymie said, joining her friend, placing one calming hand on her shoulder. "We'll find him, I promise!"

She pulled away and paced back and forth on the dew-damp lawn, cell phone in hand. "What if he's been catnapped though?"

"That's unlikely."

A neighbor's dog started barking madly. She glanced around wildly. "He's never been on his own in this neighborhood!"

"He's a smart boy. It'll be okay. Let's get looking. I want to go in the direction of that dog barking. It could be barking at Denver."

Val rounded up every flashlight she had and handed them out. The others searched Val's backyard, while Jaymie and Jocie went down the block. Val would stay close to her house calling Denver, while telling neighbors who came out of their homes what was going on.

"Mama, why would someone do that to Val?" Jocie asked as they walked down the sidewalk from pool to pool of streetlight, pausing to call the cat and search under cars and in bushes.

Jaymie shone the flashlight under a low-growing juniper bush. "Denver! Denver, come on sweetie. It's Jaymie," she cooed. She straightened and took Jocie's hand. "This was either random vandalism, or someone was mad at Val and took it out on Denver's catio."

"But why?"

"Sometimes there isn't an answer to why. People get confused and angry and they do stupid things. Let's focus on finding Denver."

They walked the streets around the block calling and calling. No Denver. When they met back up in front of Val's house the others hadn't had any luck either. "Let's go one more time down the street, Jocie," Jaymie said, after giving Val a hug of reassurance. Denver had been an indoor/outdoor cat in his youth, so he was no dummy. They set off, this time on the other side of the street, shining a light and asking every jogger and dog walker if they had seen a fat gray tabby. No luck. She stooped along a boxwood hedge as Jocie hunkered down beside her. "Let's get real quiet," she said. "I'll call, and then we'll wait for him to answer. Denver," she called softly, and waited.

There was a faint mew.

"Denver, is that you, buddy? Where are you?"

Another mew. She got down on her hands and knees, grit digging into her palms. "Jocie, hold the flashlight for me, please?" Jaymie showed her where to shine it. She peered under the hedge and saw the reflection, two bright reflective orbs. "Denver, sweetie?"

Again, the mew, unusually timid and plaintive, but it was him. A surge of relief flooded her. "Come on, darling boy. Your mom is worried." She got hold of one leg and dragged him out of the bush, then pulled him into her arms. He clawed and resisted for a moment, then settled as she hugged him close, sniffing deeply the fresh air in his fur as he trembled. "Let's get you home," she said, struggling to her feet, burdened by the heavy cat.

Jocie happily bobbed alongside Jaymie, shining the flashlight in front of them. Denver huddled in Jaymie's arms as she hustled as quickly as she could, not wanting Val to suffer a moment more anxiety than she needed to.

As they approached, Val turned and let out a screech of relief. "My baby!" she cried. Denver squirmed and reached out to Val and she took him into her arms, hugging him and burying her face in his fur. He truly was her cat now, despite how long he had lived with Jaymie before the change in homes.

Brock had, meanwhile, called the police about the vandalism and they promised to send someone out in the morning. But for now, Val's brother insisted she and Denver come home with him and spend the night. "Who knows what nut did this, and if they'll be back?"

Jakob and Jocie in the SUV, Jaymie stood by the driver's side with Val. A neighbor approached. She was an older woman with wild graying hair, robed in a housecoat and clutching a tablet in one hand. "Val, Val!" she cried, trotting across the street. "You've got to see this. I think my doorbell cam caught them, the dirty so-and-so who vandalized your place." She held the tablet so Jaymie and Val, still holding a grumbling Denver, could see it. She had a video up and hit play. It was grainy. The time stamp showed that it was six fifty-two and already almost dark.

An SUV stopped at the curb and someone got out, staggered slightly, then stomped up the walkway and banged on the door. It was a woman with wild bushy hair wearing what looked like something with a fur collar. When no one responded she stomped back to the vehicle, got something out, then returned to the house, veering around to the left side, disappearing from view. Moments later a small figure streaked past the camera's view. A dog barked, a motion detector light came on, and the woman tore back to the SUV, threw something in through the open window, got in and drove off, careening down the street.

Val, gaping, stared. Jaymie blinked and then said, "Did you see what I saw?"

Val said, "I did. Was that who I think it was?"

"Yup. Mandy de Boer."

Six

Saturday, Jakob had promised his business partner, Gus, that he'd help him move, so he would be gone all day. Jaymie called Val, and her friend said she was fine, but she sounded down. Grocery shopping at a big-box store with Jocie in tow, they talked about the food, school activities, and what gift to get her friend Noor for her birthday. Jocie was so excited about the upcoming sleepover that she did her own shopping, picking out ingredients for the treats she was planning. She was becoming, like Jaymie, a list-maker, organized and precise when it came to party planning.

Jaymie then had the usual things to do when they got home: putting it all away, walking the dog with Jocie, and making dinner. Finally, late that night, Jakob texted he was on his way home.

Sunday was family day for the Müllers.

After breakfast with his parents, Jaymie, Jakob and Jocie walked across the road, meeting Mia and her aunt and grandmother there with Bram and Luuk Brouwer to finalize the paths wending through the woods. Kim confided that they were considering moving to the house Mia and Alicia had shared. They spent most of their time there anyway, now. Kim could fix the house up for Mia's future, while renting out her own home to pay her mortgage. Her husband agreed and had offered to do much of the work himself.

"I'm happy to hear it. Mia is making a wonderful friend for Jocie," Jaymie said, watching the two girls with Luuk Brouwer. Mia was smaller than average height and wore a prosthetic leg, while Jocie was, of course, tiny. The boy towered over them both but he kindly crouched down and showed them some of the autumn delights he had discovered, dried leaves, pine fronds, acorns and toadstools. "I'm happy they both still enjoy dance class together."

The three Müllers then returned to the cabin and a slow cooker full of stew for dinner. After dinner they played a board game, enjoyed some playtime with the animals, and then it was off to bed for Jocie. Afterward, Jaymie lay back on the sofa with her head in Jakob's lap and said, "I'm working at the Emporium tomorrow so I'm going to meet Val at her place and walk over. I have to be at her place at seven thirty. Why did I agree? I don't have to start work until eight thirty!"

"Mmmm," Jakob murmured sleepily. "Then it is time for bed, my darling wife," he said. "We both have a long day tomorrow and I'm still aching from helping Gus move."

It was more like seven forty-five by the time she got to Val's and parked, so she didn't go in. Val was waiting and ready and they headed down the street, walking over to the Emporium. Jaymie yawned, wrapped her coat around her more closely and wished she'd drunk one more cup of coffee. It was too early, and a Monday.

"I took Denver back over to Brock's this morning to stay. I don't feel safe with him at my place while I'm not home," Val said as she and Jaymie walked briskly in the dim morning light.

"Have the police told you anything about their investigation into the vandalism yet?"

"Not a thing," she replied grimly. "I wish I knew for sure if it was Mandy. Though it makes no sense even if it is, I guess." She jammed her hands into her pockets as they headed around the corner and along the clapboard side toward the rear of the Emporium. Jaymie would go through to the front and open the Emporium for business at eight thirty. Val, jingling her keys in her hands, huffed, breaths of steamy air puffing out. "Today I'm going to lay low, do my job and wait for all of this to blow over."

The back of the Emporium, in the shadows of the hulking old Victorian building, was a mass of dark shapes. There was the small parking area behind the Emporium where the upstairs tenant's car was parked, the only vehicle. Then toward the building from that was a square shape Jaymie knew was the locked wooden shed where the garbage was placed, then the rickety wood steps up, damp and gleaming pale in some reflected light from a partially visible security light at the back of property on the street behind them. There was a dark huddle at the top of the shadowy steps up to the porch where the back door of the Emporium opened.

"What is that, a bag of garbage? Don't tell me Gracey Klausner lost the garbage shed key again," Val muttered.

Jaymie squinted and blinked. Something didn't look right.

"Why isn't the motion detector light coming on?" Val grumbled, waving her arms, trying to trigger it. "Probably have to get Bill to replace the darned bulb again."

Jaymie followed her friend to the steps and grasped the railing, ready to follow her friend inside, but Val screamed and tumbled backward. In confusion Jaymie thought she was falling and grabbed her friend's sleeve, but Val wrenched it away and screeched, "It's a b-body! Jaymie, get out your phone and bring up the flashlight app!"

Jaymie scrambled to do so and pointed it to the stairs. There, by the back door, was a slumped figure with bushy hair and wearing a sweater with a fur collar. With a low moan, Jaymie realized she knew exactly who it was. "Mandy, *Mandy*!" she shouted, kneeling by the figure while Val whipped her phone out and called nine one one. She babbled to the operator that there was a woman in distress at the back of the Queensville Emporium.

"She's not in distress, she's dead," Jaymie said after taking up Mandy's stiff hand and feeling how cold and lifeless it was. A piece of paper fluttered from her clenched fingers.

"No no no, she can't be dead!" Val said. A minute later, as she still spoke to the nine one one operator, sirens wailed.

Jaymie flashed the cell phone light over

Mandy. As full of horror and fear as she was, this was an awful, terrible pivotal moment. Mandy de Boer was dead on the back steps of Val Nibley's pharmacy. Of natural causes or — she prayed this was not true — murdered, people would make a connection. As the sirens grew louder she hunkered down, examining everything she could see without touching it.

There was no blood, no vomit, nothing showing a cause of death. No obvious wound, no knife, no blunt instrument. Poor Mandy huddled almost in an upright fetal position, as if she had sat down, drawn her knees up, fallen asleep, and slumped over. Her face was pale, drained of life, the bruising still showing around her face and even down to her mouth. Blood from bruises sinks, Jaymie remembered from a black eye Becca once had that turned into a purplish cheek.

She flashed the light on the paper that had been in Mandy's grasp. It was an article torn from the *Howler* on the power of social media in today's society. Jaymie frowned and stood, looking down at Mandy. Tears clouded her vision and she felt sick, her stomach doing an uncomfortable flip-flop. Recognizing she was in shock, shivering and beginning to feel nauseous, she turned away from Mandy and stared at Val, who paced steps away, still on the phone.

Was Mandy coming to try to make amends with Val? Or was she coming to do her more damage? And why the *Howler* article in her hand?

The police and the paramedics arrived at the same time, setting the place ablaze with light and raucous with sound. Val was hustled away and placed into a cruiser parked in front of the Emporium. Jaymie was sat in a separate one by Bernie, who offered a sympathetic smile and pat on the arm. Neighbors, including the new upstairs tenant, Taylor Bellwood, wandered out blinking and sleepy, to see what was going on. They gathered in clusters along the road: the dog walkers, the housecoat wearers, the early-morning coffee drinkers, mugs in hand. A few took surreptitious pictures with their cell phones while others glared at them disapprovingly.

The police had asked for and were given her cell phone, so Jaymie couldn't even call Jakob. She had left before Jocie and Jakob that morning, and both, by now, would be off on their day's tasks. The scene was a hive of activity, uniformed officers bustling about, conferring, nodding with serious expressions, heading away on secret tasks.

Vestry arrived, her usual cool, collected self in slacks and suit jacket, bulk under one side showing where she carried her gun. She was briefed by an on-scene officer Jaymie didn't recognize. She nodded, glanced at the cruisers where Jaymie and Val sat, then retreated around the back of the Emporium.

Jaymie turned her thoughts inward to avoid the uncomfortable fact that she was being stared at by the gathered watchers. Mandy looked like she had crouched down on the stairs and died. With the weirdness of her behavior in the last week it was possible there was something physically wrong that had taken its toll. Or perhaps the car accident had resulted in internal injuries that, because she refused medical care, had remained undiagnosed.

Her heart thudded as she looked toward the cruiser that held Val. This was awful, truly terrible. Her friend must be so upset and frightened, to have this happen behind her pharmacy and for them to find the body. Val spotted her and gave a mournful wave. Jaymie waved back. It was going to be a long morning.

Hours later Jaymie emerged, dazed, from the small questioning room at the police department to discover that Becca had been invited in to answer questions because of her discussion with Mandy at the auction on Thursday evening, though her interview was brief and routine, she murmured to her sister. Jaymie, Val and Becca were leaving the police station as Candy Vasiliev was arriving, supported on the arm of a good-looking middle-aged man. Her face was red, her eyes swollen, and she was slumped, stumbling and weeping. He appeared distraught but restrained, emotion showing only in his twisted grimace. It was the man who was in photos with Mandy vacationing in Vail and Belize. Her boyfriend? Candy spotted their little group and glared at Val then turned away, sagging against the man.

"Candy, I'm so sorry about your sister." Val started toward her, but a police officer guided the near-hysterical woman away. Watching her, Val said, "She looks half out of her mind. I wish . . ." She didn't finish her sentence.

They emerged from the police headquarters into a cloudy, ominous October day, wind gusting leaves across the parking lot. Becca had driven there so she guided them to her parked car and opened the driver's side. "Get in," she said tersely, glancing over her shoulder at the police station.

Jaymie took the passenger seat as Val

climbed in the back, closing her eyes. She muttered that she had been allowed to call Helen Pham to fill in at the pharmacy, though it opened late as the police had a look through first. Jaymie volunteered that she called Gracey Klausner, who found a replacement for her. She flicked a worried glance back to Val, who huddled in misery, shivering. Becca turned on the car heater.

Jaymie thought about all she had been asked, first about her activities in the last twelve hours. She had given them a detailed timetable, but she knew Val had been alone at home for the evening and night. If Mandy de Boer's death was not natural, the lack of an alibi could leave Valetta a suspect in the eyes of the police. If only she had stayed with Brock! Not that Val had anything to worry about, but it did complicate matters.

"Let's go to my place and have a coffee and talk this over," Jaymie said. "Or wait . . . I forgot. My car is at Val's place."

"Let's go to my place and have tea instead. I'd like to get Denver first, though, and then I want to be home," Val said, rousing herself from her slump. "I guess I don't have to worry now about Mandy terrorizing him," she added grimly.

A half hour later they settled in at Val's. "Vestry had Bernie with her, taking notes,"

Val said.

"Your interview was taped, wasn't it?" Jaymie asked.

"Sure."

"You didn't wait for your lawyer?"

"I didn't *do* anything. I don't need a lawyer," Val said firmly, pushing her glasses up on her nose. "And I know that's what every unfortunate person in true crime books say, but it doesn't make it any less valid in my case. Given her recent erratic behavior, Mandy likely died from undiagnosed head trauma, or some other weird thing the medical examiner will determine." She gave Jaymie a shrewd glare. "You were with me when we found Mandy. Did *you* retain a lawyer?"

"No, but I . . ." Jaymie shut her mouth. To go on would be to insinuate that Val was the one who needed a lawyer because she would be the one under suspicion. Val eyed her with a serious expression; she knew what Jaymie wasn't saying.

"There is no point in speculation until we know if Mandy's death was of natural causes or not," Becca said.

For once, Jaymie agreed with her sister. "Who was that man who came in with Candy?"

"Randall Kallis," Val said. She knew many

people from her work and her volunteerism. "He's a partner at Manor Homes."

The partner, Jaymie thought. "He's a co-owner, right?" She pondered what her editor had told her about Mandy's reputed affair with a coworker and the man's advancement after Chad Manor's death.

"I guess that's what it means."

"Did he have a relationship with Mandy?"

"I wouldn't know," Val said. Denver jumped on the sofa and lay beside her, half on her lap and half off. She stroked his head absently. "I only know he became a partner at some point after Chad died."

They chatted for a while longer, but Val was distracted and upset. She was taking a leave of absence from the pharmacy while she was a person of interest. She'd make the calls and find replacements for at least the next week. Helen might be able to work the whole time, but she had another pharmacist who could fill in, too.

"Did the police actually call you a person of interest?" Jaymie asked, startled by the step that she thought was unnecessary.

Val shook her head. "After my public confrontation with Mandy I want no questions lingering. Customers of the pharmacy have a right to feel safe."

Becca stood, shaking the wrinkles out of

her clothes. "You two have lunch. I'm going over to the antique store and check in. Georgina is off on a toot, so Kevin is looking after everything." She reached out and hugged Val, squeezing her tight. "We'll get through this, Val. Together. Call me later."

When Becca had left, Jaymie stared at Val for a long minute, while her friend fretted at her bottom lip. "Okay, are you going to tell me what's wrong, or do I have to drag it out of you?"

Val closed her eyes and rocked back, her hand tightening on Denver. The cat grumbled. She loosened her grip and met Jaymie's gaze. "I *am* a person of interest, because I gave them my phone."

"Didn't you get yours back? I did."

"They kept mine."

"Why?"

"There are text messages on it between me and Mandy, and a ten-minute-long phone call we had."

"Wait, what? When was this from?"

"Last night."

SEVEN

Jaymie stared at Val, trying to wrap her mind around what she was saying. "You and Mandy texted back and forth last night?"

She nodded.

"And spoke on the phone?"

"For ten minutes or so. At least. Maybe more. And that's not counting the times I hung up on her."

"Why? When? What —"

Val held up one hand. "Okay, Miss Reporter, let me explain."

"This calls for another pot of tea." As she put on the kettle she texted Jakob. She was supposed to pick up Jocie today, but Val needed her. She briefly explained her shocking day, ending with *I'm fine. love you. I'll explain later.* He texted back immediately with shock and concern. She replied *I'm fine* again and added a hug emoji with a string of hearts.

She carried the tea tray into the living

room. Val had her head back and her eyes closed. Understanding her friend's deep weariness, she fixed both their mugs and let her rest.

After a few moments Val said, "I got a text from Mandy late yesterday."

"What time?"

"Around dinner."

"What did it say?"

"She asked me to meet her. She had something to ask me."

"What did you do?"

"I didn't know what to think. She's been odd lately. I thought maybe she had texted the wrong person and ignored it."

Jaymie nodded. "I mean, where did she even get your cell number? I'd do the same. Go on."

She texted again and again until finally Val texted back saying she wouldn't meet her unless Mandy told her what she wanted. "She said she wanted to talk."

"What time was that?"

"Later. Maybe nine or so."

"What did you say?"

"I told her that she had endangered my professional reputation, which means *everything* to me. Given what had gone down, I didn't trust her. She said she couldn't tell me by text. She had to meet me in person."

"But you didn't meet with her."

Val shook her head. She lifted her glasses and swiped at pooling tears with a tissue. "I was torn; I was curious, I'll admit. And now I wonder, what if I could have helped her?" She sniffed and blew her nose. "If her death was from natural causes maybe I could have helped. I've seen enough in my professional life that I may have spotted something wrong and been able to get her to a doctor." She covered her face with both hands.

This was a Val Jaymie had never seen, distraught and teary. She sat down by her and put one arm around her shoulders. "Val, you mustn't blame yourself."

"I feel guilty," she cried, tossing the tissue onto the coffee table. "I should have met her. I should have talked to her."

"What about the phone call. What was said?"

Val blinked and pushed her glasses up on her nose. She took a fresh tissue and blotted the last of the tears and sniffed. "I was out late last night walking and thinking when my phone rang. It was Mandy. I thought, maybe I should hear her out. Maybe I'll hear something in her voice and know whether she's sincere or trying to trap me. I answered."

"And?"

"She sounded upset. She wanted to come by my house." She paused and looked away. "I said no." Guilt thickened her voice.

"Val, the woman was out to destroy you, as far as any of us could tell," Jaymie said, leaning toward her friend, speaking with urgency. "I would have said no, too."

"But if I had let her come to my house —"

"No! Stop." She took Val's hand and shook it with each emphasis. "Of *course* you couldn't meet her."

Val blinked and shook her head. "Mandy is dead, and she died behind my pharmacy. If I'd let her come to my house it would have been different."

"Maybe. Maybe not." Jaymie frowned. "Why *was* she behind the pharmacy?"

Val looked down at Denver and stroked his fur. "She went there to meet me."

"What? You didn't . . . I mean —"

"No, I didn't go. She wanted me to. She was troubled about something, but she understood why I had doubts."

"How did she sound?"

Val frowned. "Not good. She was crying and almost incoherent. I thought she was blotto, and I didn't want to get caught in one of those conversations with a drunk. She said if I didn't want her to come to my

95

house she'd go to the pharmacy and wait half an hour. If I met her, we'd talk, if I didn't, she'd go home." She picked a piece of fluff from Denver's neck. "I considered going, but . . ." She trailed off and shook her head. She pushed her glasses up and swiped at her eyes under them.

"But you didn't," Jaymie said, then her eyes widened. "The police don't know that, do they? That she was going there to meet you?"

"I told them the truth."

"Val!"

"What else was I supposed to do? What would *you* do?"

Grudgingly, Jaymie said, "The same."

"They needed the information. It gave them a time window for when she was there."

"*If* she went when she said she did." It took real courage to tell the whole truth, but at what cost? Who else knew Mandy was going to go to the pharmacy? Jaymie wondered. "What time did you speak to Mandy?"

"It was about ten forty-five or so. I don't have my phone now, so I can't verify the exact time I spoke to her."

Jaymie nodded, thinking hard. "And she said she'd stay there for half an hour."

"She said to give her a few minutes to get over there, but then she'd wait for me. I said I wasn't going to go, but she insisted I think about it. She'd wait half an hour."

"She'd wait for you for half an hour. That's *exactly* what she said."

"Half an hour from whenever she got there. I guess it would take fifteen minutes for her to go out, get her car and drive over to the pharmacy."

"If she went right away, after talking to you, and if she was going from her home in . . . where, Wolverhampton? So, say eleven to eleven thirty she'd be there. What do you think she wanted to talk to you about?"

"I don't know. She was worried about something or someone. She wasn't being very clear and wouldn't say more. I tried to get her to tell me, but she said she had to have the conversation in person."

"Maybe about the things she said, why she said them?"

Val shrugged.

"And she was alone?" Jaymie asked.

"I think so, but how would I know?"

"True." Jaymie thought it over. "Where was she when she called you? Was she home?"

"I don't know."

"Was there noise in the background? Think!"

Val frowned and hesitated. "There *was* noise in the background . . . muffled voices. And I think I heard glasses clinking?"

"A restaurant or bar? You said she sounded drunk."

"I don't know. Jaymie, how do I prove I *didn't* go to the pharmacy? All anyone knows for sure is that I spoke to her for ten minutes while I was out walking. I turned my phone off and went home."

Jaymie swallowed hard. "You shut your phone off."

Val gazed at her blankly, catching something in Jaymie's tone. Then her eyes widened. "Shutting down the GPS location on my phone. *Dope!*" She smacked her forehead. "*So* dumb!" It jarred Denver who, in a huff, jumped down and retreated to his room. "If only I'd left it on. But it kept pinging. I turned it on this morning and there was a whole flurry of texts, but of course that was at six, when I first got up."

"Texts from Mandy? What did they say?"

"I didn't read them all. More of the same, I suppose. I was feeling put upon and angry, like there was nothing she could say to me to make up for trying to ruin my career." She hung her head and mumbled, "I should have read them, I guess, but I put it out of my mind and got ready for work. Not that it would have helped. The whole time she was there, dead!" She looked up. "The police have to be thinking, who's to say I didn't turn my phone off, then walk over to the pharmacy, kill her, and skip home?"

"*If* she was murdered."

"*If* she was murdered," Val agreed.

"Which she wasn't."

Val was silent.

"You think she was? Why?"

"Why was she murdered, or why do I think that?"

"Either. Both, I guess."

"Murder or natural causes are not exactly the only options."

Jaymie understood immediately what she meant. Given Mandy's wildly odd behavior lately, it was possible she had taken her own life. Not likely, but barely possible.

Val went on. "I spoke to Ti yesterday about Mandy. She couldn't talk long, she had some kind of meeting to go to at the Queensville Inn."

"Meeting?"

"With Manor Homes executives."

"Would that have included Mandy?"

"Oh, you know, it likely did. That's probably where she was when we spoke. Ti agreed there was something wrong with her friend, but not in a way of deathly ill or anything. She said she was 'loopy.' "

"Would she have spoken to her at that meeting?"

"I don't know. I'm sure the police will ask her."

"Will they?"

"Well, sure," Val said, but doubt crept into her tone. "Won't they?"

"I don't like to take things for granted. You're friends with Ti. Why don't you ask her if Mandy was at the meeting last night, and if so, how she was? And how late it ran. I mean, maybe that would confirm that she called you from there."

"Won't it seem ghoulish to approach her now?"

"Of course not! I'm not saying to call and demand to know if Mandy was still loopy last night. Ti was a friend of hers, and she's a friend of yours. She'll be grieving. Commiserate. Sympathize. And *then* find out what happened at the meeting."

"You're good at this, Jaymie. I don't know if I can do it."

"I didn't used to be good at this. You know me. I was always shy. Getting nosier was self-preservation." Her friend shook her head. "Val, you're good with people."

"Not in this case. This is intrusive. I wouldn't be able to ask her the hard questions."

"Yes, you *can.* Do you want me to go with you?"

"Would you?"

"Where can we find her?"

"I don't know whether she'll be at home or at the food bank headquarters."

"Her home is the first place to start. Let's go."

"Now?"

"Yes, *now,*" Jaymie said firmly. She was not going to let Val wallow. This was too important.

They freshened up, then took separate cars, as Jaymie had to run home and check on Hoppy. Ti lived in one of the older Manor Homes developments in Wolverhampton. Her house was a bungalow, garage to the right, a breezeway separating the garage and house. Val, who had led the way, pulled into the wide drive and got out of the car. She waited for Jaymie, who parked behind her, and the two approached the front door together. There was no car in the drive, but the garage door was closed. Leaves scuttered up the drive, rattling on the pavement, gathering in piles along the low stone wall that lined the drive.

However, as they approached, the front door opened, a woman came out, fished keys out of her huge purse and hustled down the steps. She stopped when she caught sight of them. She was about the same age as Val but shorter, with black shoulder-length hair shot with silver. "Val," she said slowly. She jingled her keys in one hand. "What are you doing here?"

"Oh, Ti, I know how close you are with Mandy, and I wanted to —"

"I'm on my way to the police station. Is it true?" she asked, her dark eyes searching Val's face, flicking around the visual triangle, right eye, left eye, mouth, then back. "She's dead? And you found her?"

Val nodded, her lip trembling.

"I'm Jaymie Leighton Müller," Jaymie said, stepping forward. "I work at the Emporium sometimes. I was walking to work with Val and was with her when we found your friend."

Ti nodded, but she hardly glanced Jaymie's way. She looked uncertain.

Val stammered, "I w-wanted to express . . . I wanted to say . . . I'm sorry, Ti."

"Sorry for what?"

"For what happened to Mandy."

This was awkward and not going well. Jaymie glanced at her friend. Val, normally confident and calm, Jaymie's rock in life, had been shattered by the day's events.

Ti shifted and stepped back, clicking her garage door opener. The door groaned to life and started to rise. "Look, I have to go. I have an appointment with a detective and —" She glanced at the phone in her other hand. "I'm already late. I was detained. I had to call Trina."

"Trina?" Jaymie said.

Ti glanced her way, then returned her gaze to Val. "Trina is Mandy's daughter. Poor kid is in England studying architecture. She's on her way home now. Tough to hear your mom is dead by phone."

"I can't even imagine. Ti, can we talk later?" Val said, regaining her customary composure.

"Sure." She entered the garage and got in her car as Jaymie and Val headed toward their vehicles. Ti passed them, backing down the drive and waving as she went.

"That didn't go as expected," Jaymie said, glancing at her friend.

"What in life does? It's okay." She squared her shoulders, seeming more herself again. "I'll sort it out with her."

With Val having regained her equilibrium, Jaymie was confident that she could leave her alone. They hugged and parted. Jaymie drove home in a contemplative mood. Once again she was in the middle of an investigation, but this time it wasn't even clear how the victim had died. It left her feeling uneasy.

EIGHT

Was there anything about Mandy's lonely death that could reveal what happened in the minutes or hours before she died on the back step of the pharmacy? Jaymie, sitting on the sofa in the cabin living room with Hoppy at her side and Lilibet napping, laid her head back and closed her eyes.

Mandy had been worried and wanted to ask or tell Val something. She died where she had arranged to meet Val. She was only supposed to be there a half hour, so that gave an approximate time of death. Maybe she huddled there and died of natural causes, or someone accompanied or followed her and killed her. There was no blood. There was no sign of blunt force trauma, no bruising or lacerations. Mandy had looked peaceful, like she sat down and fell asleep.

Maybe it *was* natural causes. The accident Mandy had may have led to internal injuries, like a slow bleed. The autopsy would reveal that.

What else was possible? Poison? Were there poisons that caused behavioral changes and then killed the victim? And who would be close enough to poison Mandy? That possibility raised more questions than it answered.

Given the woman's weird behavior of late, they'd surely test for drugs. If it *was* drugs causing her behavior, were they drugs she took on purpose? Prescription clashes? Were there drugs that could have changed her behavior *and* lead to death?

So many questions.

She gently moved Hoppy, got her trusty notebook, and wrote down everything she was thinking. It was time for a phone call. "Mrs. Stubbs, it's me, Jaymie." The elderly woman, one of her closest friends, was delighted to hear from her — after she adjusted her hearing aid — and agreed Jaymie could come see her the next morning bright and early for tea.

"I'll be looking for you by ten a.m. I assume you'll want to get to the bottom of this new murder."

"Murder?" Jaymie gasped.

"Don't we have to assume Mandy de Boer's death is murder until we know

106

otherwise?"

Jaymie grimaced. Mrs. Stubbs was right. That's what the police would be doing, certainly. "I was hoping for everyone's sake that it was death by natural causes, though I don't think that would make Val feel any better."

"You and Valetta found the poor girl, I understand?"

"We did."

"And Valetta had a run-in with her before her death?"

"Some days before, yes."

"Now don't you worry about this. No one with a halfwit's IQ would think Valetta Nibley would have anything to do with murder."

"The police may not think Val did it, but the gossip mill may decide otherwise."

"She'll be all right. I still say no one important will believe Val did it."

"I'd still rather have it solved, if it's murder. You would have known the de Boer sisters, right?" From her time as a volunteer working in the school library. "What was your opinion of them? Which was smarter, do you think?"

There was silence for a moment. "Both girls were clever, in different ways and different subjects."

"Who was more popular?"

"Mandy. She had an instinct for what people needed to hear."

"I don't trust people who tell you what they think you want to hear."

She hesitated, the sound of her breathing gustily the only indication she was still on the line. "Am I being fair to her? Let me think about it. It was a long time ago, dear."

"Okay. Can I ask a favor? Before tomorrow can you find out about the meeting last night at the Queensville Inn in the dining room?"

"You mean between Ti Pham, from the food bank, and the Manor Homes group?"

Jaymie smiled. Of *course* Mrs. Stubbs would know about it. "Was Mandy there?"

"She was."

"Do you know how long she was there and who she spoke with?"

"I'll tell you all tomorrow."

There would be no cajoling her to speak sooner. "I'll see you in the morning, then." Hoppy barked. "And I'll bring your friend. He knows who I'm talking to." The little dog yipped again. Jaymie hung up as Hoppy waggled his whole body. "Yes, we'll go and see Mrs. Stubbs tomorrow morning. But right now we're going to pick up Jocie."

Late that night Jaymie lay in Jakob's arms.

108

Normal routine had, until then, kept her grief at bay, but once the horrendous day's necessary strength had drained, sorrow swept over her for the life lost that morning. He knew she didn't need words. He held her and stroked her hair, murmuring those soothing nonsense words that whispered through her down to her core.

Finally, the tears ebbed. She blew her nose and sat up. He sat up too, and regarded her calmly, his beautiful brown eyes holding all the love and empathy he had conveyed to her with his whispered words.

"What a lonely way to die," she said, a sob catching in her throat. "Alone, in the cold, behind a pharmacy." She blew her nose again.

"It shouldn't happen to anyone. It sounds like she has had a rough time lately."

She turned and brought her knees up to sit cross-legged on their cozy bed. The slanted walls of their upstairs bedroom, steps from Jocie's, made the space feel warm and safe, everything poor Mandy had lacked in the last hour of her life. She pulled the pine tree quilt up over her knees and traced one design with her finger. "What happened, Jakob? Why did Mandy go crazy in her last days?"

"I'm sure it will all come out in the days

to come."

"I'm worried for Val. She's scared and she's lost faith. You know, she has always been the strong one for everyone around her. She went away to school, graduated top of her class, apprenticed as long as she needed to, and even though she could have lived anywhere, *worked* anywhere, she came back to Queensville. Home."

"Valetta is one of the best people I've ever met," he said softly. "I'd trust her with my life. With your life. Even with Jocie's."

"I'm worried that with it happening right behind the pharmacy, and after Val had those run-ins in public, people will think she did something."

"Anyone who knows her won't."

"I'm not so sure about that," she said darkly.

"I know you're going to investigate," Jakob said gently, wrapping one arm around Jaymie's waist and pulling her down to him. "Be careful, as you always try to be. Call on me if you need me. I will drop anything anytime to help you. I hope you know that." She stretched and he covered her with his heavy body, kissing her with a lingering sweetness that had her forgetting her own name for a moment.

"I do know, and I'll be careful," she

whispered against his lips. "And I'll call you if I need you." She smiled against his mouth. "Jakob?"

"Mhmm."

"I need you. Right now."

NINE

Tuesday morning, Jaymie and Jakob shared a smile, the memory of love in the dark of night sweet in both of their minds. Jocie looked up at them both, her gaze going from one to the other. She squinted her eyes. "I heard something last night."

"Oh? What did you hear?" Jakob said, stifling a laugh.

"I heard a thump. And Mom laughed."

"We had a tickle fight and I fell out of bed," Jaymie said with a prim smile. Jakob snorted in laughter and went back to scrolling through messages on his phone. She finished packing Jocie's lunch bag. One day soon she would have a frank chat with Jocie about adult love, but not right before school on a hurried morning. Choose your moments for important conversations, her mother-in-law had urged her. "Gather your things and get going. Dad's driving you this morning. I have things to do, starting with tea with Mrs. Stubbs. Any messages?"

Jocie's eyes were still narrowed, but she said, "It's Noor's birthday in a couple of weeks."

"You may have mentioned it." Many times.

"She's going to have a tea party at the inn and I said I'd have Mrs. Stubbs come to our table to talk to us."

"You'd like Mrs. Stubbs to come talk to your friends?"

Jocie nodded.

"Why, honey?" Jakob asked, setting his phone aside.

"I told Noor that Mrs. Stubbs was cool and lives at the inn, and Noor asked would she come talk to us, and I said I'd see."

"What would she talk to you about?" Jaymie asked, glancing at Jakob, who looked as puzzled as she was.

"Did you know she had her own car way back? She said it was a Dodge La Femme. Weird name, huh? It was pink, with pink upholstery. She called it Pinky Lee."

"That can't be true," Jaymie said, staring at Jocie. "Honey, I think she was teasing. Mrs. Stubbs would never . . . I mean, can you picture her driving a pink car with pink upholstery? And why would she call it Pinky Lee? I don't get it."

"Nu-uh, she wasn't teasing. She said she hated the car, so she named it after some kid's show she hated too. She said it was the last time she chose . . ." Jocie screwed up her face. "What did she say? It was . . . oh, yeah . . . it was the last time she chose style over substance. She was telling me friends should be substance, not style. Whatever that means."

"She meant you should choose your friends because of their real worth, not how pretty they are, or how rich, or what their house is like, or what they can give you."

She nodded. "Okay. She said that she never again let a salesperson talk her into buying something that was wrong for her."

Jaymie smiled; her reliable friend. Sometimes cranky, she was often right about things she had learned in her long life. "I will talk to Mrs. Stubbs this morning and see if she will be a guest at Noor's party." She kissed Jocie especially hard and held her close.

Jaymie parked behind the Queensville Inn and leashed Hoppy, who eagerly bounced about in the front seat. "You know where we are, don't you, buddy? We're going to see Mrs. Stubbs!" She was one of his favorite people, a source of cookies and a lap that was always a lap. Jaymie got out, helped Hoppy down, slung her purse over her shoulder and started through the parking lot, crunching brittle brown leaves. She noticed, parked in a spot near the back, a familiar car and swerved, approaching and tapping on the glass.

Detective Vestry looked up from her laptop and nodded, then lowered the glass. "Jaymie, what are you doing here?"

"I'm visiting Mrs. Stubbs. What are *you* doing here?"

"Working. Good to see you. I wanted to talk off the record. I have something important to say that I should not be saying to you, and that I don't want spread about." The solemn woman stared at Jaymie with a stern though not unfriendly gaze. "I know you, Jaymie. I know how you feel about Val. This is what is off the record: I do *not* believe Valetta Nibley murdered Mandy de Boer, despite her having motive, means and opportunity."

"So, you're saying Mandy de Boer was murdered?"

"I'm saying nothing of the kind. Listen carefully. Whatever we believe, we know there were interactions between the two that were less than friendly. We must take that into consideration and investigate if this turns out to be a homicide. We don't base investigations on feelings and intuition, we base them on facts."

"Val has told me everything, Detective. I know she was out walking, and that she spoke with Mandy on the phone, and what they texted and spoke of, as far as Val remembers because you still have her phone."

"Look, I know you're going to be uncomfortable with this, but we'll be looking into your friend's movements." Jaymie was about to answer, but Vestry held up one hand. "If it's murder, every second we are *seen* to be investigating Val Nibley is a second the real killer gets more comfortable, lets down their guard. We may be interviewing the real killer as we investigate Val. It's not like we're ignoring leads or failing to look into other aspects of Ms. de Boer's life. Eventually — *if* it's murder — the killer will slip up and say something, contradict publicly known facts, reveal something they shouldn't know. So don't interfere."

Jaymie bristled. "I would never interfere."

Vestry rolled her eyes and smiled grimly. "You say that now, but at some point you'll be in it up to your eyeballs and —"

"And what?"

"I'm going to leave it there. Say hi to Mrs.

Stubbs for me. At least you're safe talking to her."

They parted ways. Hoppy wobbled over to a grassy spot to piddle, then led Jaymie to the side door. She picked him up and walked through toward the reservation desk. Edith bustled out from behind the registration desk to make a fuss over Hoppy, who she adored. Jaymie then proceeded down the hall in the newer section to Mrs. Stubbs's room, with Edith's promise of pastries from the kitchen wafting down the hall after her.

She entered and greeted her old friend, who had a mystery novel in her hand but set it aside when Jaymie and Hoppy entered. They exchanged hugs, then Jaymie made tea at the kitchenette tucked away in a nook in the corner of the spacious suite. She told Mrs. Stubbs about Noor's birthday tea party and Jocie's invitation to Mrs. Stubbs. She asked her about the car story.

"I will gladly attend," Mrs. Stubbs said, her creaky voice crackling. She cleared her throat and took a sip of water. "And despite your sly insinuation that I fibbed, every word I told your daughter is true. I had that awful car, Pinky Lee, and —"

"Is Pinky Lee a real person?"

"He *was* a real person." She explained

that Pinky Lee was a TV personality in the fifties who had a children's show. His antics and manic personality irritated her.

"Sorta like Pee-wee Herman?"

"Oh, that fellow! I disliked him too and suspect he stole the character from Pinky Lee."

"So that line from the movie Grease, *'to you from me, Pinky Lee,'* was a real reference!"

"It was. Any baby boomer likely recognized it, or at least had a vague notion that Pinky Lee was a real person."

Jaymie told Mrs. Stubbs all about the last few days, Val's trouble with Mandy. "I'm stumped by Mandy's behavior. When I saw her at the auction she seemed angry. Confused. But more scared than anything. I've found a body or two in my time but this one got to me. Mandy died cold and alone." She dashed tears away from her eyes, shivered, then jumped up and retrieved the teapot and poured for both of them. Edith bustled in without knocking, a platter of pastries in one hand. Mrs. Stubbs stiffly thanked her. The woman paused, looking between the two of them, then left.

Jaymie stared at the door. "What was that about, Mrs. S.?"

She flapped one arthritic hand. "Oh, nothing." She sighed. "Edith is a nice woman, and she's good to me and Lyle. And she tries hard."

"But . . . ?"

"But I can't chatter at her like she'd like. I think she wanted to be invited to have tea with us. She's . . ." She shrugged.

"Lonely?"

Mrs. Stubbs nodded, and the strangest thing happened — a faint bloom of pink appeared on her weathered cheek. "I've been shabby toward her. She brings out the worst in me, I don't know why. I'm old enough to know better, but the closer she tries to get to me, the more I pull away." She paused, then burst out with, "Oh, I may as well admit it. I *do* know why! She's inane. Her inconsequential chatter is infuriating. And she's clingy. I can't abide clingy people!"

Jaymie smiled. It was nice to see her wise friend flustered. It rarely happened. "I think, for once, I can give *you* advice. I can't help you with the clingy part, but I do have a way of dealing with that kind of talker. It's soothing if you look at it the right way. People like Edith don't expect a lot, and that's nice. They get brushed away so often that to have someone listen is a treat. Listen, nod, smile, and let the sound wash over you like waves."

"I don't have to think about what she's saying?"

"Respond occasionally, but you don't have to say anything earth-shattering. A *how interesting* or *imagine that* every once in a while is enough. Consider it white noise. People pay for machines that do what Edith does for free." She paused and stole a glance at her friend.

"What are you thinking? Say it."

"If you don't mind me saying, you have ready excuses for not engaging, and yet being pleasant. If she asks if you heard her and you don't feel like engaging, say, *oh, I must have dozed off, dear* or *No, I couldn't hear you* or *I think I'm tired now, maybe I'll take a nap.* Nobody will fault you for it. In fact, they'll get a bonus hit of good feeling for being compassionate toward you."

"Because I'm old?" Mrs. Stubbs's tone was acerbic, but her mouth twitched in a smile.

"Grandma Leighton is the one who told me that secret."

Grudgingly she smiled. "I suppose if it's good enough for Lucy, maybe I'll try the doddering old lady act."

"*She* said it's about embracing the perks

120

of every age."

"Your grandmother is a wise woman."

They finished their treats and discussed the murder. Talking with Mrs. Stubbs allowed Jaymie to organize her thoughts. She related the details of the last few days.

"What I don't understand," Mrs. Stubbs said, "is why, when she knew Val was not working, and she drove past Val's home and saw you both there, she *still* accused Val of poisoning her. She picked up the prescription; she knew Valetta had nothing to do with receiving it, dispensing it, labeling it, handing it over. It's irrational."

"I don't get it either."

"Something or someone had to have started her thinking that."

"Maybe Candy had something to do with it, since she was the one closest to her."

"Do you *know* her sister had that kind of influence over her?"

"I don't know it for a fact." She then swore Mrs. Stubbs to secrecy and revealed what she had learned about the events of Sunday night, that Mandy had called Val begging to talk to her, Val's refusal and them finding Mandy's body together Monday morning.

"So, do you usually walk over with her on days you work?"

"Not generally."

Mrs. Stubbs, after ruminating for a few moments, said, "Anyone would think she'd be alone, going in the back. If the killer set Mandy up to die — I suppose we're speaking of some kind of poison or fatal ingestion of narcotics or other drugs — and influenced her to go to the back of the pharmacy, Val was intended to find the body alone."

"Val goes in an hour early to sort and fill prescriptions before she opens. I suppose it's general knowledge she goes in the back door."

"Whomever it was must have known Mandy was going over to talk to Val Sunday evening, then. Either she told someone, or she was overheard making the plan."

"Or it didn't matter where she died. Maybe her being behind the pharmacy was coincidental."

"If so, whomever killed her is rubbing their hands with glee today. The police will focus on Val's public run-in with Mandy."

"I suppose. At first Mandy wanted to come over to her place. Val said no way, understandably, so Mandy then told her she'd wait for her behind the pharmacy for a half hour."

"Everyone knows Valetta's work schedule.

She works from Monday to Friday, and every other Saturday."

"How do you know?"

"She calls me every Friday morning to say my filled dosette will be delivered Friday afternoon. Sometimes she even brings it over herself, and we have a nice visit."

"Then if we conjecture someone convinced Mandy to meet Val behind the pharmacy, Val was intended to find Mandy dead the next morning. She was *meant* to look guilty."

"It seems far-fetched, I suppose."

That scenario would require a twisted mind in a person with a lot of control over Mandy. And yet . . . "Someone was feeding her lies, telling her Val was trying to poison her, or some ridiculous tale. Who would it be? That has to be her sister, doesn't it? How well do you remember them?"

"Once I set my mind to it, quite well. They're a year or so apart, and similar in looks, or at least they were."

"Who's older?"

"Candy is the older sister. She was in a grade above Valetta and Rebecca. I told you yesterday that both girls were smart, and that's true, but in different ways. Mandy was smart but lazy. Candy was not quite as smart, but she was clever, good at things.

Both girls were popular, Mandy more than Candy." She clasped her arthritic hands together, surreptitiously rubbing the swollen joints. "Their mother was very nice. She died too young, poor thing. Candy was in her last year of high school, if I remember right, and Mandy was one year behind her."

"Were the sisters close?"

"I suppose. But there was tension sometimes. I got the idea their mother favored the older girl, Candy. Caused some trouble."

"What kind of trouble?"

"They would feud and be mortal enemies for a while, both girls would gossip and degrade the other to their little cliques of friends, there would be a huge blowout, and the next day they would be best of friends again. And then the cycle would continue."

Time to get down to what she really wanted to know. "About the meeting —"

"The food bank meeting? Let me tell you what I know. Chef was making pot roast so Dee and Johnny came for dinner. Dee never could cook a pot roast to save her life and Johnny loves it, so whenever it's on the menu I call them. We were in the dining room early, about five thirty. I saw the Manor Homes people and the girl from the food bank come in. At the same time there was a Dickens Days organization meeting."

Dickens Days was the annual winter and Christmas season festival that spanned all of December in Queensville.

"Everyone on the planning committee was there: Imogene Frump, Tree Bellwood, Mabel Bloomsbury, Cynthia Turbridge, Jewel Dandridge and Bill Waterman. Bonnie Smith was there too. She announced at the meeting that it will be her last year. She's selling the Knit Knack Shack and moving to Florida." Mrs. Stubbs, one eyebrow arched, sat back.

"Really! That's big news." The Knit Knack Shack, a yarn store along the main street, was a venerable Queensville institution, the oldest shop other than the Emporium, having been opened in the late sixties by Bonnie's mother. "Is she selling the business as well as the building? Will it stay a yarn shop?"

"I don't know, but I do know that she was furious when she arrived late."

"Furious? Bonnie Smith?" That seemed impossible. She was a vivacious great-grandmother who soothed her worries with perpetual knitting, her needles clicking at every gathering, even a dinner meeting. "What was she angry about?"

"Someone hit her car. And guess who it was?"

"I can't guess."

"Mandy de Boer. Bonnie confronted her right there in the dining room. Mandy denied it."

TEN

"Wait, What?"

"Bonnie confronted Mandy, who was with the Manor Homes folks. She stomped over to their table and lit into her, saying — loudly, I might add — that Mandy had been swerving through town and hit her car. You know how fussy Bonnie is about her vehicle."

A vintage Caddy in impeccable condition. "What did Mandy say?"

"She looked befuddled but —"

"Befuddled as in drunk?"

"I don't think so."

"Was she drinking?"

"She was guzzling liquid from a plastic bottle, but I assume you're asking if she imbibed alcohol, and that I cannot tell you. She seemed woozier as the evening went on, but I went back to my room about eight."

"Who was tending bar?"

"I didn't notice but Tree Bellwood's granddaughter Taylor was waiting tables. Matter of fact, she waited on us *and* on Ti Pham and the Manor Homes folks, *and* the Dickens Days committee table. The larger tables are along the far wall, as you know, and Johnny, Dee and I were tucked into the small table in the corner, nearest the window. If you talk to Taylor, she can give you far more information than I can."

"I'll go and see if Taylor is around. I need to speak with her anyway," Jaymie said, relating what Mabel had said about the autumnal overload. "Although Mabel may have said something to Taylor Sunday evening."

"I wouldn't bet on it," Mrs. Stubbs replied drily. "You know how Mabel is, she frets. Tree Bellwood was right there, and she becomes as feisty as a rat terrier where her kids or grandkids are concerned. You go on. I'll keep Hoppy here for a snooze."

"I'll take the treat plate out with me and see if I can catch Taylor to transfer the autumn stuff from my car to hers. It'll give me an excuse to talk to her alone about what she may have observed between Bonnie and Mandy."

Jaymie carried the plate out and put it in a bus tray in the servery behind the back wall of the dining room, then looked around. The place was empty except for lunch staff, who were setting tables with linens, vases of chrysanthemums, and napkin-rolled cutlery. Another was filling sugar bowls and sweetener holders. Taylor was in her waitstaff attire of black dress pants and a crisp white shirt, tucked in, with a black Queensville Inn waist apron tied with a bow, her abundant frothy hair re-strained in a clip at the nape of her neck. She had the menu board on a table easel, colored chalk laid out neatly beside her on a small table. She wrote the lunch specials in ornate script, blowing chalk residue away occasionally, and dusting her hands off on her apron.

Jaymie stood a moment and admired the absorbed young woman's lovely work. "You're good at that, Taylor!" she finally said.

The woman jumped and whirled, but laughed. "I get into it and don't hear or notice a thing." She took a deep breath and let it out, shaking off her jolt. "You're early for lunch. We don't start service until eleven."

"Say, Taylor, I was out at the historic house the other day reviewing our displays for the next month or so. You kindly donated autumnal décor items, but we're going for a more muted look. Your cute modern items don't quite fit."

"Okay. Mrs. Bloomsbury should have told me. I'll take the stuff back, if you like. My new apartment looks bare. I was gonna have to hit the dollar store for more!"

"I have the box in my trunk. Do you have your car here today, or did you walk over?"

"My car's in the parking lot. I can grab my keys and we can transfer the stuff now, if you like."

Taylor returned from the back kitchen with a black hoodie over her shirt and her car keys in hand. They exited together to the windswept parking lot. As they walked, the girl glanced over at Jaymie. "Hey, I know you and Val found that poor woman behind the Emporium. I'm sorry. You must have been . . . I mean, I can't even think of it . . ." She trailed off and bit her lip, turning her face into the wind.

"It was awful," Jaymie said. "You live right upstairs, above the Emporium. Did you see or hear anything that night?" She led the way to her SUV, unlocking it as they walked. She opened the hatch, handed the box to Taylor and grabbed the loose wreath that had tumbled out, then slammed it shut and locked up.

Taylor led the way toward a green hatchback and hit the trunk opening button on her remote. It popped open. She slid in the box and turned around as Jaymie put the wreath on top. "I talked to the police. Do you think it's okay if I tell you what I told them?"

"I don't see why not."

"Okay." They walked back toward the inn. "I worked night before last, as you know, the dinner shift, which goes until about ten, or whenever we get done cleaning up. By ten thirty-ish people were still lingering, but I wasn't supervising and there was other staff. Me and another girl left. She's having boyfriend problems. I went back to her place for an hour or so to talk. We had a glass of wine so I didn't get back to my place until eleven fifteen, I'd say. Maybe more like eleven thirty."

That placed her there in the critical timeframe, if Val's recollection of talking to Mandy at about ten forty-five was accurate. "Were you driving or walking?"

"I drove."

"You parked behind the building and walked around the side to the stairs."

She nodded. "I'll swear on a stack of Bibles there was no one on the back landing behind the Emporium then. It was pitch dark but my headlights shone right in that direction."

"Did you hear anything then? Or later?"

She shook her head. "Not a thing, at least not then. I turned the TV on while I had a bath. I don't like silence, it creeps me out. I think it was a movie or something, I don't remember what. After my bath, I was getting out my clothes for the next day and I thought I heard a car door slam. Weird that time of night. Queensville is always so quiet. I came out of my closet, turned the TV volume down and looked out the window, but there was nothing that I could see."

"Which window?"

"Overlooking the street."

In front of the Emporium. "What happened then?"

"I turned the TV off and went to bed."

"What time would that have been?"

The girl frowned. "It had to be after midnight."

"Nothing else?"

"I thought I heard a car gunning it down the street. I'm not sure." As they entered the dining room she pulled off her hoodie. "Sorry I'm not more helpful."

Jaymie put one hand on her arm and said, "Before I let you get back to work, I was going to ask you one more thing. I understand you served the large tables Sunday evening, the ones where two meetings gathered. Did they all come in for dinner?"

"Most of them," Taylor said. "The Dickens Days folks first, and the rest a little later."

"Who? Do you recall?"

She closed her eyes, her eyeballs moving under the lids, then she nodded and opened her blue eyes. Mrs. Stubbs's party came in early and lingered through dinner, she said. All of them had the roast beef and Yorkshire pudding, with coffee and dessert afterward.

The Dickens Days table was as follows, Taylor said: her grandmother was there early, as were Mrs. Frump and Mr. Waterman. The ladies, as she called Cynthia Turbridge and Jewel Dandridge, came in together. Mabel Bloomsbury arrived but appeared to be avoiding her; Taylor didn't know why. Jaymie didn't say that was because Mabel was worried about how Taylor would feel about the return of her fall décor. That was around five thirty or so; she noticed because her grandmother asked if the early bird special was still valid, and it was, until six.

The food bank meeting table was next: Ms. Pham was first. She was followed by Mr. Kallis and Olivier Ricci, who worked for him as a receptionist.

"You recognized them?"

"I've seen Mr. Kallis here before and I know Olivier. We have some classes together at college." Taylor was in the hospitality course part-time. "Olivier is taking business management, but there's some crossover."

"And he works for Manor Homes?"

"Work placement. Olivier came in with Mr. Kallis, and they joined Ms. Pham. Mrs. Vasiliev came in about then."

"Do you know why Candy Vasiliev was there? Was she part of the food bank meeting?"

"I don't think so. She was looking for her sister."

"Mandy de Boer wasn't there yet?"

"She came in a bit later."

"What time?"

"Shortly after six; maybe a quarter after, or twenty after."

"And then Mrs. Bonnie Smith, who was with the Dickens Days group. How long after Mandy arrived?"

She screwed up her face and looked to the ceiling. "Oh, couldn't have been more than fifteen, twenty minutes tops?"

"I understand there was a confrontation between the two women, Mandy and Bonnie. Did you hear anything?"

Taylor's bright blue eyes focused, and she

regarded Jaymie carefully as she slung her hoodie over a chair. "You're not saying . . . I mean, Mrs. Smith would never —"

"I'm not suggesting Mrs. Smith would have killed Mandy de Boer. I was trying to figure out what exactly went down." She paused, then said, "There was some suggestion that Mandy de Boer appeared intoxicated. Was she drinking alcohol?"

"No, uh-uh. Our bartender was running late — her car broke down — so I tended bar as well as serving until about eight. It was mostly cocktails and wine; nobody was drinking hard." She put her head to one side as she took up her blue chalk. "Did someone say she was drunk?"

"Bonnie Smith said that Mandy ran into her car and drove away, and I wondered."

"I'd swear she wasn't drunk when she came in."

"Did you see the confrontation when Bonnie accused Mandy of running into her car?"

"I did. It was heated, but over quick, like, *super* fast. Mrs. Smith marched over to the food bank meeting and like you said, she called Ms. de Boer out, saying that she — Mrs. Smith, you know — was stopped at a light, and Ms. de Boer dinged her, then sped up and took off. Ms. de Boer said no way, it

135

never happened. She said she was in a meeting before coming to the inn."

"*Another* meeting. Who with?" Taylor shook her head; she didn't know. "And Mrs. Smith was very angry?"

"She sure was!"

"What happened next?"

Taylor sketched a blue iris, then took up the green chalk and drew a slender, elegant stalk, with swirling vine-like leaves that lined the left side of the menu board. She looked sad, making a final flourish then turning back to Jaymie. "Ms. de Boer looked like she was going to cry, and Mrs. Smith got upset. She took Ms. de Boer aside and they chatted for a minute, then hugged. That was all."

What did Mandy say to Bonnie that ended the quarrel? Jaymie retrieved her little dog from Mrs. Stubbs and exited to the parking lot. As she put Hoppy in the car, a dirty white sedan pulled into a nearby spot. Candy Vasiliev climbed out. Busty and thick through the middle, she was dressed fashionably in jeans and a tunic that showed under the shorter jean jacket she wore over it. She looked wretched: pasty, weary, her tan fading, her skin blotchy. She retrieved her bag, checked her phone, and, not seeming to notice anything or anyone, headed toward the inn.

"Candy!" Jaymie called as she walked toward her. The woman halted and turned, staring at her without seeming to recognize her. "Remember me? Becca's sister. I was with Val when we found Mandy. I'm sorry for your loss."

She blinked, frowned, shook her head, then opened her mouth, closing it again without speaking. Finally, she said, "I have to . . . the inn." She wearily flapped a ring-laden hand. "Funeral catering. I have to go." But she stopped and stared for a moment. "Wait, you're Valetta Nibley's friend, aren't you."

"Yes."

Her expression twisted. "You said at the auction that someone had faked a social media account in Val Nibley's name. I want to believe it wasn't Valetta stalking her, but that's crazy. There was not a soul in the world who didn't love Mandy."

"We all have people who don't like us. You must know someone."

"Not a soul." She shook her head and angrily said, "You're covering for Val. Your buddy killed my sister."

"She didn't. *Please,* Candy . . ." Jaymie pleaded, wanting to reach out but not sure she should. "Please think about it. You *do* think it was murder?"

"I'm certain of it." Candy took a step toward Jaymie and poked a finger at her. Jaymie saw the resemblance between the sisters, as the elder's face, in sorrow, had become pouchy and drawn, like Mandy's was in the days before her death. "If Valetta Nibley is responsible . . . you tell her I won't rest until she pays." She turned and started to walk away, hoisting her purse up on her shoulder and shoving her hands in her jean jacket pockets.

"Wait a minute," Jaymie said, anger rising to replace the sympathy she felt. "Stop!"

Candy turned back and glared at her.

"As far as *we* know, this all started with someone sending a prescription request to Val's pharmacy in Mandy's name, one, I might point out, that she didn't fill. She wasn't even there and Mandy knew it because she picked up the prescription herself, and then drove past Val's place. I saw her! Val and I were together all day that day at her place. It was Helen Pham who dispensed it. I don't know where Mandy got the idea that Val tampered with her prescription."

Candy Vasiliev blinked at Jaymie's vehemence. "I only know what my sister said."

"Your sister was confused. I'm sorry, but it's true."

"What do you know about what she was going through?"

"I know she was having a rough time for some reason. But that's no reason to blame it all on Val."

"I'm tired of Val this and Val that. You'd think people would get sick of how perfect she is. I have never believed it, not for one second. I knew her in high school. You didn't!"

"What does that mean?"

"It means you don't know as much about your friend as you think." Candy whirled and stomped across the parking lot with new vigor, pain and anger blending into action.

Jaymie got in the SUV, drove to the middle of Queensville and parked. She carried Hoppy into her sister and brother-in-law's store and set him down. "Hey, Kevin," she said, leaning on the cash desk. "Do you mind if I leave my little guy here for a few? I shouldn't be more than a half hour.

"You know he's welcome here any time," Kevin said, setting aside his sheaf of orders and coming around the desk to pet the Yorkie Poo.

She thanked him, then explained what had

happened with Candy. He sympathized. "But what could she have meant, saying I don't know as much about Val as I think I do?"

Kevin straightened and met her gaze. "She's in pain. She was lashing out at who she suspects inflicted that pain."

Jaymie nodded, feeling pity in place of anger. "I think you're probably right. Thanks, Kevin. It's nice to have a big brother." She exited and walked down the main street to the Knit Knack Shack. As she entered, the jingle of bells greeted her.

The Shack, as it was called for short, was one large room lined with yarn bins up to the ceiling. Woven baskets filled with pattern books, needles, hooks, yarn bowls and other accoutrements were scattered along the aisles. A rotating rack near the cash register held more pattern books adorned with images of happy people wearing perfectly knitted sweaters and carrying knitted bags.

Bonnie, a stout florid woman, bustled forward. "Jaymie, how are you? I don't need to ask. You look lovely. Hey, are you okay? I heard what happened, you and Valetta finding that poor young woman behind the Emporium." She surged forward and took Jaymie's wrist in a firm grip, dragging her along. "Come and sit with me. How is Valetta? I don't believe a word of all this nonsense about her making a prescription mistake, and no one worth a penny would believe it either."

After replying to the torrent of questions and comments, Jaymie perched on a high stool and accepted a cup of tea. They talked about Bonnie's upcoming retirement, something she was looking forward to with a vivacious grin. Florida was full of "silver foxy hotties," as she called them, and she'd been widowed several years. It was time for a man.

But after gossip punctuated by tea and homemade cookies, Jaymie got down to business. "I heard you spoke with Mandy de Boer Sunday evening about her running into you. You ended up hugging her and chatting. Why?"

Bonnie frowned. "I know Mandy. We've worked together on a charity fundraiser for the food bank before. I'm a bit of a car fanatic so I know she drives a maroon Dodge Journey."

"Banged up, right?"

"It had some front-end damage, now that you mention it. I was sitting at a light, got clipped, and got out — I know, not smart when it was pretty close to pitch dark out

141

— and who should I see but Mandy. She suddenly revved the motor and sped away!"

"You saw Mandy?"

Bonnie nodded. "I saw Mandy at the wheel, sure as I'm sitting here. That mop of red hair? Can't miss that do nowhere. When she screeched off I pulled over and called the police, but after about half an hour with the cops a no-show, I toodled off to the inn. When I got there, I checked the parking lot and there was her SUV, big scrape along the passenger side. I was blazing mad — I don't get that way often, but when I do . . . hoo boy — so when I saw her in the dining room I let into her. She had some nerve showing up at the inn after a hit-and-run, I said, along with a few nastier words. She looked like I'd told her her pet bunny died. She started crying, big gusty sobs, you know? Anyhoo, I took her aside and she said she didn't *think* she hit me. She looked scared, my gosh."

"Scared."

"Yup. She had no memory of hitting my car."

"No memory." Jaymie sat back, puzzled.

"She had driven herself to the inn, she told me when I asked, and no one else had her vehicle. Anyhoo, she promised to write me a check rather than ding our insurance, but I don't suppose I'll see the money now that she's gone. That's the least of anyone's worries. Poor kid." She narrowed her eyes. "She seemed so strange, out of it. Was she a drinker?"

"I don't think so." Mandy didn't remember the accident but didn't deny it could have been her. She drove her own car to the inn. "Did she say anything else, anything at all?"

"Lemme think." Bonnie got up, bustled around the shop, tidying the bins and taking one out-of-place ball of yarn and tucking it in with its purple sisters. Finally, she turned. "I don't know about you, but when I get mad I kinda run right over the person I'm mad at. I know I talked over Mandy at first, but it seemed to me that she said . . ." She scrunched up her face again, trying to remember. "She said she'd been forgetting a *lot* of things. People had told her she had done things that she didn't remember."

Was Mandy abusing drugs or drink to the extent that she was having blackouts, or was someone sabotaging her by doing bizarre things pretending to be her? "You should tell the police."

"I didn't want to call the cops about the accident. I only did it because the driver drove off. That's why I didn't stick around,

143

though. I knew who I saw, and I prefer to settle things face-to-face."

"So, if you hadn't seen Mandy at the inn . . . ?"

"I'd have hunted her down to settle up, sure."

"But you should tell them about it now. They need every scrap of information to figure out what happened to Mandy."

"What does that have to do with the accident?"

"It happened the same night."

"What *did* happen to Mandy? I mean, I know y'all found her on the back step of the Emporium, but how did she die?"

"There was no obvious cause. Please, call the police and tell them what happened. They like to build a timeline of events. It could be important." A customer came in the store. "Please think about it."

ELEVEN

She emerged into the gloom of an autumn day. In Michigan one could experience the panoply of seasonal adventures in one day: hot sunshine, wind, rain, snow, sleet. Today was simply gloomy with gusts of wind that scurried leaves along the main street. She huddled in her jacket, but as she was walking away from the Knit Knack Shack she noticed Detective Vestry walking toward it. The detective had probably heard about the altercation and was following up on it. Jaymie was glad she'd put a bug in Bonnie's ear. She had to trust that Vestry, as a good investigator, would get what she needed from the store owner.

Jaymie returned to the antique store. Becca, who had replaced her husband, was in the front showroom helping a customer accessorize a rosewood dining set she had purchased with china and silverware. When Jaymie asked about Hoppy, her sister put one finger to her mouth in a shushing mimicry, then pointed back to the office off the payment area. Jaymie crept to the door to find that Hoppy was happily curled up in Georgina's office chair snoozing while the woman sat on a low stool crooning a lullaby.

Even the steeliest heart has a melting point, she reflected, watching the older woman with the little dog. Jaymie carefully backed away and returned to the front showroom, where Becca finished writing up the order for all the items the customer, who had already left, was purchasing. "Wow. Just . . . wow," she murmured, glancing back toward the office.

"I know, right?" Becca said, eyes wide. Georgina was a tough bird, but the scene in the office proved the flinty exterior cloaked a marshmallow heart.

Jaymie perched on one of the dining chairs in the showroom and glanced around at bare spaces and items stacked together. "Looks like you're clearing stuff out?"

"We've got a new shipment coming. Kevin is taking care of the details right now. This table and the chairs were sold to that customer, and a whole set of the Royal Imari I bought forever ago. I don't know if you even remember me buying it. It was at

146

an auction maybe three years ago now, where you bought the Hoosier, shortly before your first murder."

"My first murder? You make it sound like I'm a hazard to people's health." She shrugged off the irritation. "I thought people weren't buying dining sets and good china anymore. There are articles written about how today's generations aren't into fancy dining."

Becca finished her list and glanced around. "It's getting tougher. What it takes is finding the right buyer. I was lucky to unload this stuff. I didn't get what I wanted for it. As much as I love this kind of product, we need to reevaluate our direction. I may need to stock more mid-century modern furniture and accessories for all the people who were going to buy those crap homes Mandy de Boer was planning to build and furnish. What was she calling it? Vintage Estates?"

At the mention of Mandy, Jaymie fretted at her bottom lip. She told her sister what she'd learned at the inn and from Bonnie Smith.

"I can't believe it's murder," Becca responded, setting her order pad on the dining table. "Why would anyone want Mandy de Boer dead?"

"I don't know. If we find out the why, we'll know the who. I need to get to the bottom of her recent obsession with Val, all the wild accusations. And why she suddenly came to Val's pharmacy for one medication. It doesn't make any sense. Why did Mandy transfer one prescription over to Val's pharmacy, pick it up from Helen, and then accuse Val of tampering with it?"

"Maybe there will never be an explanation. Maybe her behavior has nothing to do with her death."

"I can't stop looking into it, not with Val in danger."

"Danger?"

"If Mandy was murdered, what happens if the police never discover who did it? People are going to suspect Val. I want to get to the bottom of what set Mandy off. That feels like it's at the heart of the mystery." She watched her sister. "Do you have any ideas?"

"Me? Nope. That's your department."

They heard clicking nails on hardwood. Hoppy wobbled cheerily out to them, alerted perhaps by the sound of Jaymie's voice, followed by Georgina, who had donned her sweater and best snooty expression.

"Oh, good, you're here," she said to Jaymie in her haughtiest tone. "I've been keeping the dog from coming out to bother customers."

Jaymie and Becca shared a smile. "I'll get him out of your hair," she said and left, accompanied by her pup. She sat in the car for a few minutes making notes and then jotted a string of questions, as she often did, to try to identify key puzzles within the larger problem of who killed Mandy de Boer.

1a) Why was Mandy's prescription sent to the Queensville Pharmacy? 1b) And why did she accuse Val of tampering with it when she knew it was Helen who dispensed the medication?

2) She's being sued by homeowners. Could any of them be irate enough that they'd construct an elaborate plan to kill her?

She grimaced, shook her head and added a note: *This doesn't seem likely. For some reason the murder feels personal, so . . . *note to self: check who is suing her.*

3) What about her personal life? Her relationship with her sister? Was she dating? What about her late husband's family? Anyone in the Manor Homes business with beefs? What about Randall Kallis, who had arrived at the police station with Candy? What was his and Mandy's relationship like?

Her cell phone rang. It was Bernie. They

chatted a minute, and her friend wanted to know of the plans for the trail clearing, and if she and Heidi could contact Bram Brouwer directly to offer their help clearing brush.

"Be my guest! I'd welcome folks to jump in and take care of things." She hesitated a moment, and then said, "Say, Bernie, I heard that Mandy's death has been ruled a murder. Do you know why? I mean, what evidence led them to call it homicide?"

"You know I can't tell you," Bernie chided. "I'd lose my badge."

"I'm sorry, I get it. I do have a question you may be able to answer, though."

"No promises."

"What kind of tests would have been done on Mandy's body? I hear the words *tox screen* on the cop shows Jakob watches, but what does any of that mean? And what other tests would be done?"

"*Tox screen* is short for toxicology screen, a report on the presence in the victim's blood of legal or illegal drugs."

"Would it find *any* kind of drug or poison?"

"Not exactly. I mean, they'll screen for the usual, but they can't screen for every known drug or toxin." Bernie hesitated, then said, "I'll tell you a little more, but this does not specifically apply to Mandy de Boer or anyone else in the case. Don't quote me on this!"

She then explained the difference between the blood tests done on a suspected intoxicated person in the emergency room, and forensic toxicology done when a body arrived at the morgue for an autopsy. Very different things. In the first case known intoxicating substances would be looked for, legal and illegal.

But in the case of someone for whom no obvious cause of death could be discovered, more extensive testing would be done beyond the toxicology screen. Multiple samples would be taken, including but not limited to blood from the femoral artery, heart blood, and tissue samples from the liver, brain and kidney. There were other tissues and samples taken that Bernie sped through, including stomach contents. The hope was they could determine Mandy's drug use, legal or illegal.

Bernie would not — could not — confirm or deny that the death was murder.

While talking to Bernie Jaymie had missed a call from Val, so she called back and related what she had learned, which didn't seem like much.

Val had been doing internet deep dives,

and with her pharmacological knowledge had come up with some possibilities. Hoppy crept onto Jaymie's lap as she listened. She scruffed his ears until his hind leg was going.

"I took all the symptoms we've seen and heard about Mandy displaying over the last week and wrote them down. I've identified paranoia, irritability, impulsiveness, memory loss, lack of coordination and lost ability to perform tasks previously accomplished. My first thought was that many of these can be the result of head trauma, explained by the car accident —"

"But some of these things were evident before the accident."

"Let me finish. I investigated other explanations, singularly or more than one."

"More than one?"

"Combinations, like head trauma along with drug abuse."

"I get it. So, what's the consensus, Doc?"

"Any or all of these symptoms can be caused by TBI — traumatic brain injury — and we don't know if she suffered a previous head trauma. But abusing some drugs can cause any or all of the symptoms too. So, we're back to square one." She sounded defeated.

"Not necessarily. Let me keep working on

it, and you find out anything you can about Mandy's last days. I want to put together a timeline of where she went, with whom, and who else did she see. I don't know if it will help, but it's a start."

"I can start that. I know of a few possibilities right away." She sounded heartened by having something to do toward her own exoneration.

"Good. Write everything down and keep your chin up," Jaymie said.

TWELVE

Jaymie took Hoppy home. Lilibet greeted him with an all-over sniffing and then a chase game. She ate lunch, and then put the makings of beef stroganoff in the slow cooker. At her favorite spot, the kitchen counter that looked out to the woods across the road, she assembled everything she needed for the next "Vintage Eats" column.

One of her favorite old-fashioned desserts was apple crisp. She had her grandmother's simple recipe, but this time of year she wanted to put a fresh spin on it, something to bring it forward. She got out her stool and climbed up to the upper cupboards, hoping she had what she needed. So many things were still at the Queensville home and she never knew what was where!

Ramekins . . . she had some somewhere. She searched for fifteen minutes and finally found them tucked away in a lower cupboard. Hoppy meanwhile sat watching her in puzzlement, and when she triumphantly said "Aha" he yipped in excitement. She washed the cute little dishes, adorned with rural scenes, and thought how nicely they'd photograph.

Now, ingredients: rolled oats, butter, flour, apples, cinnamon, brown sugar. Apple pie spice, maybe? Though apple pie spice was simply a blend of cinnamon, nutmeg, and allspice. What could she do to make this jazzy besides making individual crisps?

Oooh, *cranberries*! That was the perfect tie-in to the coming season. She turned the radio on to an oldies station and hummed along while she baked. Soon the kitchen was full of the fragrance of oats and apple and spice that combined deliciously. She curled up on the sofa in front of the fire with one of the apple crisps. She'd call it lunch. A balanced diet! She tasted it, and it was perfection.

After lunch she photographed the dish, using her beloved vintage utensils as props, including her lovely, red-handled serving spoon, which was older than her mother, a vintage apron that belonged to her grand-mother, and some fall leaves in a vase. She looked through the photos and sat with her laptop, writing the article and recipe to ac-company the photos. It was good to ground herself and take this break.

Jakob and Jocie came through the door together. Her husband looked weary, Jaymie thought, enveloping him in a hug that restored his smile. As Jocie played with Hoppy and Lilibet, she chattered about a friend's piano recital on Saturday — to which she and her other friends were invited — then revealed her and Mia's plans for a dance performance for the winter festival in December. She showed them a part of the routine they had worked out, ending with a bow, applause, and barking. They ate dinner at the table — the stroganoff was good, though not spectacular — then devoured warm apple crisp with vanilla ice cream for dessert. Then it was off to bed for all of them, humans and pets alike.

How could she ever have imagined her life would be so full? She had always been happy, but now there was a depth to her joy that was abundant. This is what life was about, and even in the midst of investigating, she must never forget that her good fortune was a precious gift.

The next morning she checked in with Val, who still couldn't get past the thought that she may have been able to prevent Mandy's tragic demise.

"You can't do this to yourself, Val," Jaymie said. "You made a decision based on your interactions with Mandy. I would have done the same."

"Would you? That makes me feel better, it really does."

"We'll get to the bottom of this, I promise," Jaymie said, hoping she was telling the truth. "I'll touch base with you later."

She dressed carefully, in gold slacks with a cranberry sweater and gold scarf scattered with fallish leaves. It was more Becca's style than her own, but not knowing what the day would hold, she wanted to look professional. She added gold hoop earrings, a gift from Jakob on their anniversary, and set out, armed with her knowledge of the construction company receptionist's name and relationship to Taylor Bellwood, and that he, too, was at the inn for the Sunday evening food bank board meeting.

The Manor Homes Development headquarters, on the outskirts of Wolverhampton, was a low brick building alone on a three-acre patch of weed-strewn land and bordered on two sides by a cracked paved parking lot. A few cars were parked in back, but only one along the side, a glossy black SUV with tinted windows. Glass windows along the front of the office were shielded by cheap-looking horizontal mini blinds and topped with blue awnings.

The glass door along the side, through which Jaymie entered, was emblazoned with a scratched logo of a house roof, over MANOR HOMES in a blocky font. She took it all in with a glance. The reception area was the width of the building. To the right was a hallway lined with office doors, and at the end of the hall was another door with an *Employees Only Beyond This Point* sign. Along one reception area wall was a table with a pyramid of plastic protein shake bottles emblazoned with a logo of a mountaintop and *Keto Kolonics* in stark lettering. In front of the shake bottles were squat containers of Keto Kolonics Shake It Off protein powder in vanilla, chocolate and strawberry, and a pile of boxes holding packets of the same, arranged in a semicircle behind a stack of pamphlets.

On the other wall in front of a window covered in peeling UV protection film was a duplicate table, this one laden with bottles of cleaning products labelled *Natur-All Kleaning.* There was window spray, oven cleaner, floor cleaner and one that promised to clean everything "but your dirty mind," whatever that meant. There was a stack of pamphlets no doubt extolling the virtues of

Natur-All Kleaning products and (probably) how you too can make a mint in selling it. It was strange that a business office would have displays of multilevel marketing. She wondered if Mandy had been unable to say no to friends or family selling the goods.

The reception desk was staffed by a slim young man with dark wavy hair that flopped over his forehead, one diamond earing in his right lobe. He was wearing a white dress shirt with a gold cross pendant nestled in his jugular notch. When he noticed Jaymie, he adjusted his telephone headset, said something, punched a key on his computer keyboard, then smiled. "Hello. What can I do for you?" His voice was pleasant, well-modulated, and professional.

"Olivier Ricci?"

"Why yes," he said with a puzzled smile. "Do I know you?"

"We have a mutual friend. You attend college with Taylor Bellwood? I'm Jaymie Leighton Müller."

His eyes widened and he jumped up, coming around the desk. He clasped her hand, covered it with his other, shaking it as he said, "Oh, I *do* know of you! What can I help you with?"

Unbidden, she sat in the chair as he took

his seat behind the reception desk again. "This is going to sound terrible. I feel awkward even asking."

He looked intrigued and widened his brown eyes. "Do tell."

"I'm truly sorry about Mandy de Boer's death. It's a tragedy."

He nodded, an appropriately solemn look on his face. "She was a nice lady."

"I'm sorry if this sounds nosy, but I understand she had changed lately. I wonder why?"

He nodded. "I haven't been here long but even I noticed." He glanced over his shoulder and kept his tone muted. "She was so put together at first, you know . . . hair done, nails done."

"And that had changed," Jaymie mused.

"It sure had. I mean, some days she dragged herself into the office and it looked like she'd slept in a back alley," he said acidly. His eyes widened and he colored, the ivory cream of his high cheekbones turning rosy. "I didn't mean . . . oh, gosh, I know she was found in a back alley. I didn't mean anything by it." He shook his hair out of his eyes and his color receded as his composure returned.

"Can you tell me how she was at the meeting at the Queensville Inn Sunday evening?"

"What do you mean?"

"You say she had changed since you first started working here, right?" He nodded. "My sister and her friends went to school with Mandy back in the day. A couple of days before she died we ran into her at an auction. She wasn't herself, it seemed. Even her sister, Candy, seemed upset by her behavior."

He glanced down at the computer, tapping at the keys. "I don't know how I can help you."

Or why he should, and yet she sensed a willingness to talk. She explained that she and her friend were the ones who found Mandy deceased. "It's troubling. I'm trying to figure things out. I think I'll feel better if I understand. I didn't know Mandy. I do know someone who had an argument with Mandy at the Queensville Inn on Sunday evening when you all were at a dinner meeting for the food bank. Mandy crashed into her car, but when confronted she denied it, claiming she had no memory of the accident. Do you remember the quarrel?"

"The brassy lady with the big voice?" He grinned. "I sure do. I was sipping my daquiri and watching the show." He sobered. "Not that I didn't feel bad. I mean, poor Ms. de Boer is gone now. Terrible."

"You heard it all?"

"I overheard her saying something about an accident, but with my boss there," he said, slewing his eyes behind him with a significant raise of his eyebrows, "I couldn't exactly listen in. They went off and talked in private and then hugged and it was over. But you're right, Ms. de Boer *has* seemed confused lately. She's missed meetings, made calls to former clients that left them puzzled, forgotten she asked me for reports."

"My friend said that despite Mandy not remembering the accident, they settled things between them. I guess that's why they hugged." She paused and eyed Olivier. "Everyone I've spoken to says Mandy had changed a lot in the last while."

"Apparently, she was a joy to work for: engaged, smart, happy. I found her so at first too. But in the last seven months or so, I'd say, since the threat of lawsuits started, she had been going downhill."

"I've heard about the class action suit being launched for shoddy workmanship."

He sighed. "I know. Nothing like being a cruise director on the *Titanic,* right? That's what I feel like being a receptionist here. I'm telling people about shuffleboard on the Lido deck while those in charge buckle a life vest."

162

"Were the company problems affecting her mental health?"

"She's been getting more and more erratic, but I don't know if it was the company troubles causing it. Her appearance had gone downhill, too. She used to be so neatly dressed, but lately she'd become sloppy."

"Did she drink?"

"Alcohol? I never saw her if she did."

"Did she do drugs?"

He shook his head. "Nope. Not to my knowledge. I heard one of the construction managers was caught buying meth and she pitched a fit, fired him the moment she learned about it. She said she'd never have anyone working for her who couldn't be trusted. The crew's safety was in his hands, and she wouldn't have it compromised."

"It's weird, the change in her. If it wasn't alcohol or drugs . . . ?"

"I'm not sure what was going on, but —" He stopped abruptly and sat back in his chair as Randall Kallis, looking trim and athletic in a navy suit, strolled out from the back accompanied by another man.

The other fellow was average height, very slim, with jet-black hair swept back from his high forehead. He turned to Kallis and said, "I'll leave it in your hands then, Randy. I have to say, I've been worried for some time

163

but —" Something in Kallis's face stopped him and he glanced at the receptionist and Jaymie, then back to the other man. "We'll talk later. I'm counting on you, Randy. I expect to hear back from you tomorrow morning, at the latest."

There was an odd dynamic between the two, a balance that was off-kilter. "Don't worry about *anything,* Win," Kallis said with heavy emphasis. "We'll take care of things."

They exchanged a handshake, the other man exited, and Kallis turned. He eyed Jaymie as he asked Olivier about the timeline of some delivery. The receptionist looked it up on his computer and replied, then answered the phone. Kallis frowned as he regarded Jaymie. "I know you from somewhere."

Jaymie introduced herself.

He jabbed a finger at her. "Your friend is that pharmacist woman who killed Mandy!"

"No, she didn't," Jaymie said firmly as she stood, unwilling to be placed at a disadvantage by looking up at him. "She had nothing to do with Mandy's death and I'd appreciate it if you would not repeat that lie."

He shrugged, frowning. "Just repeating what I've heard. But she *was* murdered, is that true?"

Olivier, his eyes widening as he stared up

at Jaymie, lost his thoughts in the phone conversation he was having, stumbled with his words, then turned away and resumed.

"As far as I know, the police have not released a cause of death yet. I was with Val when we found her," Jaymie said, with a crack in her voice. "And I want both to exonerate Val and find out who *really* killed your colleague, if it turns out to have been murder."

"Isn't that a job for the police?"

"Don't you think when it comes to crime, the community should be helpful?"

He nodded.

"I don't know if she was murdered or not, but if she was, Val didn't do it, which means someone else did. Can I have a few minutes of your time?"

He hesitated, regarding her with a solemn expression, but then nodded sharply. "Okay. Follow me."

THIRTEEN

Jaymie followed Kallis down a hall, past a closed door with Mandy de Boer's name on it. If only she could get in there. Every businessperson she had ever known kept a calendar on their desk, even if they used phone apps to schedule their day.

Kallis's office was not large or luxurious. There was a big window on the far wall behind his desk, but the vertical blinds were drawn. The other walls were covered with development site plans overlaid on aerial photographs of property. Colorful rectangles in curved lines and wedge-shaped properties around cul de sacs indicated building lots labeled *Golden Manor Estates, Livonia Manor Homes,* and a newer one labeled *Vintage Manor Estates,* among others. Color coding indicated stages of building. The room was cluttered, with file drawers open and stacks of paper sagging sideways, a blue recycling bin overflowing with paper, and a map of Wolverhampton and the surrounding counties on a corkboard covered in pins and marked with mysterious acronyms.

It was old-style clutter, Jaymie thought, the kind that was supposed to be banished with the advent of the paperless society of computers. Kallis took his suit jacket off, folded it neatly over a file cabinet, then waved her toward a chair. She sat, slinging her purse over the back as he plunked down into the desk chair.

He stretched out, practically reclining, his hands cupped behind his head, his legs thrust out, as he glared at her. "So, what's this about? You know, Candy will kill me if she finds out I'm talking to you. She is *convinced* Valetta Nibley murdered Mandy."

"That's ridiculous, and I think you know that. What do *you* think?"

"I don't know." He abruptly sat up, his chair screeching in protest. "Candy claims Valetta had been stalking Mandy online and even in person."

"I told her this in person, that simply isn't true. You know what social media is like, anyone can claim to be anyone. A fake profile was created by someone who used it to harass Mandy in Valetta's name."

"Why would anyone do that?" he said.

"That, I don't know." She sat back and

took a deep breath. "I'm worried and upset. You must be too. Mandy was your partner, your colleague. It leaves you up in the air, I would imagine." She paused to let him nod, then said, "I'm trying to find out what happened. Will you help me?"

"How?"

"The more I know, the more I can figure this out. For example, everyone I've spoken with says Mandy had changed lately."

"I don't know what was going on, but yes, she's . . . she had changed."

"In what way specifically?"

"She was distracted. Unhappy."

"Why?"

"I don't know."

"What else?"

He frowned and shook his head, then eyed her speculatively. "She had become uncoordinated, clumsy. She was always a graceful person. She walked with assurance. Until recently."

Jaymie digested that. Was it proof Mandy was taking drugs? "How did you find out about Mandy's death?"

"Candy called me Monday morning asking if I knew where Mandy was. I guess she wasn't answering her phone. Next thing I know a cop shows up at my door and asks me to go to the Queensville Township police

168

station."

"Did they tell you about Mandy?"

He nodded. "I wouldn't go with them 'til they did. I'm listed as her emergency contact on her driver's licence and with the police."

"Where did they take you?"

"I told them Candy was worried about her sister, and asked if she had been told. She hadn't, so they took me to her place. The officer and I told her together. She was devastated." He closed his eyes for a moment. "I'm still coming to grips with it. You saw Win with me. He's in shock too. He's one of our contractors and everyone is freaking out about what this means for Manor Homes."

"You were a partner in the business."

"I stepped up when Chad, Mandy's husband — a stellar guy and great businessman — died. Mandy was out of it. She didn't know what to do. She had only done the books up until then. Chad and I had run it together."

"That's when you became a partner."

"It was the only way I'd stay on," he admitted, rocking his creaking chair back. "She needed so much help. There was no upside to me staying unless I had skin in the game, you know?"

"I don't think I understand."

"Let me explain it in easier terms," he said with casual contempt. He sat up straight and regarded her across the desk. "Mandy knew nothing about running a business. If I was going to stick around to teach her and help her, I needed to be incentivized."

"Helping your friend and boss's widow wasn't incentive enough?"

"Of course not. Look, I told her, it's okay if you want to sit around boo-hooing, but you don't pay employees with tears."

"She lost her husband!"

"And I lost my friend! We went to school together, in case you didn't know, Chad, Shannon, and me."

"Shannon?"

"Chad's older sister. Private school. He was two grades ahead of me and looked out for me, like a brother. I was his best man. After he died I told her, *Mandy, what we can do for Chad is make a success of his little business.* With my help we have zoomed ahead, taken advantage of every market bubble, monetized every scrap of land."

Cheated and lied and maybe even embezzled, Jaymie thought, eyeing him. She had no proof of fiscal impropriety and no reason to think there was any, except for a gut feeling. That was not fair, but she wouldn't disregard her gut wholly. "I understand you were with her at the meeting at the Queensville Inn Sunday evening. How did she seem to you? Who did she talk to?"

"Why?"

"I was wondering how late she stayed. And if she left alone or with someone."

"*With someone?* What do you mean?"

"There has to be some reason she stayed in Queensville and ended up behind the pharmacy."

He eyed her with suspicion. "Do you know something I don't? *Was* Mandy murdered? I have a right to know."

"Do you? Why?"

"Because it affects me! It affects my business."

"I suppose you'll find out when we all do, when the police release a cause of death. But in the meantime, maybe we can all figure this out together. Group source a solution."

He nodded, then checked the time on his phone. His cooperation had a time limit.

"You were at the Queensville Inn meeting as a partner at Manor Homes."

"That's right." His tone was cool, detached.

He wasn't sad Mandy was dead, she thought. The notion startled her. Was she

171

right? "Will you go ahead with the food bank alliance now that Mandy's gone?"

"We'll review it."

"Did the meeting run super late?"

"I was home by . . . oh, shortly after eleven." He shifted in his chair and glanced down at his cell phone.

"That's quite late for a dinner meeting to run."

"People get talking. You know how it is."

"Was Mandy still at the inn when you left?"

"We headed out at about the same time, but I didn't see her drive away."

Her car was found some distance away from the pharmacy. Why, Jaymie wondered, since she had driven to the Queensville Inn? How did she get to the pharmacy? "And you went home?"

"Sure. I worked in my home office for a while. I probably didn't get to bed until two or three."

"Your wife must hate that," Jaymie said.

"Not married," he said, waggling a bare ring finger. "I live alone."

No alibi. Jaymie glanced at his nameplate: Chief Financial Officer. But in a business this small she would bet roles were combined and only loosely observed. "Mandy was CEO, correct?"

He snorted. "An honorary position. She flits around and pretends while I do everything here." He glanced at her expression and perhaps saw her distaste for his boasting. "She was still learning, that's all. CEO is a big title. She didn't have the formal training like I have."

"Ah. Weren't there any of the Manor family remaining to run things?"

"Trina is Chad's daughter," he said with a trace of impatience. "She holds a few shares."

"What about Chad's sister?"

"Shannon? When their father died she was given a minority stake in the company, along with a cash inheritance. She was well-compensated." He shifted again. "I'm sorry, what does this have to do with Mandy's death?"

Jaymie observed him calmly. Trina lived in England. With Mandy gone, did he gain more control in the company? That could be a motive for murder, she supposed. Maybe there *were* financial hijinks and Mandy had become aware of them. Nan said there was a rumor that Mandy was having an affair, then her husband died, and then her lover became co-owner. Randall Kallis, clearly. Was it true? "Was Ti the only member of the food bank board who attended the meeting?"

He narrowed his eyes. "Yes. It was just a discussion about the benefits of Manor Homes sponsoring other fundraising ventures, to raise the identity of the food bank in the public eye. I had Olivier Ricci with me, he took notes. He's got a good head for organization on his shoulders, and I thought he might be helpful. It wasn't a formal meeting, we were spitballing ideas. There's nothing binding."

"You're rethinking the partnership?"

"I have a business to run. We're in the middle of a pitched battle for our reputation in case you didn't realize it."

"I'd heard about the class action suit being filed against Manor Homes."

He held up one hand. "Not filed *yet*! And not at all if I can help it."

"Threatened, though. Mandy was upset about it. How did the construction problems occur? Manor Homes has always had a solid reputation."

He sat back and tented his fingers. "I fail to see how that is any of your business."

"I'm trying to figure out what was going on with Mandy. You must have been shocked when you found out she died."

"I was." He stared at Jaymie across the desk and there was a shift in his expression and dark eyes. He looked away. "They told us where she was found, and who found her. Candy immediately felt sure Ms. Nibley was responsible," Kallis said, sitting up straighter and staring at her again.

"It's ridiculous to try to pin this on Valetta."

"Candy isn't making much sense right now," he admitted. "She suffered a huge loss. I feel bad for her. Mandy did everything for their father and now that'll fall on Candy's shoulders. Henry is an ungrateful son-of-a . . ." He stopped and jabbed one finger at her. "You didn't hear that from me."

"You know him?"

"Sure. He's their father, after all. And he bought one of the first of the homes in Golden Manor Estates. He's done nothing but complain from day one." He straightened and suddenly said, "None of this has anything to do with Mandy's death. You should probably go."

"Just one more question. I don't know any of these folks personally. Does Candy work for Manor Homes?"

"No, of course not."

"What is she like?"

"Candy is quite the woman," he said with an admiring tone. "She has traveled, sky-

175

dived, rock climbed, you gotta respect that go get 'em *joie de vivre.* It's more than I've ever done. She throws herself at life." His cell phone chimed. He glanced at it. "Look, I hate to cut this *delightful* conversation short," he said, "but if you've gossiped enough, I have things to attend to. If this business is going to survive then I need to be on top of it before doubt creeps into the trades."

"What do you mean?"

Impatiently he stood and waved toward the door as his phone chimed again. "What I said. We exist on credit. It's vital that our creditors, including suppliers, see the business is in firm hands and we're moving ahead with projects."

"I guess I never thought of that," Jaymie said, gathering her purse.

"Of course you didn't." He pasted a smile on his face and opened the door for her as he barked "Yeah?" into the phone. "Sure. Let me get those figures."

She exited and was barely out of his office when the door slammed behind her. Such a busy, successful man. She started toward the front but hesitated in the hallway. Mandy's office tempted her. She heard Randall Kallis's voice in his office and Olivier's voice in front. He was on the phone, a

176

personal call judging from his tone and laughter.

She tried Mandy's door; it opened inward. She crept in and softly closed the door behind her. She had no idea what she'd say if she was caught snooping so there was no point in worrying about it. She took in her surroundings, a blandly decorated square office space with basic beige walls, gray industrial carpeting, and nondescript landscapes on the walls. File cabinets lined the far wall, with files piled on top, and in the corner a coat tree stood, burdened with a raincoat, an umbrella, and a windbreaker. A pair of boots leaned against the bottom.

The desk was littered with pens, paper, vitamin bottles, protein powder packets, a phone charger, a half-empty diet shake container, tape, and notepads with scribbles. An award in the shape of a house with *Builder of the Year* emblazoned on it was tipped over, holding down a stack of paper. Leaning over the desk, she moved the mouse and the desktop computer blinked and woke up, humming to life. It looked like Mandy had every intention of coming back to whatever she had been working on. However, it was password-protected.

On the keyboard drawer she found a daily calendar open to the previous week. Jaymie sat in Mandy's chair and picked up the calendar, flipping through it. The notations were in the same handwriting, but some were scrawled, some neatly written and a few almost illegible.

She noted many of the same notations and quickly identified abbreviations. *Tr* meant Trina. It seemed Mandy spoke to her often, usually on Sundays, as there was a *Call Tr* notation every Sunday. *RK* was likely Randall, *OR* indicated Olivier, *TP* was probably Ti. *C* had to be Candy. Maybe she had a standing lunch date with her sister because there was a *C* noted every Friday. There was a *GV* marked in heavy letters with an exclamation mark beside it on the Sunday she died.

Other than that, there were dozens of mystery notes with times, phone numbers and scrawled names. Maybe she was one of those people whose handwriting got worse when they were stressed or in a hurry. Jaymie got her phone out and took pictures of the desk, the office, and several pages of the calendar.

She picked up one of the notepads strewn about. *What is RK doing with Win?* one note read. *Is Win part of plan????* read another. Mandy was suspicious of Randall and Win, the man she had seen with Kallis in the outer office. She scanned the rest but couldn't make head nor tails of any of it. She got up and headed toward the door when, to her horror, it swung in. Randall entered, shouting over his shoulder to Olivier that he was getting a file from Mandy's office. He whirled but halted and stared at her.

"What are you doing in here?"

"I saw the door open and came in to grab one of these," she said, grabbing a Keto Kolonics pamphlet.

"There's a whole stack of them out in the office," he said.

"I didn't notice."

"You've been in here for ten minutes. What are you *really* doing?" She tried to scuttle past him, but he blocked her exit with one arm against the doorframe. "Were you snooping? I should call the cops on you."

Jaymie stared at the blue cotton of his sleeve and tried to think of an excuse. Olivier, drawn by the shouting, came and looked over his boss's shoulder, his eyes widening when he saw her. Randall whirled and said, "Why didn't you usher this snoop out? What are you doing up there other than painting your nails and gossiping?"

The receptionist's fresh complexion

shaded red. "How was I supposed to know you two were done? I thought you were still talking."

"I'm on my way," Jaymie said, taking advantage of Olivier's presence to duck under Randall's outstretched arm and squeeze past the two men, speeding down the hallway toward the outer office.

"Wait a minute, young lady," Randall said, storming after her. "I want to know what you were doing in there?"

"*Young lady?* Wow, I haven't heard anyone under seventy use that phrase in a long time," Jaymie snapped as she sailed toward the door. She turned, pushing the door open with her butt, as she said, "It's been real, fellows. Take care."

When she got out to the parking lot she bolted to her SUV, climbed inside, locked the door and fanned herself with the Keto Kolonics pamphlet, her face heated and her heart palpitating like a drill team drum. Who *was* that sassy woman? Couldn't have been her. Randall Kallis opened the door and glared at her across the parking lot. She started up her vehicle and headed out.

Home, now, or somewhere else? Somewhere else, she decided, determined not to let this fright stop her inquiries. She'd make a condolence call on Mandy's father, Hendrik de Boer. She found his address and drove to Golden Manor Estates, a tidy development of new homes. Seniors were raking leaves or mowing manicured lawns. There was the usual sprinkling of walkers, dog and otherwise. Service vans appeared to proliferate. A plumber and a basement repair van advertising that they'd help *keep your bottom dry*!

She checked the address. The house with the repair van was the very one she needed to visit. She parked at the curb, got out and walked up the drive as a white sedan zipped past her far too close. She shuddered. She hated when that happened but turned her attention to the scene before her. A burly elderly man stood square in the doorway yelling, red-faced, at a tall young man with a clipboard saying something was impossible.

With the defeated and yet patient air of someone who is explaining something for the third or fourth time, the young man said, "Sir, I can only give you my professional opinion. It's not like I haven't seen this before. You're the seventh person in this subdivision alone who has this problem. The concrete foundation didn't cure properly before the house was built, so the weight of the construction and instability of the surrounding earth that wasn't compacted properly is causing foundation cracks." He glanced at her, nodded, and smiled tightly, then turned back to the man standing in the doorway. "It's a problem with the construction company. Your house could still be under warranty, or failing that, you could join the class action suit that's pending. I can give you the information —"

"Bunch o' horse crap," Henry de Boer yelled, jabbing his finger at the worker. He scratched an inflamed cut on his chin where he had haphazardly tried to shave, missing much of the gray stubble. "My daughter built this house, and she'd never have sold me a lemon. Stick your goddamn opinion where the sun don't shine. I'm gonna call your boss about this."

When the basement repair fellow threw up his hands and strode away, Jaymie stepped into the space he had vacated and said to the homeowner, "Mr. de Boer, my name is —"

"I don't give a flying crap what your name is. C'mon in."

"But I —"

"Don't stand there wasting warm air. C'mon in and I'll show you the place."

"But I —" Too late. He was gone, the door

trying to close behind him whacking her in the shoulder. May as well follow.

FOURTEEN

She entered and set her purse on the floor in the tiny foyer. "Mr. de Boer?" she called out.

"In here."

She followed the voice but went slowly, taking in framed photos on the wall of a couple in a posed wedding photo, circa nineteen sixties. There followed photos of two little girls, dressed identically, growing up. Jaymie examined them closely. Two little blonde girls, one a toddler, one a baby, dressed in identical Easter best, and another, again in identical dresses, sitting on Santa's knee. Candy and Mandy, two blonde, then brunette, then — in a rebellious teen phase — redheaded girls. In later life they had finally found individuality, it appeared, with Candy's hair now dyed blonde and Mandy's flaming red hair. When she reached the living room she found their father in an easy chair with papers spread out around him.

He looked up at her and said, "Don't know why they sent another girl. Regular one isn't due until tomorrow anyway, but the place is a mess, so get started. Soap and pails and rags are in the coat closet and, and . . ." He seemed to lose the thread of his thoughts, water gleaming in his eyes. He shook his head.

"Mr. de Boer, I'm sorry, but I'm not your cleaner. I came to see you to offer my condolences on Mandy's death." He listened to her, a confused look on his face. It looked like he needed company. "May I fix you some lunch?" she asked.

He nodded.

She got her bearings in the small house and headed to the kitchen.

He followed her and plunked himself down in a creaking farmhouse chair at a dusty round wood table cluttered with newspapers, crossword puzzle books and more paperwork, insurance forms from a local broker. Shoved to one side was a clutter of drink packets, plastic paper napkin holder, salt and pepper shaker, bills, toothpicks, cream for muscle aches, arthritis pain pills, vitamin bottles and more prescription medications.

"What would you like for lunch?"

185

He grumbled that it didn't much matter.

"Would you like coffee?" she asked, noting the dregs in a drip coffee maker.

He nodded again.

As she checked the fridge, he donned smudgy reading glasses and riffled through the insurance papers. She glanced at him, wondering if he understood what he read. He appeared perplexed. Mandy had likely taken care of these things for him.

The fridge held the usual staples: condiments, milk, an opened tin of evaporated milk, crusty around the lip, take-out containers, and plastic tubs of leftovers. Someone, though, was organized. There were multiple tubs with labels lettered in a round clear hand she recognized from the office calendar as Mandy's: chili, soup, chili-mac, spaghetti. The last date was Sunday, a homemade microwave dinner of roast beef and gravy, partially eaten. She opened and sniffed other tubs, tossing anything with too old a date and adding the empty container to the sink. She turned on the faucets and watched as it swiftly filled with soapy water.

"My daughter usually takes care of things, but she's dead."

She turned and regarded him with pity, wiping bubbles from her hands. "At least you have another daughter," she said.

"She's too busy to help her old man."

"Too busy?"

"She runs a construction company. The one that built this place," he said, throwing down his smeary glasses and waving a broad gray-furred hand around him.

"Your daughter who is still alive runs a construction company?"

He blinked and frowned then shook his head. "No, that ain't right. It's the other . . ." He shook his head again and fell silent.

She turned back to the sink, washed what was left, put the last mug in the drainer tray, pulled the plug in the sink and wiped her hands dry.

Jaymie assessed what was left in the fridge and decided on a grilled ham and cheese sandwich. She put on the drip coffee maker first, then assembled the sandwich, grilling it as she dried the dishes, doing her best to put them away where they belonged.

She made them both a cup of coffee, then plated his sandwich, cutting it into triangles and putting the catsup within reach in case he wanted it. She sat down opposite him as he started to eat, tentatively at first, and then with real hunger. "What are all of these papers, Mr. de Boer?"

"Insurance."

"On the house?"

He nodded. "Don't know what to do. Damned house. First day I moved in the damned sink leaked and the toilet wouldn't fill."

"Where did you live before this?"

"House me an m'wife built new, back in the seventies."

"Why did you leave it?"

"Mandy told me I'd make money on it and could buy this piece o' crap. Smaller. Easier to look after." He harrumphed.

"But your daughter must not have known it would have problems when you moved in?"

"Guess not." He slurped coffee and ate.

"About Mandy," she said, and began to ask him questions about her.

As he spoke, he became clearer. He knew what day it was, and what day Mandy died. Yes, the police had been to see him — girl detective, he said — and he told them all he knew. His daughter had visited him Sunday afternoon about three and brought him the roast beef dinner.

"How was she?"

"Worried. Upset."

"What about?"

"Something about work, probably."

"Did she tell you what was bothering her?"

He took his last bite, chewed, then wiped his mouth and put his paper napkin on his plate in a wadded ball. He thought for a long moment and finally said, "Said someone at work was cheating, or had cheated. She was awful upset at that Randall fellow. Smooth talker. Never liked the look of him. He'd sell his grandma for spare parts."

An interesting take that confirmed her impression of Kallis.

"Poor Mandy," he said, shaking his head, water welling in his bloodshot eyes. "She had an accident, y'know. Car was banged up but she was still driving it. Awful bruises on her face. I said she looked like hell. She knew she'd had the accident but couldn't remember how it happened. Things were bad at work, too. Problems with houses, the newer ones, like mine."

"You do have problems with your house."

He blinked and looked around. "Leaky basement. Coupla other folks around here got the same thing. Bunch of whiners, the lot of them. Put in a sump pump, I say."

"That won't correct foundation leaks."

"Guess not. She said it happened on her watch. She was gonna fix it, by hook or by crook, she said, and she'd make sure the crook was out."

"What did that mean?"

"She was worried the company was going to go under, y'see. She'd been hoping to leave it to Trina, my only grandkid. Guess I'll finally see her now that her mom is dead. About time. These kids don't give a good goddamn about me. She wanted to protect Chad's legacy, she said."

Jaymie recalled Randall Kallis's derision, his implication that Mandy knew nothing coming in and had to be coached the whole way. Sort of like the fox coaching the hen on egg-laying practices, it seemed. And yet how did it benefit Kallis for the company he co-owned to end up in such trouble? It didn't make sense.

"So, she was concerned that it happened while she was in charge, meaning after Chad's death. How *did* it happen, the foundation issues in multiple homes? Did she say?"

"She said it was something about subcontractors. I dunno." He pushed his plate away. "But there was something else upsetting her. She wasn't feeling well, she said, wasn't feeling right."

"Oh?"

"Said she was forgetting to do things, and I said, now Candy, you're not forgetting me, and ain't that most important?"

"You mean Mandy."

190

"Did I say Candy? Meant Mandy. Idiot notion, naming the two girls like that. M'wife's fool idea. She thought it was cute. Dressed 'em alike too, their whole childhood, like they was twins. Couldn't hardly tell them apart when they were little. I went along because she said I could name the boy when we had one, but we never did." He shook his head and tears welled in his eyes. "We never did. Just the two girls. Lost a couple, but not the girls. My wife used to say we were lucky. *Henry,* she'd say," he said, wagging his finger, "*Henry, don't you know a son's a son 'til he takes a wife, but a daughter's a daughter for all your life?* Then she'd smile. She died when the girls were in high school. Left me alone to look after 'em. But now I'm down to one daughter, Mandy. She's all I got left."

"You mean Candy," Jaymie gently corrected.

"Candy? Oh. Yeah, I guess so." Tears spilled from his eyes and trailed down his cheeks. He swiped them away. "Last time I saw her, Sunday afternoon. She had to hurry off to some meeting in Queensville. Last time I saw my daughter."

She handed him a tissue and he blew his nose as she patted his shoulder. "Was she going anywhere first, sir?"

191

He blew his nose again and tossed the tissue aside, nodding. "Said she had to talk to someone. Had to figger something out."

"Who?"

"Some fella."

"Was it someone you knew?"

He shrugged.

"Randall Kallis, maybe?"

He frowned and shook his head. "Don't think so."

"Brock Nibley?"

"Nope, that wasn't it."

"Greg Vasiliev?"

"That's it! Rusky name. Candy's first hubby. I liked him."

Jaymie did some rapid calculation in her head. Mandy had been here at three and likely stayed for a while at least, say until four. She was then going to see Greg. Where did they meet, and for how long? "Did she say why she was going to talk to Greg?"

"Didn't hear her if she did."

There was a knock at the door. That was likely Candy, Jaymie thought, and went to answer, not sure what kind of reception she'd get from the grieving sister. But it was Ti Pham standing at the door with her arms full of grocery bags.

"Oh!" she said, physically stepping back.

"Hi," Jaymie said, moving away from the

door to allow the other woman in. "I dropped in to visit Mr. de Boer and he thought I was his cleaner. I thought he looked lonely so I made him coffee and lunch." She was half ashamed she had come to pump him for information. It could look like she had taken advantage of an old man's befuddlement, and hadn't she?

"That's nice of you," Ti said mildly, slipping off her shoes in the entry. Jaymie took one of her laden bags from her. "I brought him groceries," Ti said. "Mandy always shopped for him."

"What about Candy?"

"She's got enough on her plate right now, I'm sure," the woman said, glancing away. "With everything going on. It's going to be all on her shoulders now, her dad and everything. If you've spent some time here, you know he has memory lapses and other problems."

"Other problems?"

"Oh, arthritis that limits his movement, balance issues, mood changes. He can be difficult."

"Will Trina take over his care?"

"She lives and studies in England. He needs everyday help." Ti moved past Jaymie to the kitchen and greeted Mr. de Boer with a hug, bending over him like a protective willow. With a familiarity borne of past acquaintance, she chatted with him as she put away his groceries. Jaymie refilled his coffee mug and listened.

"I went to the flea market over the weekend and thought of you, Henry," Ti said. "I bought you some of those spicy pepperonis you like. I'll put them in the fridge. Don't eat too many at once. You know they give you heartburn if you eat more than one or two. On a healthier note, I made pho and brought you some." She set a labeled plastic tub of the broth in the fridge along with a plastic bag of veggies. "You liked it last time I made it," she reassured him. "All you have to do is pour some broth in a bowl and microwave it, then put in these bean sprouts." She held up a plastic bag of fresh sprouts. "I'll be back tomorrow and make you some spring rolls, so I'll use up the bean sprouts then. You like my spring rolls. So good for you!"

Mr. de Boer grunted, then looked at his watch. "M'show is on," he said. He lumbered into the living room and switched on the TV to a *Dateline* episode.

When he was gone, Ti turned to her. "You came here to grill poor Henry," she hissed, her tone low but sizzling with fury. "What do you think he'll know? He can barely remember his name." She turned away and her shoulders slumped. "I didn't mean that how it sounded," she muttered, palms flat on the countertop. Her voice was choked.

Jaymie put one hand on the woman's shoulder, with as light a touch as she could manage. Ti had lost someone who was probably like a sister to her. That was heartbreaking to consider. "I know this looks bad, like I'm taking advantage." She paused. "Maybe I *am* taking advantage, Ti, but I won't apologize. You've lost a good friend in Mandy. Maybe your best friend? If you think about it, aren't you willing to do anything to find out what happened? That's all I want, to find out what happened. The quicker it's resolved the better for everyone."

"You're acting like this is murder." She regarded Jaymie with a cool gaze. "The police haven't even released a cause of death yet. Or if they have, I haven't heard about it."

"Trust me, the police will be treating this like a murder, even if it may turn out to be a death by natural causes. No one has time to do otherwise."

Ti sat down in Henry's vacant chair and covered her face with her hands, weeping into them. "I can't believe she's gone. She always joked I was her 'sister from another mister.' Who would kill Mandy? And why?"

"Aren't you in the best position of perhaps anyone apart from her family to answer that? She talked to you."

Ti nodded but was silent.

Jaymie watched her for a moment. "You're worried. Mandy was in some kind of trouble. She must have confided in you."

"Can't you trust the police to take care of it?" Ti jumped up and finished putting food away in the fridge, freezer and cupboards.

Jaymie took a deep breath, sat down at the table, and folded her hands in front of her, noting the stiff spine of the other woman, her aggressive movements and jerky head tilt. "No, I can't. This is too important."

Her head jerked up and she slapped her hands on the counter. "You're right, though. If Mandy was murdered, I want the son-of-a-bitch caught. And yes, before you say anything, I *know* Val would never do anything like that."

"Okay, who could? There must be other people who Mandy had a negative relationship with."

"Maybe, but Mandy could be secretive. She worried a lot." She shook her head. "She didn't trust easily."

196

"Maybe you can help me with something else. I'm trying to figure out what her last day was like. She was here between three and maybe four. Her father says she was going off to talk to Greg Vasiliev from here."

Ti looked startled and frowned. "Really? Greg?"

"You seem surprised. Was he someone she didn't get along with?"

"It's not that."

"What is it? You know Greg, right?"

"Everyone knows Greg. My brother has worked for him before."

"Your brother?"

"My brother's a contractor and Greg is in real estate."

"I didn't know that. Why would Mandy meet with Gre—"

"Let me think about this," Ti said, holding one hand up. "I have no idea why she'd be going to see Greg, but let me think about it."

She didn't appear ready to say anything more. The TV boomed as Mandy's father turned up the volume. Impatient to make headway, Jaymie said, "Ti, we have to face facts. Mandy made some devastating accusations against Val and they have taken on a life of their own."

"I don't understand the whole thing."

"Me neither, especially since it was Helen who took the prescription, dispensed it, and handed it over to Mandy."

A cloud shadowed Ti's expression. "Helen didn't do anything wrong."

"Neither did Val. Statistically speaking, a killer is almost always a family member, a friend, or coworker with a personal — or business — motive. If it *was* murder, then almost certainly the killer was close to Mandy. You probably know them. It's someone she made angry, or scared, or unhappy. *Or* someone who benefited from her being gone." She took a deep breath. "Who were those people?"

"No one!" Ti said, but her voice trembled, and there was fear in her eyes.

"We've all made people angry. Each of us . . . our death benefits someone."

"I don't like to think that way!"

She examined the other woman's face and saw the doubt and fear and indecision. "Ti, clearing Val of suspicion also helps narrow down the list of who could have killed Mandy. It seems like she was in a bad place. Has she seemed like herself lately?"

"There was something she wasn't telling me, something upsetting her. I asked her if everything was okay and she said she was fine. I didn't believe her, but how much can you push? We were close, but Mandy wasn't one to share her deepest darkest thoughts." She took in a deep breath. "Of course, I'm a bit of a closed book too, I've been told." She paused and became misty-eyed. "She was so excited about her daughter coming home for the holidays. She had plans." Her lip trembled and her breath caught. "She was a wonderful person, warm and loving and generous to a fault. I miss her terribly."

Jaymie let it go a moment, but then asked, "Was she ever self-destructive, in the way of taking drugs?"

"Not illegal ones. Not that I know of, anyway."

"Prescriptions?"

"Nothing she would abuse. She took an antianxiety med but she was so careful! She asked me about it once, knowing Helen is a pharmacist. Helen said it was pretty common, but if she was worried, she should talk to her doctor about it." She hesitated, then said, "I did wonder . . . I mean, I know some antianxiety meds can cause a bad reaction." She stopped.

"Anxiety, paranoia, clumsiness?" Val had mentioned those possible side effects.

She nodded. "I wanted her to talk to her doctor. I almost had her convinced, but we ran out of time." She grabbed a tissue from a box on the table and dabbed, sniffing back tears. "Other than that, she took a cholesterol pill and one for high blood pressure."

"She was on a diet, too."

"Oh, you mean the Keto Kolonic stuff that Candy sells? Both of them swear by it and I must say, Candy has lost about thirty pounds in the last year."

"I notice her dad has some packets. What's in it? Is it okay with Mandy's meds? Some herbal supplements can clash with prescription meds."

"Helen was okay with it." She blew her nose and tossed the used tissue in the open garbage by the back door. "When I mentioned my concerns, she asked me to get her a packet of the stuff. She looked it over and said it was protein powder with some added vitamins. The company has an okay reputation, though I told Candy once that it sounded like an MLM scam to me, with all the pressure to recruit salespeople."

This was going nowhere fast, and yet Ti, being Mandy's best friend, must know something helpful. "You say she was different lately and I believe you. In what way, and why? And for how long?"

"Lately she had started talking about someone being out to get her but wouldn't elaborate. I kept asking but all she'd say is, she'd tell me when she could. She was afraid, paranoid." She stopped and her eyes widened. "But given what happened, maybe it wasn't paranoia. I loved that girl. She was the sister I never had, strong-minded, a bit high-maintenance, but loyal to the dirt. She was a great mom and a good daughter, even though Henry can be difficult."

"He said Mandy was worried about all the problems with Manor Homes, right?"

Ti nodded. "There was a lawsuit, and even *this* house is falling apart. Henry only moved in a year and a half ago or so and there were problems from the beginning."

"He said the plumbing leaked the very day he moved in."

Ti leaned across the table. "Whatever was going wrong with Manor Homes, it wasn't *her* responsibility."

"What about the older Manor Homes? Do they have the same problems?"

"Only the ones since Chad died."

"The ones built since Mandy took the helm as CEO of Manor Homes, you mean."

"Look, all Mandy did before he died was bookkeeping. Running the business was hard. Chad had a lifetime to learn. But regardless of who was in charge they had people who kept things afloat. It should have been enough to keep the quality up."

"Especially with Randall Kallis there."

Ti nodded. "Even though I don't like the man, he must know what he's doing. He's been there long enough. Mandy was determined to straighten things out, anyway, to come to terms with the homeowners suing her. She was meeting with them —"

"Meeting with them? Who? What day? Had she already met with them?"

Ti pulled back at Jaymie's intensity. "Not yet. She had tried before, but they weren't having it. The worst were Dina and Connor Ward. They were the ones spearheading the class action suit. Troublemakers, if you ask me."

Jaymie remembered the couple from the auction. The husband was plenty mad. Angry enough to kill? There had been slighter motives for murder. "Don't they have a right to a home without serious problems?"

"Mandy offered them solutions, but they wouldn't let the Manor Homes guys into the house to do repairs. Connor is the worst, he's some piece of work. I mean, did they want help or a lawsuit?"

He did say at the auction that there was no way he was allowing a Manor Homes worker into his house, but who could blame him for not wanting the same people who had caused the problem to try to fix it?

"I have to go," Ti said. "I have a board meeting for the food bank to brainstorm fundraising. We have to pivot, now with the Manor Homes partnership in danger."

"Is it?"

"Even if Manor Homes goes ahead with the partnership, we don't know when we can work on it, or even if it will happen with Mandy gone. It was a big part of our projected revenue stream for the next year." Unspoken was her stated dislike and mistrust of Randall Kallis.

"Who inherits Mandy's part of the company?"

"Trina, I guess."

"Not Candy?"

"I don't think so, but I don't know for sure."

First rule of investigation, follow the dollars, Jaymie thought. Who inherited? Who were the beneficiaries of insurance policies on Mandy? And who had access to her in intimate settings? Which made her wonder: "Did Mandy have a boyfriend?"

"No."

She decided to float a question she already knew the answer to, kinda sorta. "Was she close with Randall Kallis? He looked stricken when I saw him at the police department supporting Candy. Anything going on with him and one of the sisters?"

"I don't know. Honestly. Jaymie, I'll tell you this: I don't know who killed Mandy or even *if* it was murder, but I want to, and so will Trina. She loves her mother. We have to know!"

FIFTEEN

"I have to go," Ti said.

"Me too," Jaymie said as Ti gathered her things. She followed the woman into the living room.

Ti took up the remote, turned the TV down, then leaned down and gave a drowsy Henry a kiss on the cheek, a pat on the shoulder, and promised him dinner the next day. Jaymie settled for a friendly farewell. He barely responded.

Outside a chill wind blew, tugging at her clothing and tearing wisps of hair out of her ponytail. Jaymie wrapped her jacket more closely about her and turned to Ti, who hoisted her bag up on her shoulder and dug in it for keys. "You haven't known Candy as long as Mandy, correct?"

"No. I've known Mandy ten years or so. Candy only came back to stay, oh . . . two or three years ago."

"What's your impression of their relationship?"

"It was okay, I guess. Siblings are your friends for life, whether you like it or not."

It sounded like she was talking about her and her brother. "Are you good friends with Candy?"

Ti regarded Jaymie through narrowed eyes. "You're not trying to pin this on Candy, are you? Because that's ridiculous. She's got nothing to gain and everything to lose. She'll have to take care of their father now, no easy chore," she said, eyeing the house. "He was always difficult when they were growing up, from what Mandy told me."

The notion that Candy would have to take care of their father now only went so far. Not everyone felt the same level of responsibility toward aging parents. "I'm not thinking anything, I promise." Though she was. "I'm gathering information." They said goodbye, with Ti promising to contact Jaymie if she thought of anything.

"I need to talk all this over again with Mrs. Stubbs," Jaymie said out loud. She knew more now than she had the previous day and wanted the older generation's perspective on the family. "And then some research into Manor Homes and their troubles."

Mrs. Stubbs was in the dining room, seated with Mrs. Bellwood and Mrs. Frump. They were having a special cream tea the chef laid on for Mrs. Stubbs and her friends when asked. Jaymie sat with them and drank tea, nibbling on a few of the trayed goodies offered. The two guests grilled Jaymie about her "latest body," as they called it.

Jaymie shifted uncomfortably in her chair and evaded the questions. Thinking about poor Mandy dying on that stoop alone left her nauseous and faint. True crime was best enjoyed at a distance, when you didn't know the victim.

Mrs. Stubbs eyed her and spoke more lightly of the de Boer sisters. "I can tell you which of them was in the library more often," she said. "Mandy loved those silly Sweet Valley High books."

"Becca had some of those!" Jaymie said.

"I've known those girls all their lives," Mrs. Bellwood said. "They were in my Michigander Girls Troop," she said, naming a local girls' organization, now defunct. "We called them the MichiGirls. All of them were in it: Mandy and Candy de Boer, Valetta, Becca, DeeDee . . . *all* of them. It had disbanded by the time you were grown enough, Jaymie. No one wants to volunteer anymore, I guess."

"I don't know that I've ever heard of the MichiGirls."

"We had so many girls we had to have two nights a week for two separate groups. The de Boer girls belonged to the Wolverhampton chapter, while Becca, Dee, and Val belonged to the Queensville chapter. But we gathered for fundraisers, group camp-outs, parties and such. Everyone got along at that age."

"And then middle school happens," Mrs. Stubbs said drily. "Hormones kick in and everything goes haywire."

"What was their mother like?" Jaymie asked.

"Mrs. de Boer was a sweet woman, genuinely a delight," Mrs. Bellwood said. "She sewed all Mandy and Candy's clothes, identical but in different colors, blue for Mandy, pink for Candy. She made the best butter tarts around before Tansy's Tarts came along." She paused with a frown. "She always seemed sad, though."

"Sad. What do you mean?"

Mrs. Bellwood hesitated and slid a glance from one side of the small group to the other, taking them all in. "Like her life didn't turn out as she expected. I wondered at the time if Henry was mean to her."

"Do you mean hurt her?" Jaymie asked.

"Not physically. At least, I hope not. But he was such a wretch. All he ever did at gatherings was grunt and eat."

"And spit and belch," Imogene Frump added with a sniff.

"She died when the girls were in high school?" Jaymie said.

"And was ill for a long time before she died. I felt sorry for her. We all pitched in: casseroles, rides for the girls, a bit of house cleaning. Henry could never be bothered. Both girls were cheerleaders, I think?" Imogene nodded in agreement with her friend's assertion. "Only eleven months apart, sometimes friends, sometimes competitors. Sometimes mortal enemies. But they'd band together the minute anyone came at one of them."

"I always thought Mandy took her mother's death the hardest of the two girls," Ms. Frump said.

"Why do you say that?" Jaymie asked.

The woman shrugged. "Just an impression."

"Candy hid her feelings," Mrs. Bellwood said.

"You may be right," her friend replied.

Mrs. Stubbs said, "When their mom died Valetta befriended Mandy, if I recall. They were the best of pals for a while, but something happened and the two girls didn't chum around as much."

"Val didn't tell me that," Jaymie said.

"She's not one to toot her own horn," Mrs. Stubbs replied. "She wouldn't talk about it if it could appear to be bragging about her kindness."

"None of this explains why Mandy has been so odd lately."

"What happened to change her behavior?" Mrs. Stubbs mused.

Mrs. Bellwood said, "Maybe she was going through the change. Women do get grouchy while going through the change."

"Pshaw, Tree, that's ridiculous," Mrs. Stubbs said. "I didn't change one iota when I went through menopause."

Mrs. Bellwood said to Jaymie, "My granddaughter heard something when those folks were all talking on Sunday night. She heard Ms. Pham ask Mandy de Boer something about falling down stairs."

"What?" Jaymie, startled, dropped her fork. "I never heard about that."

Mrs. Bellwood, taken aback, said, "Why don't you ask Taylor? She's around here somewhere."

Jaymie found the server outside taking a break on the inn patio. She hastily butted out a cigarette and gave Jaymie a chagrined look. "Don't tell my grandmother, please!"

"Not my business, Taylor. You're an adult; you do you."

Taylor grimaced and waved away the lingering smoke. "I *know* it's bad. I only smoke a cigarette now and then when I need it and can borrow one from someone."

Jaymie pulled her jacket around her, shivering as she sat down on a patio chair across from the young woman. "Taylor, I came out to ask you a question." Jaymie relayed what Mrs. Bellwood had said about Ti's conversation with Mandy. "Do you remember exactly what was said?"

"Let me think." She gathered her thoughts, watching a dusty white car pull through the parking lot, using it as a short-cut to the next street. "I was talking to Olivier. We were in the prep hallway, where the coffee maker is kept, chatting. Ms. Pham was close by around the corner from us. I could hear her voice and she was saying something like, *Mandy, please, you have to be more careful* and then Ms. De Boer said something like, *I'm fine, stop fussing, Ti,* and then Ms. Pham said, *Remember how you fell down your basement stairs last month. I'm worried about you, Mandy. You should have gone to a doctor.*"

"Wow. You heard all that?"

"Sure."

"What else?"

"Ms. de Boer said something about a dizzy spell, but that she was fine. And then they walked away."

"Why did you mention it to your grandmother?"

Taylor flushed a pale pink. "I was worried. She had a dizzy spell yesterday, and I said something about Ms. de Boer, and how she fell, and maybe the dizzy spell was how she ended up dead. I told Grandma I was worried about her."

Made sense.

"I asked Olivier about what I heard. He remembered her talking about it when she came in to the office. She'd had a dizzy spell and fell down her basement stairs, she said, and was bruised, but she was fine and didn't need to go to the hospital or see her doctor. Olivier said she was bruised and had a black eye."

And yet no one, not Ti, not Randall Kallis, *no one,* had mentioned the dizzy spell or the fall. Not that they needed to say anything to her, but had they told the police? Jaymie would certainly tell Vestry. Maybe

212

she had a concussion and didn't even realize it. Could that, combined with the other
injuries from accidents, have ultimately led
to death from natural causes on the back
step of the pharmacy? "Was there anything
else odd about Mandy de Boer that evening?
Anything you noticed? Who did she talk to?
What did she eat?"

"She didn't eat anything."

"But it was a dinner meeting."

"First off, she came late."

"What time?"

"Their reservation was for six. She came
in after the rest had arrived."

"And had that run-in with Bonnie Smith
about the car accident."

"Sure. And then she wouldn't order. She
was hyped up, agitated. She brought her
own 'dinner' in a sippy cup."

"She was on a weight-loss program. That
would have been a keto shake. Did you see
her drink it?"

She nodded. "She complained of a headache and downed a couple of painkillers
with the shake. I said something to the dining room manager about it — I mean,
people aren't supposed to bring in outside
food, you know? It's a restaurant — but she
said if it was a special dietary thing, we

213

shouldn't interfere. We try to accommodate."

"You *saw* her drink it?" Jaymie insisted.

"To the last drop."

But was it the keto shake? What was *really* in the bottle? Was she intoxicated after all, Jaymie wondered, not from anything she ordered at the restaurant but maybe something she brought with her, concealed as a diet shake? And what pills was she taking? So many questions! "What went on in the meeting?" It had gone on for hours, apparently. "Did Mandy take part?"

"I was busy waiting tables and tending bar so I only heard their conversations when I was serving them or tables nearby, but yeah, she took part. First, she complained about a lawsuit, and how they needed good publicity, and that partnering with the food bank would help. Ms. Pham seemed put off and asked what form the help would come in, and what did Mandy mean by partnering?"

Jaymie frowned. Sounded like tension between the best friends; interesting that Ti hadn't mentioned that at all. "I thought the Manor Homes–food bank fundraising collaboration was a done deal."

"I guess not. Ms. Pham complained that Ms. de Boer kept canceling meetings on her.

I don't know, maybe she was starting to have second thoughts."

"*Who* was having second thoughts?"

"Ms. de Boer. Olivier told me that Mr. Kallis was concerned about how much it was going to cost Manor Homes and was trying to talk her out of it. He says that Mr. Kallis and Ms. de Boer had knock-down, drag-out fights over it."

"Did Mandy sit with Mr. Kallis alone at any point?"

"She may have, but she kinda floated around the whole time, real jumpy."

"Agitated?"

She nodded, then her eyes widened. "Wait a sec. She *did* sit with Mr. Kallis for a while. They had their heads together. I wondered, were they having a fling? She sat with Olivier, too, for a minute but got up when her sister came back in. They sat at the bar for a while."

"What did *they* talk about?"

She shrugged.

"How did they look?"

"Mrs. Vasiliev seemed angry, or . . . worried, maybe? She put one hand on Ms. de Boer's shoulder, like you do when you're worried about someone, you know?"

Understandable, given Mandy's behavior.

"It seems like everyone came over to talk

to Mandy while she sat with Mrs. Vasiliev. Mr. Kallis. Olivier. Ms. Pham. And there were others, too. I swear, everyone in the place that evening knew her."

Jaymie's attention sharpened. "Others? Who else was there?"

"We were pretty busy. There were all the Dickens Days folks there for the meeting, so Grandma and Auntie Frump and the others. I saw some other woman talking to Ms. de Boer at one point. I didn't recognize her and I wasn't serving her table, but I'll tell you, they did *not* appear friendly."

"Another woman? What did she look like?"

"She was older, slim, tall, *very* elegant, you know? In the way that Miss Georgina is before too many G&T's." She giggled.

Ah, yes, Georgina and her G&Ts.

"And then Mr. and Mrs. Ward came in for dinner."

Connor Ward was there? "He didn't come over to talk to Mandy, did he?"

"He sure did *and* it got heated. He was leaning over her yelling into her face, practically spitting, he was so mad. He grabbed her shake bottle and I thought he was going to throw it. But Mr. Kallis got rid of him quick. Told him to back off, or he'd call the cops."

SIXTEEN

Angry, red-faced, belligerent Connor Ward, the one suing her, was at the inn that night and yelling at Mandy? Jaymie'd need to jot all of this down soon and then tell Vestry about it. That was all Taylor recalled. Jaymie thanked her, then went back inside, seeking Edith. She was in her usual spot, the reservation and check-in desk.

After preliminary niceties, Jaymie asked about the Sunday evening dining room guest list. Fortunately Edith didn't ask why Jaymie needed that information, she simply consulted her computer and rattled off the diners Taylor had already mentioned, then said, "But there were others who didn't reserve — casual diners, you know, plus some of our inn guests."

"Do you remember any of those?"

She gave more names, but they had all since checked out, except . . . there was one name that caught Jaymie's attention. "Wait, who?"

"Mrs. Shannon Manor-Billings."

"Manor?"

Edith looked at Jaymie over her reading glasses. "She's a guest here. Manor-Billings is hyphenated. She's very particular about that."

Shannon, Chad Manor's older sister! "How long has she been staying here?"

"Oh, a week or so. She's in town on business, she said, when she asked about long-term rates. Not a very friendly lady."

Edith was talkative, and Mrs. Manor-Billings likely was not. Could she be the elegant stranger Taylor spoke of, who spoke with Mandy?

The phone rang and Edith answered, sitting down at the computer to confirm a booking, so Jaymie returned to the dining room. As the ladies prepared to break up the tea party, Jaymie questioned each then sat in her SUV for a few minutes, letting the vehicle warm up as she wrote detailed notes of everything she had learned, which was quite a bit, as it turned out. The trio of ladies confirmed and made more precise what she already knew about who arrived when. With the avidity of the Queensville gossip telegraph in triple force, the three of

218

them, with some squabbling, had been able to say who else arrived when.

Jaymie jotted down the arrivals in order. Ti Pham. Then Olivier Ricci and Randall Kallis, followed soon after by Candy Vasiliev, looking for her sister. Mandy de Boer then arrived. Bonnie Smith stomped in a few minutes later and accosted the business-woman. Dina and Connor Ward came in.

Connor was furious. He accosted Mandy, which appeared to frighten her and Candy. Randall intervened and calmed the waters. The Wards then left without having dinner, too upset by Mandy's presence, apparently. None of the Dickens Days committee knew or noticed the woman Jaymie thought was Shannon Manor-Billings and could not at-test to when the woman arrived or with whom she spoke or interacted.

Jaymie got out her phone and did a brief internet search of some local websites, including the *Wolverhampton Howler,* input-ting the name Shannon Manor-Billings, and there she was, the late Chad Manor's sister. She called Val, told her what she had discov-ered, and asked her friend a few questions, like, could a fall down basement stairs resulting in facial bruising have resulted in a concussion.

"Absolutely," Val said.

"What would happen if the person ignored the symptoms?"

"Possibly a headache, blurry vision, or even dizziness."

"Would Mandy be the type to ignore something like that?"

"*Mandy* fell down her basement stairs?" Val said.

"Apparently."

"Who knows if she'd ignore adverse symptoms? Maybe."

"Okay. I'm going to tell Vestry. Her death could still be from natural causes, like we discussed, from the fall down the stairs and repeated car accidents." She hesitated, then said, "Val, I'm hearing a lot about you befriending Mandy when you were in high school. You never mentioned that part. Why?"

There was an uncomfortable silence. Then she said, "Her mom died and I felt so bad for her. We were only friends for a while, and then Mandy changed. I don't know why."

"Changed?"

"She stopped talking to me and started avoiding me. I've never known why and I was too proud to ask."

"So why didn't you tell me?"

"It wasn't relevant. That was almost forty

220

years ago, for heaven's sake."

She called Vestry and left a message relaying all she had discovered and all she thought. She finished with a question: did Vestry know Mandy de Boer had apparently fallen down her basement steps about a month before her death?

Jaymie returned home and wrote a few blog posts, scheduled them, then replied to comments. She then wrote the next "Vintage Eats" column with the reworked vintage apple crisp recipe, recalling the delicious scent of cinnamon and apple and how it filled their home. It evoked cherished memories of family gatherings from her childhood, as she hoped it would for readers. She had come to know some of them, and it warmed her when they told her how her column took them back to childhood and learning to cook by their parent's elbow, as Jaymie had learned from her Grandma Leighton.

She was on a roll of productivity, so she continued, making notes for her next radio appearance on the Sid Farrell radio show *Old Stuff with Sid.* She then called Jocie's school to arrange for the class tours of the Queensville Historic Manor.

Finally, she turned to a task she had been

looking forward to. From under the stairs she pulled out her collection of sieves to catalogue. She had managed to gather quite an array, from a small copper sieve that fit in the palm of her hand, to a large wood mesh-lined hoop tool that may have been used to separate root vegetables from the drying dirt that would drop away through the wire screen. The whisk display at the historic house had been simple, using shadow boxes Bill Waterman had built for her to contain the collection, as the whisks were mostly flat. The sieves were a different matter entirely. Some were small, some large and most awkward. How could they display them?

Hoppy begged for attention and curled up in her lap as she sat on the floor. Lilibet followed. Jaymie put her head back and relaxed, letting her mind wander. Her thoughts drifted away from murder and sadness to love and family, holiday planning, tea parties and Jocie and her new friends. She awoke from a brief nap to a crick in the neck and two snoring animals. It had been a lovely break, but she had to move. She gently shifted the snoozing animals to Hoppy's bed and packed the sieves away again. Figuring out how to display them would have to wait for another day.

As she thought about what to do next, Val called. After a brief exchange, she said, "I talked to the detective again. I wanted to know if they'd figured out if it was Mandy who vandalized my catio, but there's no definitive answer. So then I asked her if she had found out *if* or *why* Mandy changed that one prescription from being dispensed at the Wolverhampton pharmacy to mine. That's nagging at my brain. Vestry wouldn't say. She said, shouldn't I know already, being a pharmacist?" Jaymie could hear Denver purring on her friend's lap. After a pause, Val said, "I'm still staying at Brock's place. I love my niece and nephew, but I want to go home. Even Brock seems uptight."

"Does he now? That's interesting. He said something to me that I keep thinking of." She relayed what he had said about dating Mandy in high school. "Could he have been dating her again? Or Candy?"

"Why are you asking?"

"I don't know. I'm grasping at straws, I guess. I wondered if Mandy was focused on you because she had started dating Brock, or maybe they were dating and had a tiff and she decided to blame you or . . . I don't know."

"You *are* grasping at straws," Val said with

a chuckle. "There is nothing going on between Brock and Mandy. I'd know if there was." Val reassured Jaymie that she was fine. "About the prescription thing . . ." Val said.

"Do you think Mandy changed her pharmacy online and forgot about it?"

"Maybe, though she was adamant that she didn't change to getting her prescription from us. And yet we received it online through an automated request. Helen said she didn't think anything of it because it came in 'by patient request.' Now, either Mandy did it herself and forgot or someone else with access to her devices did it."

"That's crazy."

"If the intent was to get Mandy upset, it worked. She spiraled and became paranoid."

"Who would or could do that?" But Jaymie recalled Mandy's office, and her computer. Did she use the same password for every account, as some people did? If she commonly renewed her prescriptions online, anyone with access to her devices — phone, tablet, laptop, office computer — may have been able to access it. Candy, Ti, Randall, Olivier, or anyone else who had been into the office could have done it. The person may not have even needed to know her passwords. She thought of her own desktop computer tucked away in a corner alcove upstairs. Beside it she kept a handy reference book with all of her passwords written down for every account. Sometimes she even had the account name, number and password all in one place. It would be easy for someone to grab the information.

In fact, given a password and a few minor details, the change didn't even have to come via Mandy's computer or device, necessarily. Jaymie finally said, "It's something to consider. Call Vestry back and suggest the possibility."

"I don't need to. I'm pretty sure that's what she was implying when she said shouldn't I know, being a pharmacist. Talk to you later."

The moment Jaymie hung up she made a call, ready to apply a little judicious pressure. "Ti, everyone seems to be focusing on Val right now, but we can't get past the truth: it was your sister-in-law Helen who actually filled the prescription and not Val."

"You already said that. My answer is still the same, neither one of them did anything wrong."

"Agreed. But it sure looks to me like someone was trying to set Val up. Does Helen have any ideas about what happened?"

Ti hesitated, then said, "She did some investigating. She worked at the Wolverhampton pharmacy before she started regular work at the Queensville pharmacy and still has friends there, so she had one of them check it out. The change in prescription came in on their secure portal from Mandy's account, but here's the kicker: it was verified by text before the change was made."

Verified by text? "If Mandy didn't change the prescription — and she swore she didn't — someone had to have access to her cell phone."

But her hopes of resolution were dashed in the next moment. "The problem is, Mandy was notorious for leaving her phone lying around," Ti said. "She'd lose track of it for hours. It wasn't even password-protected."

Back to square one. "And we still can't be sure, given her forgetfulness lately, that she didn't do it herself. Ti, the prescription was authentic and correct and Helen filled it correctly. And yet Mandy went nuts, saying Val was poisoning her."

"As much as I loved that girl, I feel like the only thing that was poisoned was Mandy's mind."

"Someone close to her getting her riled

up? I don't understand. That's cruel, and what was the point?"

An audible sigh gusted through the phone. "I *was* starting to worry about her."

"Why?"

"She told me a while back that someone was coming into her house and moving things around."

"What kind of things?"

"She said her junk drawer had been re-arranged."

"Seriously? Her *junk* drawer? Was that a paranoid delusion, or did someone who came to visit rustle around in it, looking for something?"

"Could be either."

"And how does anyone know when someone has been in their junk drawer?" She paused, then said, "Ti, I heard that about a month ago Mandy took a tumble down her basement stairs. What happened, do you know? And do you think her death could be some kind of delayed reaction?"

"I don't see how. She had a dizzy spell and took a tumble."

"But maybe she had a concussion and that led to other problems."

"She had it checked. There was no concussion."

"You were concerned enough to mention

227

it to Mandy on Sunday evening at the Queensville Inn."

Ti was silent for a moment. "You have good sources." Her tone had shifted to caution. "Okay, she *told* me she had it checked, but I'm not completely convinced she did. If you deduced concern from my conversation with my friend, that's what it was all about."

"You were concerned she was becoming paranoid or delusional?"

Ti murmured an agreement.

"What else was she suspicious about?"

"The lawsuit the Wards were threatening to initiate. At one point Mandy swore their complaints were made up."

"But her own father's place has the same problems."

"I know."

"The Wards were at the inn Sunday evening and he had words with Mandy."

"Randall fended him off and Connor's wife convinced him to leave. Mandy grabbed his sleeve at the last minute, though, and said something to him, I don't know what. Lately she realized that the problems were real and she wanted to investigate who in their business could have caused the problems in the first place."

Oh. *Oh!* Suspicion, like a worm, wriggled

in Jaymie's brain, popping up, making itself known. How interesting that this investigation of Mandy's into her company's problems coincided with her murder.

Or *led* to her murder. "I don't think I understand how their business works. Who actually builds the houses? I mean, I know Manor Homes does, but do they have construction crews or do they subcontract?"

"They subcontract."

"Different crews all the time, depending on whose bid is best?" Jaymie said. She did not understand how the construction business worked, but figured it was a good guess.

"You would think so. But, ah, in the last four years they've only used one company."

Ti sounded reluctant, and Jaymie's interest was piqued. "Who owns that company?"

Hesitation again, then Ti finally said, "You're not going to like this."

"Why?"

There was silence for another long moment. Finally, she said, "My brother. Win and his wife Helen own the construction company."

Seventeen

"Win?" Jaymie was taken aback. "Your brother's name is Win?" Win, the man she had seen in the office speaking with Randall Kallis. Didn't Ti think that was worth mentioning when they were together at Henry's house and speaking of the problems with it?

"I know what you're thinking," Ti said quickly. "So many connections: Helen filling Mandy's prescription, Mandy insisting the drug was wrong and then dying. Win's company being Manor Homes' main builder locally, construction problems at the newer homes, the Manor Homes lawsuit . . . it's such a jumble."

"I suppose," Jaymie said, trying to make sense of it. Queensville and even Wolverhampton were smallish towns, but this level of connectedness was a little much.

"The prescription thing is a coincidence, that Helen should be the one dispensing,"

Ti said rapidly, as if she was reading Jaymie's mind.

She was right. Any other Tuesday Val would have been the one working.

"And as far as the construction and the lawsuit and the problems with Manor Homes . . . there's more to it than appears. My brother's company is not at fault."

This must have been a discussion she had with Mandy, considering her brother's involvement and Mandy and Ti's friendship. "Okay, I'm listening," Jaymie said.

"You asked who builds the Manor Homes houses and it's true, Manor contracts Pham Construction to build them —"

"By the way, why didn't you think that was something to tell me when we were both at Henry's house?"

"It didn't seem relevant. Anyway," she said, with heavy emphasis to move the conversation along, "there's more to it. My brother subcontracts many of the trades. His guys do the framing and a lot of the actual construction, but they subcontract for site prep, foundation work, HVAC, plumbing, electrical, roofing and various other trades. If they're super busy, they subcontract interior finishes like drywall, carpet and tiling. No construction company does everything anymore."

The foundations and plumbing appeared to be the most common problems with the more recent Manor homes. "Doesn't your brother's company vet those people first?"

"He wanted to, but there was a lot of pressure. Him and his wife moved here from Ohio a few years ago and he started the business from scratch. His last construction company went bankrupt."

Oh dear.

"He's determined to make this one work. Manor Homes was such a big contract, and he tried to find other jobs, but he has become reliant on them. It was an 'all his eggs in one basket' kind of thing, and he caved to pressure from Manor to use certain subcontractors. Ultimately Win had to trust Manor Homes."

Meaning Randall Kallis? Or was Mandy in on that part of the management of Manor Homes? "I don't think I completely understand."

"I don't want anything coming back on my brother. He's a good guy and a reputable builder. A class action lawsuit could destroy his reputation."

Maybe Ti didn't realize it, but this was beginning to add up to a substantial motive for murder, if Mandy had begun to investigate the problems. Was she looking to shift

232

blame to Win's company and thus neutralize the lawsuit? It sounded like Win Pham had made a deal with the devil — to maintain the Manor Homes contract they sabotaged their own reputation. She couldn't ignore the intricate way Ti was woven into Mandy's life, from the food bank, to her brother, to their friendship. How much did she care about her brother? She said herself that Mandy was always leaving her phone around and didn't have it password-protected. Ti could easily have changed the prescription to Val's pharmacy, not knowing — or not caring — that her sister-in-law might be the one filling the prescription.

And yet the drug itself was not a problem, so what would be the motive? It didn't make sense.

"Jaymie? You still there?"

"What? Yeah, I'm here. I'm thinking."

"Have you spoken to Shannon Manor-Billings yet?" Ti asked.

"I have not. I only learned this morning, as a matter of fact, that she was at the Queensville Inn at the same time as you all on Sunday evening. *Should* I speak to her?"

"You probably know she was Chad Manor's older sister. But did you know she was furious when the business was left to Chad?"

"She was left shares, though, right?"

"Sure, but Manor Homes is huge now. Back when her father died it was a small family-owned construction company. She hadn't shown any interest in it until Chad built the company into a major local developer. She was livid at being bought out cheap and cut herself off from her brother for a decade or more. That is straight from Mandy."

"Huh." It felt like Ti was scrambling to offer alternative suspects.

"She was even angrier when her brother died and left Manor Homes completely to Mandy. Those two never got along. I don't know if you *should* speak to her — she can be unpleasant — but if you're looking for someone who hated Mandy, she should definitely be on your radar. Look, I'm going to level with you. I've heard about your little investigations. I assume you're asking all these questions to try to exonerate Val of any involvement in Mandy's death —"

"*If* the death is not from natural causes, though that hasn't even been established yet, but yes, I'm getting out ahead of any potential problems."

"I know for darn sure Val didn't do anything. Neither did Helen, and neither did my brother. There were others closer to

234

Mandy, including Randall Kallis, and there were some angry with her, including Shannon, who, as you know, was at the inn Sunday evening talking to Mandy."

"She *did* speak with Mandy."

"I saw it with my own eyes and it did not look pleasant."

"Maybe I will try to speak with Shannon."

"I'm sure staying at the Queensville Inn suits her vision of herself as an elegant not-motel kind of woman." Her tone was sour. At some point since they had last spoken, at Henry de Boer's home, Ti had decided to try to impose her theories on Jaymie. She said, in an insinuating tone, "You know she only came back because she was filing suit against Mandy to try to claw back some inheritance from the Manor family construction company."

That was news. "What is her argument for that?"

"To the best of my knowledge it is that the plans were already in place to take the family company bigger, and it was misrepresented to her when she agreed to the buyout."

"How would that work? I mean, she inherited what was in her father's will, right?"

"I don't know all the details. I only know

she's been pressuring Mandy to settle out of court. Maybe she knew she didn't have a leg to stand on if they got to court. It'll be different now with Mandy gone, especially if Trina inherits alone. Shannon and Trina have been friendly over the years."

"One more question. I've heard about Mandy's behavior Sunday night from a lot of different people. How did she seem to *you*?"

"Scattered. I told you, I've been worried about her lately. I kept telling her to see her doctor, but . . ." She trailed off and was silent.

"What did you think about her behavior lately concerning all of this trouble with Val?"

"I don't know." She sounded teary, sniffling. "I have to go. I'm picking Trina up at the airport. She's coming in on a flight in two hours. She's staying with me."

"With *you*? Why not at Mandy's house, or with Candy?"

"Too sad for the poor kid. I don't think she wants to be alone. Candy has her hands full with funeral arrangements and their father. Anyway, I offered and Trina said yes." She paused, then with a clogged sniff, said, "Trina is like a daughter to me."

After the call ended, Jaymie pondered the

possibilities. In most cases it was a matter of discovering who benefited from the victim's murder, Trina, in this case. She was clearly not a direct suspect, but could she have conspired with someone locally? Maybe even her Aunt Candy? Or her Aunt Shannon, who Ti suggested had much to gain from Mandy's death? It was yet another something to consider.

Jaymie picked up Jocie, supervised her homework, arranged with her friend's parents for a sleepover near Halloween, and made dinner. She got a quick callback from Gemma's mom, who said that as Jaymie knew, her daughter was having a piano recital Saturday morning and Jocie and all her friends had been invited. Maybe, she said, it would be nice for the girls to have a sleepover Friday night and then they could attend the recital in the morning?

Jaymie said that was a great idea, and she'd arrange for getting them to the recital from the cabin.

Once Jocie was in bed, Jakob took her hand and led her to their room. He held her for hours as she sighed and fussed and worried, and with a kiss he soothed her distress. They would sort it all out, he said. She was not in this alone.

In the dark, listening as Jakob fell into a deep, relaxed sleep, Jaymie thought how lucky she was to have such a man, who knew how important family and friends were and would go the extra mile to smooth the way for her and Jocie.

She thought about Candy Vasiliev, and how she must be missing her sister. Healing for that family could only take place once the manner of Mandy's death was resolved, and, if it was murder, the assailant caught. That was what Jaymie would want if Becca ever died in an unexplained way.

The next morning Jaymie spent three dizzying hours familiarizing herself with the local building scene, of which Manor Homes was *the* major mover and shaker. She read up on the current problems in the digital archives of the *Wolverhampton Weekly Howler.*

Perusing *Howler* articles reminded her of the newspaper clipping in Mandy's hand. Why had she been holding on to it? Was that what she wanted to talk to Val about? She thought back — it was an article on the power of social media in today's society. Okay, did that have to do with the apparent bullying she was receiving online from the Val impostor? Did she finally want to have an open discussion with Val?

Jaymie dug out the previous week's *Howler* from the recycling bin and spread it out, reading the article through. It was a filler piece with no great insights. She looked at what was on the flipside, wondering if there was something on the reverse, and hit pay dirt.

There were several smaller columns on the reverse side, plus some ads, a travel piece on pharmaceutical travel, whatever that was, alongside a travel agency ad with cheap fares to Mexico, but *then* there was the gold. "Aha!" she said, startling Hoppy, who snoozed at her feet. "This is it, Hoppy," she crowed, jabbing at the piece with her finger.

A *Howler* columnist had written a take-down of local township planners and their abuse of grandfathered usages in developments, especially by a particular unnamed developer who had recently been blamed for substandard housing. The article implied that money had changed hands with township officials to look the other way, a strong accusation to level.

She didn't know a lot about property development, but from the article she gathered that Manor Homes (the article hinted strongly that Mandy's company was the example) had abused the "prior non-conforming usage" rules. If a township official had accepted bribes to ignore the infractions, it was serious and could affect the company's future.

This had to be what Mandy was holding on to the article for, and perhaps what she wanted to speak with Val about. Except that didn't make a whole lot of sense. Unless . . . maybe Mandy wanted advice and didn't feel comfortable going to her best friend Ti because of Ti's connection to the contractor used on Manor Homes developments. The high of thinking she had it figured out crashed in the face of common sense. Mandy going to Val at eleven p.m. on a Sunday night to talk about her construction business? It didn't make sense. There had to be something more immediate worrying her.

Eleven p.m. Randall had said he and Mandy were leaving the inn at about the same time, eleven or so. She was driving, but her car was found some distance from the pharmacy. How did she get to the pharmacy then? Did someone else drive her? Maybe that was the squeal of tires and the noise Taylor heard before retiring.

She saved the newspaper to talk to Val about it. She wondered if there was anything in the text messages they exchanged to indicate what Mandy wanted to discuss. It had clearly been important to Mandy.

She then spent another hour making calls, one of the first to Dee Stubbs, Becca's best friend, who had recently gone back to work at the Wolverhampton hospital. She asked a question, and Dee agreed to help if she could. She called back a half hour later.

The short précis of a longish conversation with Dee was that Mandy de Boer never did go to the hospital for testing to see if she had a concussion: not a month ago, not weeks ago, never. Maybe she had gone somewhere else, but that was doubtful. Dee had called in another favor and mined a connection at the medical examiner's office. The ME had, at the police department's request and because of widespread reports of Mandy's recent erratic behavior and car accidents, done complete testing of all tissues in search of a variety of substances. Some reports were back, but many would take longer, in some cases much longer.

She was known to be on a variety of prescription meds, including those for high blood pressure, high cholesterol, borderline diabetes and anxiety. There was a plethora of drugs that she did *not* have in her system, including fentanyl and oxy. Medication conflicts had to be considered in her death. Tests were being redone. Though her behavior in the hours before her death was erratic, her heart was strong and she was in generally good heath. Ultimately, there was no natural reason she should have curled up and died — no undetected heart ailment or embolism or stroke. She had not been choked or beaten, nor had she been shot or stabbed. There were no needle marks on her other than a recent flu shot.

She should not be dead. Further testing was being done and redone. Were the high levels of blood pressure meds in her system a problem? Or had she taken something else that lowered her blood pressure to problematic levels? Internal bleeding from previous injuries?

So many possibilities.

But what was interesting, Dee said (interesting being a relative term when a health care professional used it) was the presence of conjunctival and facial petechiae.

"Peta . . . what?" Jaymie said, stumbling over the word.

Petechiae, Dee explained, were hypoxia-related sequelae of asphyxia. Jaymie was about to ask for a further explanation, but Dee broke it down for her. "Those are little spots, in this case in the eyes and on the face, suggestive of asphyxiation."

"But you said she hadn't been choked."

"That's the thing, petechiae are present but there are no other signs of smothering or choking or manual asphyxiation. No hematoma, bruising, contusions, abrasions, finger marks, broken capillaries. It's possible there's another explanation for the petechiae."

"A natural explanation?"

"A non-homicidal explanation."

"Like what?"

"Oh, a coughing fit could do it. Or choking on food. I'm guessing," she hastened to add. "I'm not a coroner and I'm not a doctor."

"Okay, I get it."

Dee hung up and Jaymie's phone rang almost immediately. It was Mel — Melody Heath, her old college friend who was now an author — in a state of panic. She desperately needed a personal reference for a landlord, which of course Jaymie agreed to give her should the need arise. Mel, unhappily married, would say nothing more about what was going on in her life, other than admitting it was in turmoil.

But she didn't want to talk about it. Instead she asked Jaymie what was going on in hers.

Jaymie related everything she had gone through in the last few days.

"You do find bodies, don't you," Mel said, her tone amused.

"It's not funny, Mel. Val is in trouble. If they don't solve this, it's too awful to consider."

"Jaymie, get serious. No one in their right mind is going to think Valetta Nibley, she of the sensible shoes and spotless sterling reputation, is a killer."

"Mrs. Stubbs said much the same thing, only not so rudely," Jaymie admitted.

"There is a reason Mrs. S. and I get along superbly."

"Still, it's best for everyone if we figure it out." They talked, and Jaymie raised the petechiae question, musing out loud about what it might mean.

Mel, surprisingly, was familiar with the phenomenon. "It's short-hand for every mystery writer in the world. Petechiae equals strangulation in mysteries."

"But there aren't any marks on the throat or around the nose or mouth."

Mel was silent for a moment, then offered an explanation. Jaymie, startled, admitted it might have validity given what she knew about Mandy's most recent problems. The coroner had probably thought of it, but Jaymie hadn't known enough to even consider it. But with it in mind now, it changed things, subtly.

The author had to get off the phone that minute, she said, because she was expecting a call from her agent. She was overdue with one book, almost due with another, and needed to beg for more time. Poor, dear Mel, Jaymie thought, wanting only peace to write and always in crisis.

Jaymie had one more person to call who might offer valuable insight. "Nan, do you have a minute to answer a couple of questions?"

"What, for my star investigative reporter?" Nan said, sarcasm lacing her brusque tone. "I'm in a time crunch for a story from a reporter because of some new disaster brought on by a local bribery scandal, there was a hideous school shooting in a town not too far from here and all I'm getting is the usual bulls— bullsugar pass-the-buck denial from local politicians. No, I don't have time, but ask anyway."

Jaymie brushed away anxiety at Nan's impatient tone. That was how the editor often was, and she was learning not to take it personally. She asked her questions rapid-fire, one right after the other, knowing it was best with Nan.

"Okay, so, if I understand you right, you're asking is there anything hinky with Manor Homes — any bribery schemes or investigations — and about the lawsuits, and how it might all tie into Mandy de Boer's possible murder. I won't pretend I don't know why you're spending your time on this rather than the ten thousand other things on your plate. Val Nibley is your best friend. I'll answer in exchange for any info you have."

"I'll give you what I can, but I can't promise."

"Deal." What followed was a quick and precise breakdown of Manor Homes, their history, their family, and Mandy's part in it, as well as Randall Kallis and where the company likely stood now in the wake of this tragedy.

Jaymie blinked. "Randall Kallis is crooked as a paper clip and would do anything to hide it. Someone in the company is on the take and it's likely him. He's smart enough to have positioned someone else for the fall, maybe Mandy. Mandy's murder, if that's what it turns out to be, will have complicated things for Randall. As long as she was alive and he could manipulate her, he would come out smelling like a rose, therefore he likely had no business reason to kill her.

But since the rumor was that they had been having an affair before Chad Manor's death and continued it afterward, while he moved up to partnership in the company, there may be personal reasons." She took a deep breath. "Whew."

"You got it," Nan said. "However, if Mandy was beginning to push for answers, killing her may have been Kallis's only recourse. As for the lawsuit, I don't think Dina or Connor Ward had a reason to kill her. What would it get them? It'll delay things."

"But Connor Ward seemed, from what I've observed, to have a *personal* vendetta against Mandy."

"Then go visit them. Tell them you're from the *Wolverhampton Howler* and want some quotes on what they think about the chances of their lawsuit now that Mandy de Boer Manor is dead."

"Can I do that?"

"I'm giving you permission. If they call, I'll support it. I gotta go." She hung up abruptly.

EIGHTEEN

Jaymie drove through cold gusty rain to the outskirts of Wolverhampton and toured various Manor Homes subdivisions. Over the years they had managed to corner a substantial portion of the bedroom community market share, and were now, apparently, looking to move into the senior living sector. With the volatility of the real estate market it must be chancy, but potentially lucrative.

She exited the cookie-cutter subdivisions back onto the highway and followed signage indicating another Manor Homes Development ahead. The sign for Vintage Manor Estates crowed "Built to last like your grandparents' bungalows." Gravel roads had been laid in a grid, and surveyors' stakes marked plots. She steered down the slope, along the graveled road that bumped over a culvert and ditch, and into the development. She followed the lane, the windshield wipers slapping a rhythmic beat swiping away raindrops, and examined the development, an undulating patch of land with a dry creek bed that cut the property into halves. There were cul-de-sacs and courts, turning and twisting, cleverly following the hilly land. Anachronistically, a couple of buildings left from when it was farmland, and a corrugated metal storage silo, squatted in a patch of weedy brown grass tumbled with thistles and nettles. It looked like the construction company was using the old drive shed for storage because some of the weeds had been cleared and a shiny padlock fastened the shed doors.

Mandy had big plans, but today there was not a single soul around, no workers, no trucks. Would her work continue, or was this the end for Manor Homes? Jaymie tapped her thumbs on the steering wheel and hummed an unhappy tune. Everything in Mandy's life had been going great in recent years, if one judged by her social media presence. Despite the loss of her husband she seemed to be on a good track, with a happy daughter, friends, vacations, community volunteer work and a business she loved. Or was it all a sham, a social media show?

What had changed in her life to make it

fall apart?

On to the Wards' home. They lived near Henry de Boer in the senior bungalow community Manor Homes had finished most recently, Golden Manor Estates. Their tidy gray brick and blue-shuttered home was dominated by the two-car garage thrust aggressively forward. A walk circled a black mulched garden with decorative mossy river rocks in place of shrubs. The glass outer door protected a blue-painted door adorned with a woven wreath sporting blue and gray silk flowers and foliage with a blue raffia bow jauntily poking off to the side. She pressed the doorbell and heard the remote chime.

The neat gray-haired woman she had seen at the auction opened the inner door and peered through the glass at Jaymie. "Yes?"

"Mrs. Ward, I'm Jaymie from the *Wolverhampton Weekly Howler.* May I come in and speak with you?"

"No, no, I don't think so." She started to shut the door.

"Mrs. Ward, with Manor Homes' new Vintage Homes development about to begin construction we're, uh, investigating the company's shoddy practices and getting quotes from those who live in a Manor Home. You and your husband are named in the pending lawsuit against the company. Would you be willing to help us out with a little info?"

She shook her head, but paused, inner door half open.

Jaymie fished in her purse for Nan's business card. She held it up to the glass and said, "Call Ms. Goodenough, the editor in chief, if you'd like to confirm my credentials. With Mandy de Boer dead, do you think your lawsuit will run into delays? It must be awful living in a house with so many problems. Are you worried you won't get the satisfaction you need to fix your home in a timely manner?"

Dina appeared conflicted. It must have been tempting, going through a battle against larger forces, like a big development company, to lunge at the opportunity for some public leverage. She stared at Nan's card for a long minute, then opened the door. "You may as well come in. Connor and I *have* been worrying about this, about what's going to happen now with our lawsuit. It can't hurt to get it all out there."

Jaymie followed her in, slipping off her shoes and leaving them in the entrance once she saw the white carpeting in the blue and white living room.

"Come to the sunroom," Dina said. "I'm

making tea. Would you like a cup?" Once she had made the decision to invite Jaymie in, Dina became friendly and charming in an instant, like a switch had been flicked.

"Sure. Your home is lovely," Jaymie said as she slipped her jacket off, glancing around at the tidy space, white walls, tasteful paintings framed in blue wood frames, everything in its place.

Dina turned and stopped. "You're only seeing the surface. Do you want to see what we're dealing with?"

"I would." What followed was, Jaymie discovered, a homeowner horror show. In the basement, because of flooding from backed-up drains, wallboard had been cut and removed up about two feet from the floor, which had been stripped bare to expose cracked concrete. Ruts and mineral-crusted cracks radiated from a point where a section had heaved, an inch or more difference in the floor level from one cracked section to the other. A persistent smell of mold and earth assaulted Jaymie's twitching nose. Because of the floor heaving the downstairs bathroom, which they had paid to have completed when they moved in, was unusable, the water to it turned off for fear of cracked pipes.

Dina listed numerous other problems that

they corrected at their own expense to live in their home. "But we can't keep up with the problems. Our contractor said the products used were shoddy and the workmanship equally bad. It was bait and switch! We were shown a model home with lovely finishes and then got this . . . this *mess*!" she exclaimed, waving her hands around. "It will all be in the lawsuit."

Jaymie followed the irate woman to a pretty sunroom off the back of the house. It was furnished with vintage white rattan furniture adorned with floral cushions. Taking pride of place in a matching doggie bed was a long-haired tan and black dachshund. "Oh, so cute! What is her — his? — name?"

"That's Schatzi, my little boy. Isn't he darling?" she said, bending down and stroking the silky-haired dachsie. Her mood improved with her dog's wuffling pleasure at her caress. Jaymie pet the little dog, who intently sniffed her hands. "He's smelling my little dog, a Yorkie Poo!"

Dina disappeared and came back a few minutes later carrying a tray laden with a pretty tea set — white porcelain, with pale blue borders and garlands of rosebuds — that had the look of vintage, but Jaymie recognized it as a new set made in old-fashioned style. Schatzi begged sweetly, and

Dina lifted him up to sit beside her on the rattan sofa, then poured tea. The sun emerged from clouds and warmed the sunroom, which looked out on a view of the compact backyard kept immaculately tidy, a few stray leaves the only disarray. "This is lovely," Jaymie said. "I wish I had this kind of sunroom for my dog and cat. They'd love it!"

"It's Schatzi's favorite spot. He'll sleep out here all day unless a wind comes up. He's afraid when branches fall."

They spoke of pets for a few minutes, and then Dina said, jabbing her finger in Jaymie's direction, "I know now where I've seen you before! You write the 'Vintage Eats' column for the *Howler,* right?"

"I do. Do you read it?"

She nodded. "And I follow your blog. That's where I've seen your photo, I suppose."

She didn't appear to feel it was odd that a food columnist would be writing a news story on construction woes. They talked about cooking for a while, but inevitably the problems with the house came back up when Dina related trouble they'd had with the wiring for the electric stove. The problems were serious, Jaymie realized, not the complaints of disaffected whiners. And it was expensive. They had sunk their retirement into the house.

"We sold our old home. We intended to travel but my mother got sick, and we couldn't be out of the country for any length of time. She lives at Maple Hills Retirement Community." She stared out the window. "That's when we got Schatzi and bought this house. It was supposed to be our reward for all the years of hard work and sacrifice. Thought we may as well enjoy life if we're stuck in Michigan."

"I'm sorry about the problems you've been having with the house," Jaymie said with sincere sympathy.

"I thought we were getting close to a resolution, but now it looks like Mandy de Boer's death will make this a mess." Hastily she added, "Don't get me wrong, I'm not heartless. I know this is a tragedy for her family. I understand she has a daughter. And I know her sister, Candy, from years ago."

"You know Candy?"

"I do. My parents lived near their parents. I babysat them sometimes."

"What were they like back then?"

"The girls? Sweet kids. Pretty. Their mom sewed all their clothes and they'd look so cute in their matching outfits."

"I heard their lives got much more difficult after their mother died."

Dina nodded, sadness in her eyes. "She was such a sweetheart, but the dad . . ." She shuddered. "Anyway, we didn't stay in touch over the years, but still . . . I trusted her. When we bought this house Mandy was so helpful. We thought we were doing the right thing." She shook her head. "Connor blames me for that, but how was I to know Mandy had changed so much?"

"You think this is all her fault?"

"Well, who else? She was the owner, right? The boss? The face of the company? She kept promising a resolution but . . . Connor got fed up, finally. It was making the whole mess worse. She can say all she wants that she offered repairs, but who's going to trust those bozos they have working for them?"

"I get it."

"You don't know the half of it. It's ridiculous how their lawyers have been stalling for time."

"Stalling for time? What do you mean?"

"Oooh, that Randall Kallis! I could *kill* that man! We would have preferred a settlement and then we could have had the repairs done by a reputable company. Taking it to court is going to be a nightmare. But every time we thought we were making

256

headway, he'd call and say their lawyers needed this, or needed that. He'd like to settle, but Mandy was making things difficult." She paused a beat. "Do you know what happened to her?" the woman asked, casually pouring more tea, her gaze flicking up to eye Jaymie, then back down to the tea. "I hear she was murdered on the doorstep of the pharmacy right in front of Valetta Nibley by some drug fiend."

"Good Lord, where did you hear that?"

"It was a cashier at the grocery store in Wolverhampton, I think," she said vaguely, sipping her tea. "Or maybe it was at the retirement home."

"That's not what happened," Jaymie said, without elaborating. "I understand you and your husband ran into her at the Queensville Inn Sunday evening." Dina jolted, like an electrical shock had passed through her. She clasped her hands between her knees, holding them still, Jaymie noted. She was hiding something, but what? "That was hours before she died. How did she seem to you?"

"It was chance, running into her there." Dina wasn't answering the question. Jaymie stayed silent, and after a long pause the woman elaborated. "Connor and I have a schedule: bowling league on Tuesdays; my art class on Wednesday mornings at the senior center. Other things. We're very busy. And every Sunday we have dinner at the retirement home with Mother."

Jaymie stayed silent.

"But Sunday Connor decided . . . I mean, *we* decided to, uh . . . treat ourselves and get dinner out at the inn."

Decided to treat themselves, thus denying her elderly mother their company at their once-a-week dinner. "Why Sunday night and not some other night?"

"An impulse on his part." She shifted uneasily. "He gets these whims and I go along with it." She looked down at Jaymie's ring finger and saw the wedding set nestled there. "You know what it's like, when your husband makes a decision you go along to keep the peace."

"Did you know Mandy de Boer was going to be there?"

"No, I didn't," she replied tartly.

The implication was clear — she didn't, but Connor did. "Did your husband try to talk to her about the lawsuit?"

"With their lawyers dragging their feet, we want to get this settled so we can move on with our lives. How would you like a finished basement that's no longer finished? Half your house you can't even use anymore. It's disgraceful."

"He *did* talk to her?"

"He thought . . . *we* thought it would be better to do it face-to-face, to settle things like civilized human beings."

"Did it get heated?" Jaymie remembered what had been said about Connor getting in Mandy's face, and Randall Kallis having to intervene.

"Not at all. But we soon realized it was not a good time to take care of things. Mandy was . . . we didn't know she'd be with . . . that there would be so many people in her party."

"Your husband knew Mandy was going to be there. How?"

"He heard something about a meeting at the Queensville Inn with Mandy de Boer and the director of the food bank," Dina admitted.

Connor wanted to confront Mandy, but didn't realize Randall Kallis would be there to fend him off. Jaymie was about to raise the subject that Randall had been seen having an argument with Connor, who had gotten in Mandy's face, but there was a bang in the house. Schatzi jumped and so did Dina.

A moment later, Connor Ward stomped through the sliding glass doors, saying,

"Dina, who the hell is in our driveway? I didn't know you were —" He stopped and stared at Jaymie as little Schatzi tumbled off the wicker sofa and careened toward the door into the house, his little legs moving him as fast as he could. He bumbled against the man and Connor shoved him with his foot. It wasn't a kick, but it was impatient and irritated. Schatzi disappeared through the sliding door. Dina made a sound of protest in her throat but didn't complain. He put his hands on his hips and demanded, "I've seen you before. Who *are* you?"

Dina tensed and leaped to her feet. "This is Jaymie uh . . . Jaymie from the *Howler*. She's doing a piece on the trouble we've had getting help for our house."

He glared but paced anxiously and for the next ten minutes expounded on the perfidy of Manor Homes, Mandy de Boer, Randall Kallis, and even Olivier Ricci.

"Mr. Ward, is it true that you threatened Mandy de Boer? Got in her face and screamed at her, and that it took Randall Kallis to pull you away?"

He turned an even darker red and lunged at her. She skittered away, aware she had pushed him too far. Dina put herself between them, trembling but defiant.

"Connor, settle down! She didn't mean

anything by it. You know what reporters are like, with their gotcha questions and goading." There was a communication in her eyes as she stared at her husband that got to him more than her words. "I know you're upset, but go have a drink and calm down."

Jaymie, trembling, cast a wary glance between the two. What *was* Dina saying to her husband with her eyes that she couldn't say out loud? Maybe that he was revealing the violent side of himself? But Mandy had not been beaten to death. Despite her anger it had been foolish to provoke him. The tension, though, which had been sizzling like a frayed electrical line, fizzled out. Connor, his shoulders slumped, turned away.

Moments later, despite Dina's intervention and reassurance as Schatzi whimpered and cowered at her feet, Jaymie headed toward the front door with the woman still half apologizing for her husband's behavior, half defending it. Jaymie was exasperated. First Kallis and now Ward threatening her. What was up with everyone?

It was good to breathe fresh air and hear the door close behind her. Searching for her keys in her purse, Jaymie turned and stared back at the house. Maybe Connor Ward should climb the ladder to the top of her stack of suspects. He had not become violent, but he wanted to. If Dina hadn't intervened, maybe he would have struck out. The energy it took for him to restrain his rage had left him quivering. If that was him restraining his ire, what would happen if he unleashed it?

Jaymie unlocked the car and tossed her purse in. The garage door opened. Connor slunk out, old-fashioned glass in hand, a finger of dark liquid swirling in the bottom. He cast a hasty glance back at the house. Jaymie took in a swift breath and considered jumping in the SUV and locking herself in.

"No, look, there's nothing to be afraid of," Connor said, striding toward her, one hand out in a plea to hear him out. "You surprised me, is all." He wrestled with some decision, his glance sliding away, then meeting her eyes again. "Look, I'm going to tell you something, but you have to swear not to tell Dina."

"Why would I tell your wife anything?"

He came close and muttered, his breath smelling of whiskey. "Look, yes, I got in Mandy's face and sure, Randall Kallis had to haul me away. But not before Mandy de Boer begged me to meet her later, in the parking lot."

Jaymie stared at him, squinting her eyes. Why should she believe him? And yet

Mandy did catch his sleeve and say something to him before he left.

"I know it seems odd!" he exclaimed.

"What time were you supposed to meet her?"

"She wanted me to meet her at eleven."

"Did you do it?"

He stared at her. "I went, but she never showed. She never goddamn showed."

Because she was dead, over at the pharmacy, waiting for Val to show up. "You waited how long?"

"An hour. Maybe two. I don't know! I'm standing there in a dark parking lot at midnight like a fool!"

He was alone in a parking lot in Queensville blocks away from where Mandy died. What were the odds? Did this make him hover at the top of her suspect pile, or go down it? She was confused. "What about Dina?"

"Dina? She was home, sleeping. She takes pills, or she doesn't get an hour of sleep."

But Dina knew, Jaymie would stake her life on it. She knew and she was trying to protect him from himself, but he had to blab to Jaymie. "So, you took Dina home and saw her to bed, then came back to Queensville?"

He stared at her, panicked and yet defiant. "Looks bad, but it's the truth."

It could be an elaborate attempt to frame an alibi. She squinted and stared at him, considering his tale. Maybe he knew he was seen in Queensville and needed to get ahead of the suspicion. He would have been better off heeding his wife's wordless admonition, but she wasn't going to tell him that. "I saw you at the auction yelling at Mandy."

"I was mad. She's planning these other homes and couldn't damn well fix ours." His words were angry, but the liquor had done its job and taken the edge off his rage. His expression was more reflective than enraged. "I think I know why she wanted to talk to me that night. She wanted to offer us a deal. Maybe she wanted to tell me out of Randall Kallis's earshot that she was going to help us out."

It could have happened like that. She almost believed him but stayed silent.

His lip curled in a snarl. "I don't care *what* you think," he said, pointing his glass at her, sloshing his drink. "I've got no motive to kill her."

"Who said anything about you killing her?" The way Connor Ward was zinging up and down Jaymie's list of suspects it was like he was dangling on a rubber band.

He froze and whirled, stomped away a few

feet, then turned back to her. "If I were you, I wouldn't . . ." Panting, his expression twisted in anger, he shook his head, whirled away again and stomped back into the garage. He glared at her and swigged his drink as the automatic garage door descended. She stared back until all she could see were his booted feet. The door clunked closed with finality.

NINETEEN

Jaymie had been home considering what to make for dinner when Val called and asked if they could get together to talk things through. Jaymie texted Jakob and learned that he had planned to take dinner to his folks from their favorite restaurant. If Jaymie wanted to go over to Val's he would pick up Jocie and take her with him so she could see her Oma and Opa and they'd eat dinner together.

Jaymie and Val cooked together, then sat down to eat at the kitchen table. She told her friend about the confrontation with Connor Ward. "I didn't know what to think. Was he going to issue a threat, then thought better of it, or what?"

Val frowned down at her plate of quickie chicken fettucine alfredo: bottled alfredo sauce, grocery story rotisserie chicken and fettucine noodles. She stabbed a piece of chicken. "He seems to have a hair-trigger temper, but why would he threaten *you*?"

Jaymie picked at her salad. "If he's worried he'll be suspected of killing Mandy it could make him angry that I was looking into it, I guess."

Val chewed and thought. "You *are* wondering if he's the killer."

"He has motive — maybe — and now we know he had the opportunity." She had told Val about his shady story/alibi about why he came back to Queensville late that Sunday night.

"This was not a spur-of-the-moment crime," Val pointed out. "She wasn't beaten to death, or shot or stabbed."

"True. There seems to have been some planning involved."

"I wish we knew how she died," Val said. "It would tell us a lot."

Jaymie related her conversation with Melody, and the writer's theory. "So, given that he was at the restaurant and got pretty close to her, and then has no alibi for later that night, he may have had means, too. A hair-trigger temper doesn't necessarily mean he isn't capable of planning."

"I guess I always figure that someone who is impulsive doesn't have the capacity to plan ahead, but I suppose that's not always true."

"Maybe it's both true and untrue."

Val lifted her brow and paused, fork raised. "What do you mean?"

"I wonder if some impulsivity results in a plan of action being concocted and seen through . . . like the person literally can't see anything but the plan they've decided on."

"Isn't that the opposite of impulsive?"

Jaymie shook her head. "I don't know. This whole thing feels both calculated *and* scattered. I can't make sense of it. But at the heart of it I have this sense of a vindictiveness, a cruelty. Connor's behavior makes me suspect him. He blames Mandy for his problems. She has to go, so he comes back to Queensville while his wife is sleeping and stalks and kills her."

"No, that doesn't work. Why would he tell you he was in Queensville meeting her, then?"

"To cover his tracks if he realizes he may have been seen, or be on CCTV." She paused and frowned. "Problem is, we don't know if Mandy's problems in the days before she was murdered were part of the plot, coincidental to the plot, or a cause of the plot. If they were a part of the plot, then it took a great deal of planning, but if they are coincidental, the killer may have taken advantage of her state of mind to make her seem sick."

"Like her death was the inevitable end to her previous episodes of unwellness."

"Right. Or maybe someone close to her got fed up with her antics and decided to put an end to them once and for all."

"Who do you mean?"

"Kallis. Mandy was unstable. Maybe he saw enough of her erratic behavior that Sunday night and decided she needed to go. Maybe he was afraid she was onto his schemes."

"If schemes there are."

Jaymie nodded and took in a deep breath. "I'll tell you, I've had quite the time with angry men lately, first Kallis, and now Connor Ward. If looks could kill, I'd be dead." She took a long drink of her wine. "I can't believe he's telling the truth. It's bizarre."

"Who, Connor? What part?"

"About Mandy asking to meet him in the parking lot at eleven, after the food bank meeting at the inn," Jaymie said. "I mean, why? Why not arrange to meet in the open the next day?"

"Maybe what she had to say couldn't be said in front of other people."

"Mmm. Maybe. He says he suspected she

was going to propose a settlement that Randall Kallis wouldn't approve of. If that's true, then why did she blow him off and ask you to meet her behind the pharmacy?"

"It can't be both ways, can it? She can't have been planning to meet Connor Ward in the inn parking lot and me behind the pharmacy. And we *know* she was planning to meet me behind the pharmacy, so that means . . . he's lying?"

"Probably. Maybe I'm right and he was trying to establish an alibi in case anyone saw him in Queensville. I don't know what to think. He *seemed* sincere. Maybe she planned to keep both appointments."

"What do you mean?"

"She thought she'd talk to you and then to Connor? Or maybe she did say that to him but then changed her mind," Jaymie said. "I called Vestry and told her what Connor Ward said about Mandy asking him to meet her behind the inn, and him going to keep the appointment."

"Despite him asking you to keep it on the QT."

"I didn't promise to keep it to myself, he assumed I had. Besides, he only specified not telling Dina." She ate the last of her pasta and drained her wineglass.

A half hour later, dishes done, tea brewing

and everything else moved to the living room, Jaymie curled up in the corner of the sofa leafing through her notebook. Denver jumped up and kneaded her leg for a moment, before retreating to the far corner of the sofa, where he proceeded to nonchalantly lick his undercarriage. Val plunked down in her easy chair.

"I've been working on a timetable of Mandy's movements that Sunday," Jaymie said. "Mandy called you about ten forty-five and asked to come over, to which you did not agree, understandably. She was still at the inn; we know that now from other confirmation. According to Randall they both left the inn at about eleven, at which time she *should* have been on her way to the pharmacy to await you, which is what she said she'd do. However, according to Taylor, there was no one on the back porch of the Emporium when she parked her car behind the pharmacy at eleven thirty or so. Val, that means if you'd gone there to meet her, you wouldn't have found her anyway. And Vestry knows it."

"I don't have an alibi for later, either," Val pointed out. "So it's immaterial."

"I guess that's true."

Val brought out her tenth-grade yearbook. Jaymie set aside her notebook for the moment as her friend joined her on the sofa and flipped the yearbook open to the pages she had marked.

"This is Mandy," she said, pointing to a picture of a pretty girl with a radiant smile. She gazed into the distance with a dreamy, hopeful, happy expression, far removed from the frowzy frantic woman Mandy had become of late. Val then found Candy in the eleventh-grade group dressed identically, and pointed her out. The elder by some eleven months or so, she was attractive, with a sharp knowing and direct gaze into the camera.

"They're wearing the same clothes, for heaven's sake!"

"They always did that, dress alike, but in different colors. Mandy complained about it loudly, but I understand their mother had always done that."

"You'd think by their teen years they'd have put their feet down! There are good things about being years apart from your sister. At least I wasn't dressed like Becca, or even worse, in her hand-me-downs."

"Theirs was an odd relationship. Candy was clever and got better grades than Mandy." She frowned and shook her head. "I always thought Mandy downplayed her intelligence, but I don't know why."

"She was popular. She probably down-played her intelligence so people would like her, especially boys. I may be a lot younger than you all, but even in my day I knew that boys were intimidated by smart girls."

"That was never true of the smart guys, the ones worth anything," Val said. "Let's work more on this timeline."

"There are gaps in the earlier part of the day, between visiting her father and the meeting at the Queensville Inn."

"We know she was careening down a Queensville street at one point, because she hit Bonnie's car."

"Shortly before the Queensville Inn meeting." She jotted it down with an approximate time, then tapped the pen on the notebook.

"I wish we knew why she'd been so forgetful lately. It's got to be a drug, a medication interaction, or a condition. I've read something lately, I know it." Val frowned.

"Something to do with Mandy?"

"Not exactly," Val said. "But something. If I leave it alone, it'll come back to me."

"I need to fill in the rest of Mandy's timeline, where she was, who she saw or interacted with. The missing hours bug me."

"How can you find more out?"

"I'll ask around. I did make one discovery." She brought out the newspaper and pointed out the article she had been reading about the local building scene, and the implication of dirty tricks between a developer and the township zoning board.

"Interesting," Val said. "Can I keep this?"

"Sure. I've read it over a few times and got everything out of it I can. Mandy would need to talk to someone about her fear that Randall Kallis was up to no good. She certainly could not talk to anyone she knew well, or it might get back to him. Maybe that's why she wanted to talk to you. Or maybe she was going to talk to Connor Ward about it but was afraid of what he'd do if she confided in him, so ditched that appointment."

"It's possible. I can imagine her talking to him about what she suspected, I suppose, since he was directly affected. That's *if* he's telling the truth."

"Agreed." She thought for a moment. "I mean, if we're looking for a culprit, Connor Ward could be it. We're assuming, based on what he said, that she ditched the appointment, but what if she did meet him, and she told him she was on her way to the pharmacy. He killed her and dumped her on the pharmacy step. Could account for the delay."

"The same could be said for Randall Kallis." Val's phone chimed. She looked at it and answered. Jaymie listened to her side of the conversation. "Yeah. Oh, okay. *Now?* Jaymie's here. Okay, all right, come on over then." She hung up. "Brock wants to talk to us." Reacting to some shadow or expression on Jaymie's face, she said, "He said it's important and that he was glad you're here."

His kids were at a friend's mother's place, where she was hosting a "make your own Halloween costume" night, so he was over in minutes. He hunkered on the sofa with a coffee cup in hand, Denver keeping an eye on him from a distance. Glancing uneasily at Jaymie — she didn't like him much, never had, and he felt it, even if he didn't understand why — he addressed himself to his younger sister. "Back in high school, I dated Mandy. Well, we stayed friends and lately I've been working with Mandy and Manor Homes."

"You've *what*?" Val stared at him.

"It's a small town, Val. Manor Homes is a big player in real estate, like it or not, and I need to put food on the table and pay the mortgage. I've worked mostly with Mandy. She trusted me because we dated in high school."

Val pushed her glasses up on her nose. "So . . . you worked with them. On what?"

"I'm a consultant, developing sites, offering expertise on the market, trends, that kind of thing."

"How could I not know this? Why wouldn't you tell me?"

He ignored her and went on. "The master's I got in real estate and infrastructure served me well. I helped them put together packages of property for their developments. I've even brought buyers to their homes."

Jaymie glanced at her friend. Val was confused and hurt. "I drove through their plot for Vintage Manor Estates, their next development. Did you work with them on that?"

He nodded.

"Why did they leave the silo up? And the buildings? Are they going to be repurposed?"

"The sheds close to the ravine are being used for storage. They'll come down, eventually. The silo is staying up. It's grandfathered into the land usage, so even after rezoning for residential it can stay."

"That doesn't sound right," Jaymie said. "We had to do backflips when we rezoned land for commercial use. Surely that silo would not even be safe."

"It's going to be a central feature in the community," he said, ignoring Jaymie's protest. "My research showed the demographic being targeted want something a little different, something that harkened back to the past in this area, so . . . it's staying."

"You never told me any of this," Val said. "Brock, I'm your sister. Why didn't you tell me?"

He hung his head. "I'm sorry, Val."

"Don't say you're sorry, tell me why."

"You gals were friends, and then you stopped being friends. I thought that was because I started dating her."

Val stared at him in stupefaction. "Seriously? Brock, not everything is about you. Mandy stopped talking to me, not the other way around. I don't know what was going on with her, but I doubt it had anything to do with you."

"I'm sorry! I was an idiot."

"Don't let it happen again." This was Val at her huffiest, when she had been undervalued.

Jaymie suppressed a grin. "You were in on the development stage of Vintage Manor Estates."

"I collected stats on how many seniors

were local, or who would move here from as far as Ohio or Indiana if incentivized. I did market research on who else the homes would appeal to, the age range, the amenities expected. Mandy and I had gotten close, but in the past month or two things changed. She's been weird. Distant. She'd leave me messages and then forget about them. I'd see her drive up to my house, I'd go out to talk to her and she'd take off, and then she would deny it happened."

"What do you think was going on?"

"The industry is small locally," he continued. "It's pretty clear that not all was well at Manor Homes. Someone on the inside was cheating."

"Cheating? How?" she asked, not saying anything about Randall for the moment.

He met Jaymie's gaze for the first time. "It's easy enough for someone crooked. There are a half dozen employees that could cheat the company. Someone in the financial department could have embezzled: expenditures, payroll . . . there are ways to cheat in even a small company. Or the crook could enlist the help of others outside the company, like contractors."

"How would that work?"

"Kickbacks to ensure bids were accepted. Or working with those contractors to use inferior products in the homes, while charging the buyers premium prices."

"Maybe that's it," Jaymie said.

"What is?" Val asked.

Jaymie held up one hand, considering what she knew, thinking it through. Val and Brock went off to the kitchen, where they talked in low tones, him pleading for understanding, her impatient, with exclamations of irritation. She said it was fine, she was not angry, just annoyed that he didn't feel comfortable telling her. He kept saying she was angry, she said she wasn't, and he said he knew her better than that. She was angry.

Finally, Val strode back into the living room, eyes gleaming. If she hadn't been angry, she was now. "Whatya got, kiddo?"

She wasn't ready to reveal all she had heard from Ti Pham about her brother's construction company. She had to think it over first. However . . . "Listen to this," Jaymie said. She went over all the news items she had read, and about the lawsuits that were expected to be filed against Manor Homes if an out-of-court settlement could not be reached. "But to your point, Brock, that you don't think Mandy would be involved, I agree. I mean, how likely is it that she would knowingly let her father buy a faulty home?"

"It wouldn't happen," Brock said.

"Maybe Mandy was figuring things out," Val said. "And suspected someone in the company of . . . what?"

"Financial improprieties, at the very least. Fudging the books, embezzling, or the things Brock described, like faulty contractor work. And who do you think would be most likely to do any of this?"

"Randall," Val said.

"Right. And who was close enough to her Sunday evening to introduce something into her diet shake? Something to kill her."

"Randall. But to be fair, plenty of other people too, from what we've learned," Val said.

Jaymie nodded. "It's a good motive for murder, though. Randall is now at the top of my list. But she was with others, among them Candy, Ti Pham —"

"Ti has no motive!"

"Are you sure?" Jaymie said with a troubled glance at her friend. "I'm wondering, what is Ti's position with the food bank?"

"It's a small organization, so the structure is probably simple. I imagine she's in charge of several areas."

"Finances?"

Val nodded slowly. "What are you saying, Jaymie? Are you hinting that Ti could be

280

. . . ?" She shook her head, lips pressed firmly together.

"Cheating the food bank? It's possible, right? Nothing is off the table." Val stubbornly shook her head again. "All I'm saying is, let's not jump to conclusions that Mandy's murder could *only* have to do with Manor Homes. She has other things in her life, among them personal ties and her food bank involvement. That's what the meeting was about, right? Manor Homes was planning to enter into a special promotion with the food bank, and if I know anything, it's that a company like Manor Homes wouldn't partner with them unless they had investigated the charity to be sure there were no hidden problems that would damage the company brand."

Reluctantly, Val nodded. "I know you're right, Jaymie, but I would bet a lot of money that Ti is as honest as I believe her to be."

"Okay, that's fair and there is no one's judgment I trust more than yours. However, even the best of character judges can be wrong, on occasion."

"She's right, Val," Brock murmured.

"Let's not rule it out, anyway. And to follow that up, Ti was with her Sunday evening as well as the others."

"So now she's not just a cheat, she's a

killer?" Val closed her eyes and sat back, taking a breath. "Okay. All right. I'll leave it open as a possibility. If we do that, then we have to admit even Candy is a possibility, right?"

Jaymie smiled. This was classic Val, forcing herself to be levelheaded and completely open. "When I spoke to Randall he said he'd never seen two sisters as close as Candy and Mandy."

Val snorted. "He didn't know them in high school."

"What are you saying? I thought they were close even then?"

"They were," Brock said.

"But there *were* tensions," Val interjected. "One time they had a huge blowup in the school gym over . . . what was it?" She frowned and stared down at her hands, interlaced between her knees. "Oh, I remember! Whose day it was to wear a certain dress they both owned in different colors!"

"They fought over *that*?"

"They sure did. Candy decked her right in the bleachers while the guys were playing basketball."

Jaymie said, "We've established that Candy, too, had access to Mandy and her diet shake that night. And she's the one selling the stuff. So . . . how many possibilities are we up to?"

Val counted on her fingers. "Candy, Randall, Ti . . . who else?"

"The Wards. They were there and Connor has no real alibi." She didn't elaborate in front of Brock.

"Agreed," Val said.

"What about Shannon?" Brock said.

"Shannon . . . oh, yes, Chad Manor's sister!"

"You mentioned her to me," Val said.

Brock said, "Mandy told me she and Shannon were having a difference of opinion over how the whole thing went down after Chad's death. Shannon wanted a bigger piece of the pie."

"I've heard about that but I haven't followed up on it yet. Interestingly, it was Ti Pham who was pushing her name at me the most," Jaymie said.

"So?" Val urged.

"So either there is something there, or Ti would like me to *think* there's something there."

"You seem set on suspecting Ti," Val said.

"I'm keeping an open mind and exploring every avenue."

"Chad and Randall were buddies back in the day, I guess, back when they were all younger. Shannon ran with their group too,

283

Mandy told me once," Brock said.

"When Mandy married Chad?" Val asked.

"I need to find out more about Shannon Manor-Billings," Jaymie murmured. Mandy's death may have cleared the path for Shannon's inheritance suit.

"Who do you think did it if you had to guess right now?" Val asked.

"Randall Kallis," Jaymie said with no hesitation.

"Why?"

Jaymie considered. "Motive and opportunity. I think he probably has the best access to Mandy."

Val quirked a smile. "Then it definitely isn't him."

"What do you mean?"

"It's never the most likely suspect in a whodunnit, right? At least not in any book I've read or movie I've seen."

TWENTY

"How did you leave it?" Jakob murmured hours later as he folded Jaymie into his arms in their cozy bed.

Jaymie curled into his embrace, snuggling up to him, absorbing his warmth. "Brock insists that he wants to help. He may be able to find information for us that I wouldn't even think to look for."

"Like what?"

Jaymie explained about the potential for malfeasance at Manor Homes, the various ways Brock had explained someone could be cheating, things Mandy may have discovered, especially if Randall Kallis was involved. "He said he'll investigate other things, stuff I don't fully understand. Something about . . ." She thought back to what Brock had said before he left his sister's. "About subcontractors charging journeyman wages for work done by apprentices, and how Randall could maybe take a kickback. I don't understand."

Jakob thought for a moment. "I think I get what he means. Say you are paying to have work done in your house by a licensed electrician and you're paying electrician fees, right?" She nodded against his chest. "Then the electrician goes off to another job, while he gets the apprentice, who he pays apprentice wages, to do your job. You're paying top dollar and getting lower cost work."

"Ah. That electrician could take on ten jobs at *his* fees, shop it out to apprentices, and skim all the profit between what he charged and what he pays his apprentices."

"Right."

She thought it through to its logical conclusion. "So, if Randall okayed that, the subcontractors would kick a little back to him for every worker hour charged."

"Yup."

"Then if Mandy found out that was why there was substandard work done — and I have to think unsupervised apprentices' work may be substandard — even on her own father's place, and if she discovered that Randall was benefiting, what could she do?"

Jakob took in a deep breath, his chest expanding and deflating, Jaymie soothed by the rocking motion. "She'd sue him. She'd have to, or risk being held accountable. Her company's reputation is on the line, and it will soon be dirt, with a class action suit being filed against Manor Homes."

Jaymie sighed and felt Jakob's chest hair tickle her lip. She murmured, "If Randall Kallis had been murdered I would have suspected Mandy. That's a pretty good motive right there, that kind of fraud. With him gone she could maintain — true or not — that he had done those illegal acts without her knowledge. Maybe she'd pay some fines and move on. However, she's the one who ended up dead. If he's doing that kind of thing —"

"And we don't know that he is —"

"— and we don't know that he is, but if he was and she found out, maybe he eliminated her so she wouldn't turn him in, or . . ." She shook her head. "I'm confused," she admitted.

"It'll all look clearer in the morning." He kissed her softly. "Get some sleep, my love."

She awoke refreshed on Friday morning. After going over some of the details with Jakob and getting him to explain again what he had said about journeymen and apprentices, she saw him and Jocie off to work and school and made plans for the day. Somehow, she had to meet Shannon Manor-Billings. She needed to fill in the missing moments of Mandy's Sunday before she died. There had to be something of consequence, someone she spoke with, something she did. Right now, if things were slightly different she would have pegged Connor Ward as the most likely murderer, but this death was too subtle. If Connor had killed her it would likely have been with his fist or a blunt instrument.

Her phone rang with a number she didn't recognize, but she answered it anyway. It was Ti Pham. "Jaymie, I'm happy you answered. I picked Trina up at the airport and she's staying with me. She has something to tell you and something to ask. Can we meet?"

"Absolutely. When and where?" There would be no better insight into Mandy's life and mind than her daughter, surely. The woman suggested a hole-in-the-wall coffee and tea place in downtown Wolverhampton.

Jaymie took Hoppy out to let him do his business. The day was clear and bright, but so cold she could see her breath, a good day to wear a new red-and-gold plaid coatigan she had bought to go with her favorite knitted hat and scarf, a gift from her

288

mother-in-law last Christmas. With Hoppy yipping excitedly, she burrowed in her cedar trunk and brought out the bright, cheery scarlet set that went marvelously with the coatigan. She donned the set and headed out.

They were meeting at Wellington's Retreat, in Wolverhampton. Jaymie arrived first and took her favorite table by the front windows. While she waited, she perused the menu for breakfast offerings.

The glass door swung open, and the bells over the top of it jingled merrily. Ti entered with a slim reddish blonde young woman, spotted Jaymie, waved, and guided her companion toward the table. Introductions were made. Jaymie examined Trina Manor with interest as she offered her sincerest sympathy on her mother's death.

The young woman was beautiful, her glowing face devoid of makeup, one sculpted eyebrow pierced, as was her septum. A gem winked from a divot on the left side of her nose. Her earlobes were pierced multiple times.

Trina's cheeks were pink from the chilly breeze outside, her manner brisk and businesslike. She wore black leggings with a long plaid "jumper" and a ratty cardigan over it all, her footwear black lace-up ankle boots that looked clunky bottoming her slim legs. She shivered and rubbed her hands together as they chatted about the weather — Trina had lived in London for two years and claimed to have forgotten how cold a Michigan autumn could be — and local news as she looked over the menu. When the server approached they were ready. Trina ordered a vegan quiche, Ti a muffin and coffee, while Jaymie decided on the eggs Benedict topped with something new to her, avocado Hollandaise.

By mutual agreement they ate first, keeping the conversation light. The avocado Hollandaise was very good, but not truly *Hollandaise*-ish. Trina explained her studies in England, how she decided to pursue a degree in architecture.

"My father was a genius," she said softly, staring down at her cup. She sipped it tentatively, tasting the herbal tea she had ordered and nodding. "You know these vintage homes my Mom is — was — planning?" Jaymie nodded. "Those were my father's idea. He thought any company ought to diversify so when the market turned, you could pivot more easily. Back in the fifties his grandfather foresaw the boom in cheap tract housing for the young families of soldiers coming back from overseas. They were a small company back then, just Great-grandpa and a team of builders. Then my grandpa saw that those families would want to move into larger more individual homes as their families got bigger. *Dad* saw that all those baby boomers would be downsizing, not ready for retirement homes, but not needing the space of those larger homes."

"I'm intrigued," Jaymie said. "I like the notion of smaller homes with amenities close by for senior living, a nod to the idea of aging in place."

Eagerly, Trina said, "Exactly! Dad drew up a planned community map, with a wellness center, recreation center, and an attached plot of land that could be rewilded —"

"Rewilded?" Jaymie interjected.

She blinked and Jaymie could see her backtrack to explain, deciding where to begin. "Uh, let's see . . . urban planners are starting to understand the benefits of letting nature reclaim urban landscapes." Trina spoke for five minutes, and Jaymie was mesmerized. She explained that once, urban planners thought that nature should be ruthlessly controlled, directed, planned. Nature was confined to groomed parks that served a purpose, with playground equipment and sterile graveled areas. Water features were limited to cement-bottomed pools.

A more modern approach, she said, hands sketching in the air as she explained, was to acknowledge that nature itself understood what was needed better than planners. The concept was to set aside areas that allowed minimal human interference — groomed paths were allowed, for instance, but not pavement — but then let nature take its course. Planned ponds would become wild ponds. Planned gardens and landscapes would make way for wildscapes, areas given over to natural species. "The only interference from humans, optimally, would be to remove invasive plants like Brazilian elodea or Asiatic sand sedge that crowd out native species."

"If you're going to be in Queensville for any length of time, I'd love to pick your brain concerning a project I'm a part of." Jaymie explained about her involvement in the Queensville historic house, and how they were in the process of planning the exterior gardens to be tackled the next summer. "But also, across from our family cabin we're creating a wooded walking trail area. I'm struggling with the balance issue: how much wildness is appropriate in a walking trail area that I want to be accessible to people with ability challenges."

Trina glowed even more brightly until people were casting covert admiring glances at the woman, as her heightened excitement filled the dark café with her light. She was enthusiasm embodied. The whole time Ti watched, her face a study in teary pride in her friend's daughter.

But finally, it was time to talk turkey, Jaymie decided. She had questions she hoped Trina could answer. "Don't mind me being blunt. You asked Ti to set up this meeting. What did you hope to learn?"

The young woman composed herself, folding her hands on the scarred tabletop in front of her. She turned a small turquoise ring around and around her index finger as she said, tears welling, "I want you to find out who killed my mother."

No one had ever asked her outright to solve a crime. "I'm no professional. Why don't we leave that up to the police?" She smiled to soften her words. "I try not to step on their toes."

"It's not an either/or situation," Trina pointed out, her tone urgent, her incipient tears drying. "I've read all about you in the *Howler* and on social media, and I have friends here in town who think you're pretty neat. Taylor Bellwood and I go way back."

Jaymie paused, but then admitted, "I *am* snooping around. You don't think your mother's death was of natural causes?"

"I do *not.* I know you and your friend found my mother on the back step of the apothecary." She held up one hand against Jaymie's almost-interjection about their innocence. "I don't believe either one of you had anything to do with it, but something happened, and I want to know what."

"There was no sign of violence that I could see," Jaymie said gently, verbally dancing around the suggestion Mel Heath had made about cause of death.

Trina crossed her legs, bent forward, elbows on the table, and lowered her voice as she said, "No, I believe my mother's downfall is more insidious, and perhaps more long-term. You may have already thought of this, but I'll explain." She took a deep breath. "I haven't been home in a while, not since last year, Thanksgiving, I think. With school and work it hasn't been possible. I was planning to come home for Christmas this year. But I talked to my mother at least once a week, besides texts and video chats. She has looked *awful* lately!"

"For how long?"

"Months . . . at least a couple. I wanted

her to see a doctor, but she said she had and was taking care of it."

"Did you speak to anyone close to you concerning your mother's health?"

She exchanged a look with Ti, who nodded. "I talked to Ti, and I called my aunt."

"What did *she* say?"

"Aunt Candy? She was worried too. She tried to talk to her, but Mom wouldn't listen. When I talked to Mom she complained that Aunt Candy was on her case, but she was not going to take anyone's advice about her own affairs."

Jaymie bit her lip and regarded the young woman. "Was there any chance . . . did your mother ever have a problem with prescription drugs or anything else?"

Trina didn't leap to defend her mother. Instead, she thought it over, staring at the glass door and checking her phone. Then she said, "In the normal course of things I'd say no, but lately, I don't know. She's been unhappy. I don't get it. She had everything she wanted! What was there to be unhappy about?"

"You know about the problems with the company."

Trina nodded.

"Could it simply be that? She apparently wanted to pass the business on to you.

295

Maybe it was bothering her more deeply than anyone suspects."

Trina took up a paper napkin and systematically tore it into triangles. "I hope that's not it, because . . . I'll feel terribly guilty." She piled the triangles neatly. "Maybe that sounds selfish, but I hope it's anything but that."

"Maybe it's something as simple as her love life. Trina, did your mother date Randall Kallis?"

"For a while."

"After your dad died."

She colored and a mulish expression marred her lovely face, her cheeks reddening. "The rumors aren't true, you know. I've heard people say that she had an affair with him before Dad died, but it's not true."

"I wonder if they say it because he became a partner after your father died."

"Mom didn't know what else to do. Randall held the company hostage, in a way. He knew *everything.* She knew *nothing,* or next to nothing. Without him, she was afraid Manor Homes would crash and burn. She told me at the time she considered it a sacred trust from my father to me." She sighed. "Yes, I know that sounds like the company crashing and burning may have been behind her recent . . . weirdness. But I hope not."

"About Randall?" Jaymie urged.

"I think he asked her out to try to influence her, but she realized it was a bad idea and broke it off. He didn't need to sweet-talk her into the partnership. She was scared to run the business on her own. She had no one to rely on except him, and he threatened to ditch Manor Homes. Whatever anyone says, she did what she thought was best."

Jaymie nodded. So no romance there, just desperation. That aligned with Kallis's explanation about how he made sure Mandy gave him the partnership.

"Ah, there she is!" Trina said, jumping up and waving out the plate glass window.

"Trina invited her aunt to join us," Ti murmured.

"Candy?" This was good. She wanted to speak with Mandy's sister again.

"No, my other aunt, my dad's sister, Shannon," Trina said as the door opened, letting a gust of cold air into the café.

TWENTY-ONE

As Shannon Manor-Billings grabbed Trina in a strong, long, affectionate hug, Jaymie examined the woman. She was probably in her mid-to-late fifties. Her gray hair was cut short in a gleaming silvery cap and she was spare, high jutting cheekbones dotted with darkening age spots uncovered by concealer. She did wear makeup though, brown eyeliner, mascara, and coral lipstick. She was stylishly garbed in slacks, brown suede boots, and a camel peacoat, a silk scarf knotted at the throat and tucked into the neck. A warm spicy fragrance drifted from her, something woodsy and powdery . . . ah! Jaymie recognized the perfume, L'Air du Temps, a classic.

Once their greeting was done — in the depths of the embrace the two women murmured to each other, expressions of condolence from the older, teary appreciation from the younger — Mrs. Manor-

Billings slung her purse over an empty chair Ti had pulled over. She removed her coat and scarf, taking the time to hang them on a nearby coatrack. Under the coat she wore an expensive Shantung silk blouse, olive-toned. The color echoed in the scarf, which was a blend of the olive of the shirt and the camel of the coat. She turned and regarded Ti with a chill gaze and nodded, then turned to Jaymie with a furrowed brow.

Trina introduced them and Jaymie stuck out her hand. The other woman took her hand and gave it a single shake, withdrawing her cool bony fingers abruptly. But when she turned back to her niece her arctic expression warmed, the lines of her face softening. "It's good to see you, my dear. I wish it was under better circumstances."

Trina knuckled a tear off her cheek, then reached out and touched the woman's shoulder. "I'm happy to see you, Aunt Shan. We'll get together again but this was important, so I wanted to loop you in."

"It's been too long, since early summer." She reached out and touched Trina, tucking a stray lock behind her ear, her finger lightly trailing over the eyebrow piercing. "New?"

Trina nodded, smiled, then said to Jaymie, "Aunt Shan was in England in June. She stayed with me for a few days and we hit the theaters, restaurants, everything, everywhere."

"We went on a couple of day trips. I've always wanted to see Glastonbury Tor. Remember the book I gave you when you were twelve?"

"*The Sword in the Stone!*" Trina said. "I'll never forget it. It started me reading Arthurian legend and obsessing about England. Our trip to the tor was a highlight of my two years there!" She turned to Jaymie. "I've always adored reading. And Aunt Shan knew exactly what books to get me."

Jaymie listened as Trina explained why Jaymie was there. The older woman consulted her phone as she listened. Something puzzled Jaymie. Ti Pham almost disappeared, withdrawing into the shadows left by the darkening sky outside and the dim glow of the light that hung low over their table. What was there between these two women, Ti and Shannon? Antipathy, evidently. Ti had said something to that effect, that Shannon was unpleasant and hated Mandy. That she was suing to increase her inheritance. That would have been enough to turn Ti against her. And Mrs. Manor-Billings was at the Queensville Inn on Sunday evening and in fact had spoken to Mandy.

"So, Jaymie Leighton Müller," Shannon Manor-Billings said, turning to her. "Trina is asking you to investigate, or some such nonsense. I would be happy to hire a proper investigator. There are two in Wolverhampton alone. I just looked it up."

"Aunt Shan!" Trina groaned in an agony of embarrassment.

Jaymie could see the relationship and she smiled. Shannon Manor-Billings was a replacement mom. She'd be a fierce tiger if it came down to danger to Trina. Surely, she wouldn't kill her beloved niece's mother, though . . . would she? "I said the same thing, Mrs. Manor-Billings. I'm no professional, though I've had a few successes locally. I'll step aside if Trina wants me to." She wouldn't, but it cost nothing to say. She added, "It's not up to you." Ti, over in the corner, hid a smile behind her hand and coughed discreetly. To soften her bluntness, Jaymie asked, "Do you live locally?"

"No, I live in Arizona. I travel a lot, though, so I come to Michigan often."

Jaymie opened her mouth to say something but the woman held up one hand.

"Yes, I've been staying here, in Wolverhampton, for two weeks so I can go on your little list of suspects, I suppose," she said, flapping her bony hand dismissively. "I *was* contemplating suing Manor Homes. Contrary to what some people are saying, I have not initiated a suit yet, and I'm *not* suing to alter the outcome of my brother's will, or further back, my father's decisions. I've never made it a secret, but neither have I blabbed: I own ten percent of Manor Homes. Lately I've been deeply concerned about the decision-making coming from not only Mandy but the whole company. Monies owed to me from my ten percent ownership have not been paid. If I were to sue, that is what it would be about."

That would change a lot if it was true.

"We were scheduled to meet Monday morning," Mrs. Manor-Billings said.

"You were to meet with Mandy?" Her name had not been on Mandy's office calendar, but maybe there was a reason for that. Did the woman have proof?

"Mandy's death has thrown everything into confusion. She requested the meeting, she told me, because she had learned some information that might help us resolve our differences. She was willing to consider offering me a larger stake in the company in lieu of the outstanding payments if things went how she thought they were going to go."

"What did that mean?"

302

"I have no idea what she meant. We were not on chatty terms. But I know she had spoken to a business lawyer confidentially and there may be a way, she said, to restructure going forward."

A business lawyer? Jaymie's eyes widened. This sounded like Mandy may have expected Randall Kallis to be out of the company and if so, that would be Kallis's motivation to murder her. "But why would you even consider it? A larger part of what may become a failing company, if a pending lawsuit against them resulted in charges and fines and pricey restitution?"

"I was willing to hear her out. I had nothing against Mandy," she said with a smile for Trina. "We were good friends while Chad was alive." Ti sniffed loudly from the shadows and the older woman cast her a quick glance. "I didn't like how she had done things after he was gone, bringing Randall Kallis into the business. If I declined the offer we might have been in for a legal battle, I knew, so this may have been better than the possibility of getting nothing at all, ultimately. But I told her up front if I did agree to her deal — and I hadn't heard what it was yet — I'd only do it under the proviso that I could have my lawyer and accountants look at the Manor Homes books."

"What did she say?"

"She said she'd expect nothing less. And I told her I might want to have some influence on the direction the company took in the future. She said we'd work something out."

"Mom said she was going to make an offer to the Wards and other homeowners with significant problems," Trina said, meeting Jaymie's gaze.

Jaymie caught the surprise on Ti's face and knew she'd have to follow up with Mandy's best friend later. But right now, she'd focus on the matters at hand. "What kind of an offer?"

"Nothing was decided. Mom thought it would be expedient — and I agreed — to have a third-party adjudicator, a contractor, maybe, or an engineer, come in and survey structural issues and advise on a cause," Trina said.

Which is why Ti would not have known the plan. Her brother would have been cut out, potentially, and maybe even in trouble.

"If it was Manor Homes' fault," Trina continued, "they would pay an independent contractor to do the work."

Ti froze, her expression alarmed.

"What did you think of your mother's idea?" Jaymie asked Trina.

"It was the only way to move forward," the young woman answered. "Manor Homes might win the lawsuit, but at what cost? Reputation is all-important in the building trades, like it is in life. I'll speak with Randall."

Jaymie paused. How could she express her concern without being accusatory? "It sounds like Mandy had things under control," she said. "But maybe it would be unwise to speak with him? Or maybe you should take someone with you if you go, maybe even your aunt?"

Shannon nodded. "I agree."

Ti said, from the shadows, "I know Randall well. *I'd* be happy to go along with you."

Jaymie eyed Ti with concern. Given her brother's connection to Manor Homes, that would surely be a conflict of interest. "I have to say something," Jaymie said. "The Mandy I saw lately, and that others dealt with, was far from this business-savvy together woman you report. I don't mean to be disrespectful, Trina, but she was forgetful, paranoid, and had multiple car accidents, at least one of which she walked away from and another she *drove* away from."

Trina and Mrs. Manor-Billings exchanged looks. The elder spoke up. "Trina and I spoke about it last week. I had met Mandy already — this would have been almost two weeks ago now — and she seemed fine to me, though she didn't look good. She had gained weight, but not in a normal way. She was puffy and pale. Her hair was not styled. One thing she always was, in the past, was well groomed. I was worried."

"I was thinking of coming back early for a visit," Trina said, glancing at her aunt. Her eyes watered. "I wish I had."

Mrs. Manor-Billings pressed her lips together and shook her head. Ti reached out and touched Trina's arm. It was like a competition, who could offer the best nonverbal comfort.

"We shouldn't keep Jaymie too much longer," Ti murmured, and Trina jumped up.

"Oh, gosh, yes! Will you go on looking into it?" Trina asked, gazing down at Jaymie.

"Of course," Jaymie said without hesitation. "Trina, I don't want to be pushy, but could I see Mandy's house?"

"Sure. I'm going over there later. Let's exchange numbers," she said, grabbing Jaymie's phone and entering her number into Contacts.

"One thing," Jaymie said as Trina tapped away. "Mrs. Manor-Billings, I've heard you were at the inn on Sunday night and spoke with Mandy in the dining room."

The woman gazed at her coolly. "I had finished dinner and did speak to her in passing, but only to confirm our meeting for the next morning." Her tone was frosty and forbidding, even if the words were plain.

"Oh." Jaymie got her phone back from Trina and slipped it into her purse. Maybe this was what Ti had warned her about. "Aunt Shan," as charming as she was to Trina, could make one feel stupid and awkward.

They paid and left the restaurant, the three walking away with Trina between the two older women. Jaymie donned her scarlet hat and scarf and huddled in her coatigan as she watched them. She had been all confidence to them, promising to do what she would do anyway, continue to investigate the odd death of Mandy de Boer, but she was puzzled how to move forward.

And yet as in most of life, you kept putting one foot in front of the other, even when the way seemed hazy. Even when you didn't feel you would ever get to the end.

Even when you felt all hope was lost.

And that is when the universe — or chance — plops a hint to the path forward down in front of you, Jaymie thought as she saw Candy Vasiliev park her white sedan in one of the curbside spots, get out, and head to the donut shop down the street. Jaymie followed.

The place was a hum of activity, the scent of sugar and oil and dough perfuming the air as a counterpoint to the strong scent of good coffee. This was the most popular spot in town with both farmers and townees alike, the hub of gossip, the center of news spreading, better than the cyber highway and the telephone combined.

Jaymie glanced around, trying to find where Candy had gone. The woman emerged from a back hall where the restrooms were located. Did that mean she had only popped in to use the facilities? But no, as Jaymie hung back, Candy checked her cell phone, then headed toward a booth. The waitress, a tired-looking woman of sixty-something, swiped the dirty dishes from the table onto a tray and with her free hand used a cloth to wipe up the coffee rings and scattered sugar from the laminated surface.

Candy gave the woman a brief smile, said something, then slid into the booth with a weary slump. She got her phone out and set it on the table in front of her, cradling her head in her free hand as she idly swiped though text messages. Jaymie threaded her way through the tables and past the booths lining the walls and slid into the booth opposite Candy. "How are you, Candy?"

She looked up, startled out of her reverie, and gaped. "Oh, Jaymie. What do you want now?"

"I wanted to say . . . Candy, Becca is my only sibling, like Mandy was for you. I can't imagine losing her in such an awful way. I'm so *very* sorry." Her voice caught on the last words.

The woman's face squinched and she sobbed. "It's been harder than I ever could have imagined," she said, in that clogged voice when you're doing your best not to cry. "You know, you think something is going to be one way, and then it's not. It's . . ." She shook her head.

"It's harder than anyone knows or understands."

Candy nodded and sniffed.

"And worse when it's such a puzzle. Do you have any idea what was going on with Mandy in the last weeks?" Jaymie asked. "Everyone I've spoken with says she was different, that something was off."

"I wish I knew." Candy stared down at her phone. The waitress came and Candy ordered a coffee and carrot muffin, while Jaymie took off her hat and scarf, undid her coatigan — it was steamy in the shop — and ordered black tea.

"I'm haunted by it all," Candy said, her tone low, more in control than she had been. "What could I have done differently though?" The musing felt like a question she asked herself.

"I don't know. Did she say anything to you? Tell you what was wrong? I know she had been in a couple of car accidents, and yet people I know say she either didn't remember or wouldn't acknowledge the accidents."

"I can't explain it. Yes, she's been weird lately. She's under a lot of pressure —"

"Work-related? I know there is a lawsuit pending against Manor Homes."

Candy eyed her. "Why are you asking me questions? Are you spying for Val Nibley?"

"Val didn't kill Mandy. I think you know that."

"Then who did?" Candy shot back, her tone hostile and carrying. "Mandy thought Val was persecuting her. I wasn't so sure, but what else can I think now, with my sister *dead* on the pharmacy back step?" Folks nearby swiveled to stare.

"There must be a reasonable explanation, something we haven't thought of yet, or aren't aware of. Some complication in her life, or health challenge."

"There's nothing! Mandy was starting to get back on track," Candy said with a teary smile. "I was helping her. She had gained weight, but we were on this shake diet and both of us losing, me more than her, but I always did have more self-control than she did."

"What is the deal with these diet shakes?" Jaymie asked as the waitress delivered their orders.

Candy tore into her carrot cake muffin as she explained that the shakes were a convenient way to take control over your weight. "They're even keto-friendly. I've lost thirty pounds, and you can too!" She fished in her bag and handed Jaymie a colorful pamphlet extolling the virtues of the plan. "Buy it now and it comes with a shake container that makes it handy to take with you to the gym or work!"

Shake container, like the one Mandy had with her the night she died. "So, you have to drink the shakes . . . how often?"

"Twice a day — breakfast and lunch — then a regular dinner."

Jaymie knit her brows and tilted her head to one side. "I was told Mandy was drinking a shake Sunday evening when she was at the Queensville Inn for the Manor Homes

311

and food bank meeting. The waitress is a friend, and she said your sister wasn't eating, just drinking from the shake container."

Candy frowned. "Maybe she had switched it up to breakfast and dinner with a normal lunch."

"Didn't you notice her drinking from the shake bottle? You were there."

"I wasn't particularly paying attention. She could have been using the shake container for another drink. I do that all the time when I need to get in my water for the day."

"Good point!" Had the police found the shake bottle? Analyzed the contents? Did they even know about the shake bottle? Jaymie made a mental note to call Vestry the minute she was done with Candy, but first . . . "I'm curious, how was Mandy and Randall Kallis's relationship? Was there any friction there?"

"Why are you bringing Randall into this. Oh, wait!" Candy's eyes widened. "You'd do anything to get Val off, wouldn't you?"

"Whoa, Candy, I didn't mean anything."

Mulish, her eyes glittering with pooling tears, she set her mouth in a straight line and looked away, glaring out the window. "I feel alone," she whispered. "I don't care what you say, Val is the only person in the world who didn't like Mandy, and then my sister ends up dead on her doorstep!"

"Val didn't dislike Mandy, and she didn't do anything," Jaymie insisted. "You went into Val's pharmacy the Wednesday morning before Mandy died and accused Val of stalking her, but that simply wasn't true. We tracked down the fake social media account that was trashing Mandy." Candy's expression was set in a stubborn frown. "Val didn't kill your sister!" Jaymie said, exasperated. "I'd think you'd want to leave no stone unturned to find out who *did.*"

"Of course I want to know who did it, but I'm not going to let Val off the hook on your say-so. That girl always was holier than thou, smarter than everyone."

"Even if that was true — which it's not — how does that make her a killer?"

The waitress approached with a look of consternation, bunching her apron in her hand. "Candy, is everything all right? Is this woman harassing you?"

The fight went out of her. "I don't *know* what was going on with my sister," she groaned. "I wish I did. She told me Val was stalking her. She said Val sent her the wrong medication, that she was trying to hurt her. It didn't make sense, but I believed her. *That's* why I confronted Val in the phar-

313

macy. Wouldn't you if it was your sister? I was trying to help." She put her head down in her arms on the tabletop and wept, big gusty sobs. "I miss my s-s-sister! I want her back."

"Of course you do," Jaymie murmured, nodding to the waitress that all was well. "If you'll help me figure it out, we can make sure whoever is responsible pays."

TWENTY-TWO

Once Candy stopped sobbing — nearby diners had offered condolences and paper napkins, and then went back to their coffee — Jaymie explained why she had mentioned Randall Kallis, though she carefully avoided alluding to someone in the company cheating. She simply said she understood they had once had a relationship, and an ex is always an obvious possibility. "You seem pretty sure it wasn't him though."

"I don't know anymore. Maybe?"

Jaymie's heart ached for Candy. She was broken, her life forever changed, shattered in one night. It would have felt like there was plenty of time to reel in Mandy, to correct the path to ruin she was on physically, but all hope was now gone.

"If you say it wasn't Val, I mean . . . maybe she had a heart attack or something? I don't understand why she ended up huddled on the back step of the pharmacy. You've got to see how that looks!" Jaymie didn't reply. "Mandy has been acting weird lately. Maybe . . ." She shook her head and looked away.

"Maybe what?"

"No. Nope. I'm done. I don't know who I can trust, but I will *not* talk about my sister's murder anymore, especially not with *you.*" She slid out of the booth, hefted her bag on her shoulder, and bolted, leaving without paying for her muffin and coffee.

Puzzled, Jaymie paid, left a generous tip, gathered up her accessories and headed out, as confused as when she had approached Candy. As she walked toward her SUV she saw Candy on the sidewalk by her car with a man. The two were talking, and Candy was weeping. The man reached out and touched her shoulder, then pulled her into a tight hug. They stood like that for a long moment. He said something to her and gave her a final squeeze. Candy moved out of his embrace and got in her car. As she drove away the fellow stood watching, his expression puzzled.

Jaymie approached. "Is . . . Is Candy okay?"

He turned and stared at her.

"I'm sorry. I'm Jaymie Leighton Müller. I was speaking with Candy in the donut shop.

She was upset and left in a hurry. In case you didn't know, her younger sister died a few days ago. The poor woman is devastated."

"I know all about it," he said. "I'm Greg Vasiliev, her first ex-husband."

Greg Vasiliev. *GV* from Mandy's calendar? Curiouser and curiouser. Why had she been meeting him the very day she died?

He was coming to the donut shop to meet a client, he explained — he was a real estate agent — when he saw Candy and stopped to offer his ex-wife his condolences. Jaymie clarified her involvement and he looked startled.

"Oh, you're *that* Jaymie, Val's friend." His phone buzzed. He got it out of his jacket pocket and checked a message. "My client, putting off our meeting until later. Can we go somewhere and talk? I've been speaking to Val and there are a few things I'd like to explain."

"Sure. I have a call to make first, and then I'd love to chat."

She strolled a few feet away toward her own SUV and called Trina's number. "You said I could come have a look at Mandy's house. Is there a good time today?" She would be there for a few hours looking for insurance policies and choosing burial clothes for her mother, Trina said, and would welcome the company. "I'll be there in an hour or so." She hung up and went back to Greg.

"Let's walk over to my office," he said. "It isn't far."

She took a moment to throw the hat and scarf into the SUV, locked it back up, and they walked. His office turned out to be a converted detached garage behind his own house, a small, neat, older bungalow on a side street. The garage door opening had been closed in and installed in the center was a glass door with his company name, G. Vasiliev & Associates. The associates were his nephew and niece, he said, who had started as real estate agents in Wolverhampton but had since moved on, one to Livonia and one further afield in Ohio.

They sat down on a comfortable sofa along one wall plastered with a listing board of local properties. On the coffee table in front of them was a binder with a more complete list of properties for sale.

"You must know Brock," Jaymie said. "Val's brother."

"I do," he said, caution in his tone.

She waited. There seemed to be more. And she was right.

"I have nothing against Brock," he said.

There was a "but" coming.

"But we have different ways of operating. Don't get me wrong, he's actually a good real estate agent. I think he's more . . . ambitious than I am."

Ambitious: code for something unsavory? "In what way?"

"I was supposed to work with Manor Homes, helping them put together land packages for their housing developments, but the next thing I knew, Brock was in and I was out."

He had to be irritated. "Why do you think that happened?"

He hesitated.

"I understand you and Val are friends?" she said, to prompt him to talk.

"We are," he said with a smile. "*Good* friends. I never mention Brock to her."

Aha. "Greg, who messed it up for you? You and Candy were married. Do you think Mandy thought it might be awkward?"

"No, I think it was Randall that put the kibosh on me working with them."

"Why do you think he would do that?"

Greg still looked hesitant and shook his head.

"You can tell me. I'll keep it confidential if you prefer."

"That's not fair to ask of you. You're Val's

best friend. I'd never ask you to keep something from her. What I was about to say is a matter of opinion."

"If I think what you have to say would be distressing for her, I'll keep whatever it is a secret. I've got no problem with that."

He considered for a moment, then looked away. He had a bony face, not attractive in the usual sense, but there was a thoughtfulness behind his gray eyes and a firm set to his lips and jaw that spoke of intelligence and sensitivity. He looked back with a direct gaze. "Okay, but this is my impression, and I could be wildly wrong. I don't like Randall Kallis. I think he's a fraudster and a cheat. It is my opinion that he didn't want me involved in Manor Homes because he was afraid I'd see right through him and whatever shady deals he was putting together, and wouldn't stand for it. He talked Mandy out of working with me, or more likely levied some pressure against her. If I discovered anything wrong with the business — and I'd be more likely to find things out if we were working closely — he *knew* I'd tell Mandy. She was my sister-in-law once, and I value the connection. I wouldn't see her cheated." He sat back and watched her anxiously.

She nodded, thinking it through. "What

you're *not* saying is that Brock might let ambition shade his thinking. He'd let things slip if it meant keeping the gig."

"I didn't mean it quite like that," he said with a grimace, flattening his big hands out on the book in front of him. "I've no reason to think him unethical."

"It may relieve you to know that Brock was getting concerned and suspicious. He felt there was something going on at Manor Homes. Randall was his chief suspect. Others have mentioned Randall's name with suspicion too."

"I'm relieved to hear it. Maybe I've misjudged Brock. If so, I'm sorry."

"But Brock did say it could be Mandy who was causing the trouble in the company."

"No way," he retorted immediately. "She cares . . . *cared* . . . about Manor Homes and its legacy. She'd never ruin their reputation. She was trying to keep it afloat partly for Chad's sake, but even more for Trina, who will inherit her portion of the business."

"I understand she saw it as a legacy for her daughter, from her husband. It doesn't make sense to cut corners and mess it up, especially since she convinced her own father to buy a Manor Homes house that now has problems." He nodded with a thoughtful look. "Her life seems complicated," Jaymie said. "It feels like someone set Val up to be the one to find her body. It's vital to find out who killed Mandy."

He took in a sharp breath. "So it is murder?"

Jaymie had stepped too far. "There's no official word, but that's my suspicion. To put it bluntly, healthy people don't usually curl up and die." She paused, took a breath, then said, "I have to ask . . . I'm considering everyone as a suspect while looking at the murder. You were married to Candy and probably know her better than anyone. Would she kill her sister?"

He reared back and blurted, "Impossible!"

"Is it? I've heard their relationship was volatile. They fought all the time."

"Nope, no way. Look, I had knock-down, drag-out fights with my brother when we were kids. Almost killed each other. I pushed him off the garage roof once. Boy, did I get a blistered behind for that. But now we're best friends. It would wreck me if he died."

Jaymie nodded. "I feel the same about my sister."

"You may not know this, but I briefly dated Mandy in high school."

"You dated Mandy first?"

"She dumped me," he said with a rueful chuckle. "But then Candy asked me out for a Sadie Hawkins dance and we hit it off."

"How long were you married?"

"Two years."

"Only two years?"

"We were too young." He left it there.

Jaymie had a sense there was more. "But you stayed in contact."

"It's a small town. Everyone knows everyone." He smiled. "She moved away for a while, and the stories she told when she got back! She was a hell-raiser in her twenties, a wild woman. Traveled to Cali, hung out with rock bands. She's been married four times. Three fellows since me." He chuckled. "I *wish* I had Candy's guts and gusto for living. She would pick up on a whim and take off, then come back with great stories. She went to India once just because she got a good deal on plane tickets. Landed and didn't even have the right clothes or anything! She stayed a year. What a gal! She's something else."

"It sounds like she can be a little erratic."

"I call it bold. She's whip-smart. She's fun. She's energetic. She's passionate about those she loves."

"Like her sister?"

"Like her sister. When she loves, she loves

hard. If she thought someone was out to hurt Mandy . . . that's why she was angry at Val. She's got it in her head that Val is the killer, and she only sees black and white, never gray."

"But Val didn't do anything!"

"I know. It'll be hard to convince Candy."

"I get that." She'd react the same way if she was sure someone had hurt Becca. "You don't like Randall Kallis."

"I do *not*. He's crooked, but he's also a jackass. Ask any woman he's dated, and there have been many."

"Could he be the killer?"

"If it benefited him? Sure. I can't believe I'm talking this over so calmly, but I know for a fact that he bullied Mandy into making him a partner when she was mourning Chad." Jaymie kept a neutral expression. This was her conclusion too. "I have more proof than my dislike of him. She as much as told me once that she had no choice, that he backed her into a corner. It was give him a share of the company or . . ." He stopped and his eyes widened. It looked like he regretted saying too much.

"Or what? There is no point in holding anything back at this point."

"I don't want this getting back to Trina."

"I won't say a word to her."

He vacillated, waggling his head back and forth as he made up his mind, then said, "Okay. Mandy wouldn't elaborate, but Candy told me everything. She was mad!" He paused, looking like he was still thinking it over. He shrugged and said, "Okay, I don't want to leave anything secret. If it nails that son-of-a-b to the wall, then I'll tell. Nobody else except Candy knew what really went down between Mandy and Randall, and why ultimately she *had* to give him the partnership at Manor Homes. Randall seduced Mandy, took photos of her, then threatened to take them to the press. It would have looked awful, Chad dying like he did, and then these pictures coming out soon after. She *had* to cave."

Jaymie was set back and sickened. "Oh, wow. I thought he was a crook, but that's disgusting. Why didn't Candy tell me that?"

He gazed at her and raised his brows. "Why would she? I'm only telling you because I know how Val trusts you, and how highly she thinks of you. If this will help solve Mandy's murder, then I had to say it." His phone buzzed. "That's my indecisive client, he's ready now! Look, it's been good having someone to talk to, but I gotta go. I'll walk you back to your car."

She followed him, but his long-legged gait

325

was hard to keep up with. "Wait!" she said, gasping, as they approached her car. "One thing more. I've been tracking down everyone who saw Mandy that Sunday evening."

He turned. "Okay."

She hoped he'd volunteer his whereabouts, but she'd have to be more pointed. "Did you happen to be at the Queensville Inn that evening? It seems like everyone who knew Mandy was!" She played it off as a joke but was genuinely interested in his response.

"No, I wasn't there." He looked at her quizzically, tilting his head to one side. "What an odd question."

Henry de Boer had said, though, that Mandy was intent on speaking to Greg that Sunday evening, and she had seen that *GV* notation on the desk calendar. It was not clear if it was at the Queensville Inn or if they were meeting elsewhere. And why *were* they meeting? There was still some time to fill in between Mandy being at her father's and the car accident in Queensville, and the meeting at the inn. Was she with Greg? She sighed, exasperated and unwilling to let it go. "So, *did* you meet up with Mandy at all on Sunday? I only ask because someone said she had planned to see you."

"You know, I've already spoken with the police."

But that didn't help Jaymie. "Did you see her?" she pressed.

He regarded her soberly and narrowed his eyes. "Look, I'm not going to say any more. I gotta go." He turned and walked toward the donut shop and his meeting.

She got in her car, plunking her purse on top of the scarf and hat, and sat, running the SUV for warmth. How interesting that he was willing to divulge about salacious pictures of Mandy taken by Randall, but he drew the line at confirming or denying his own actions. She got out her phone and looked at the pictures of the calendar. There were the notations . . . *GV* stood out. They did meet, she was certain of it. Why not tell her when and why? Was it more than a meeting? Were they having a fling?

She shook her head. You don't pencil your fling in on your business calendar.

She scanned the other notations, wondering what they all meant while she pondered his story of Randall Kallis blackmailing Mandy. It had the ring of truth, but could that be colored by her dislike of the man?

Maybe.

But the question Mandy had posed was interesting. *What is RK doing with Win?* What did that mean? And then, *Is Win part of plan????*

What plan? Frustrated, she headed to Mandy's house.

TWENTY-THREE

Mandy's house was a gracious two-story white clapboard home with a wraparound porch. It was probably once the farmhouse for the surrounding land but now was in a mid-century subdivision of Wolverhampton known as Greenbrook. Jaymie got out of the SUV. To her surprise Mandy's maroon SUV, battered front end taped up, was parked in the drive.

Trina greeted her and showed her around.

Jaymie marveled at the beauty of the home. "This is exactly the kind of house I dreamed of as a kid." She turned in a circle, taking in the sunny kitchen, renovated in sparkling white, with a butcher block island, shiny copper pots above it on a pot rack. "I'd never keep it this uncluttered though," she added.

"My mom was not one to collect. Dad was. After he died she tore through the house and tossed stuff."

Jaymie followed the young woman back to Mandy's office in one of the bedrooms. She was searching the oak file cabinets for a copy of the will and insurance papers. "I'm surprised, given how confused she seemed in the last month, that she kept the house tidy. I expected a bit of a mess."

"Ti has been over," Trina replied. "She said it was a mess, so she went through and cleaned."

"She had a key?"

"Sure. She and Mom exchanged keys since they both lived alone."

Jaymie felt a prickle of unease at the back of her neck. Casually she said, "Did she throw things out or just tidy them away?"

"What do you mean?" Trina looked up from her chair in front of the open file cabinet drawer.

"Didn't the police go through first?"

"They've been here and taken what they wanted. I've spoken to them already and they told me some of what they took away, but it was a fair amount. They gave me an itemized list. It's here somewhere. And I know they've spoken to everyone Mom knew."

Jaymie relaxed. Okay, that was good. "I was a little startled to see your mother's

SUV in the drive. Didn't the police keep it?"

"Nope. They checked it out, but there was no reason to hold it."

"Isn't it too damaged to drive? She did have a couple of accidents."

"Fender benders, from what I understand, and nothing high-speed. It's drivable."

"You're going to drive it?"

"Me or Aunt Shan, I guess." Trina studied her face. "Why the interest in the car?"

"I thought it was totaled."

"Nope." She glanced around the room like she might find the car keys floating somewhere close by. "There should be another key fob for it somewhere."

"Maybe in her desk at work."

Trina's eyes widened and she snapped her fingers, pointing at Jaymie. "What a good thought! I'll look there."

"I'm wondering if your mom left any notes, any scribbled thoughts. Does she have a calendar or a notebook here at home? Anything that might give some hint as to what was happening to her?"

"I'll have a look around and see if I can find anything. First, though, I have to sort out the insurance and the will."

"Who is her executor?"

"I don't really know. I think maybe Ti."

"Hmm."

"Anyway," she said on a sigh. "There are a million things to do. Mom had power of attorney over Grandpa de Boer's medical and financial affairs, so I need to sort that because there are some bills she was about to pay."

"Power of attorney?"

"He's not well. Mom took care of things. Aunt Candy will have to take over, no matter how little she likes it, because I can't. I wouldn't even if I could."

"You don't get along with your grandfather?"

She made a face but continued walking her fingers through the files, pausing every now and then to check one more closely. "I can't stand the old man. It sounds horrible, but he made Mom miserable. No matter what, her whole life she had to jump when he said jump. Aunt Candy got to take off to California, but Mom stayed to take care of Grandpa."

"She did what she thought was right," Jaymie said mildly. "There may have been satisfaction in that."

"Not for me." Trina found an envelope, read it, and set it aside with a murmur of satisfaction. "Insurance, good."

"I'm curious about something," Jaymie

said, strolling the perimeter of the room, snooping on the desk, which was mostly tidy aside from a vitamin dosette, pens and the usual desk necessities. What had Ti tidied away? she wondered. "When we were at breakfast, there was tension between Ti and your Aunt Shannon. What was that all about?"

"Ti warned me about that. Aunt Shan can be fierce. They had an argument Sunday night when they were all at the Queensville Inn. Aunt Shan took Ti aside and asked her to intervene with her brother, Win. It was something about Manor Homes."

"What was it?"

"I don't know. I didn't pry. Anyway, Ti told her that was none of her business, that she didn't interfere with her brother's work."

"But what would your aunt want her to intervene about?"

"I don't tell Aunt Shan what to do and I don't ask her what she's up to. You saw what she's like. Total girl boss, born and bred."

A girl boss who wasn't given a position at Manor Homes when their father died. It was all left to Chad. If she was trying to influence Ti about Win, maybe it had to do with the lawsuit the company was facing. She frowned and shook her head. Considering the tangled web of interactions among Ti, Win, Helen, and Mandy, could any of this turmoil have led to murder? It came down to this: who was better off with Mandy dead? She didn't know if that was Shannon, but it was possible. The motives were there, and there was opportunity aplenty, as far as she could tell, but it felt like a giant snagged ball of wool with truth at the tangled heart of it.

"I have stuff to do for my daughter today," Jaymie said, getting up and hoisting her purse. "I almost forgot in all the jumble, but kids come first!"

Trina looked up, fingers inserted among the files, pausing in her work. "Don't let me stop you from looking around. Be my guest!"

Look for what? There didn't appear to be any calendar or appointment book. "I may take you up on that later, but I don't think I'll find the solution to the problem here." Especially since both the police and Ti had plenty of time to denude the place of clues. "I do have to get going to take care of my daughter's plans."

"Tell me about it," Trina said wistfully. She cleared her clogged throat and sniffed. "I need something to think about other than my mother's death."

Jaymie sat down. "Jocie has a group of friends . . . sweet girls, all of them. They made a pact to attend each other's recitals and competitions. Gemma plays the piano, Noor competes in spelling bees, Peyton does jujitsu, and Jocie and Mia are in the same dance class. Tonight, we'll have a sleepover and then go to Gemma's piano recital tomorrow morning."

Wistfully, Trina's eyes welled. "What a great mom you are. My mom was like that. She and Dad came to every game. I played soccer." She stifled a sob. "I always told her I looked forward to doing the same when I had a little girl, and she said she'd be there for those games too."

"I'm sorry, Trina," Jaymie said softly. "I'm glad you have your aunts."

The young woman didn't answer, turning her face away and swiping at her eyes. Having her aunts was not the same for Trina as having her mother and Jaymie knew it. The lame phrase had popped out of her mouth, but apologizing would only make it worse.

Jaymie left the house feeling melancholy, but she couldn't dwell on it. She had things to do, among them picking up Jocie from school. Shopping first, though.

She walked up and down the aisles of the grocery store in Wolverhampton puzzling out all the information she had received over the course of the week as she piled dog food, cat food, cat litter, milk, margarine and bread into the cart.

Motives for killing Mandy de Boer: everyone seemed to have one. Opportunity was a problem too because there was an ever-expanding circle of people who had a grudge against or problem with Mandy and Jaymie didn't know yet where they were on Sunday afternoon and evening. It may depend on access to Mandy's shake bottle, if that was indeed the weapon, as she suspected. There were other possibilities, but it seemed most likely that Mandy was killed with an overdose of drugs of some sort. She'd start there, then, those who had a motive to kill Mandy and access that Sunday evening to her bottle.

She pulled her cart over in the vitamin section of the grocery store and got out her notebook, checking her notes and adding to them.

Ti Pham: Motive: to save her brother's behind if Mandy was threatening to expose something hinky going on with his construction company. One of the notes in her calendar referring to Win and RK, Randall Kallis, wondering if Win was part of some plan. Would Ti go so far to protect her brother if she felt he was in danger from Mandy? *Means:* with a sister-in-law who was a pharmacist, Ti might know what to use and maybe even how to get what was needed to kill Mandy. *Opportunity:* she was closer to Mandy than anyone, even closer than Candy, and could easily have drugged the bottle.

Shannon: Motive: this was trickier if she believed that Mandy was trying to resolve the issues with her sister-in-law without going to court. But what if Mandy said something that Sunday evening to indicate she had decided she wasn't willing to settle with Shannon? Maybe the older woman figured if Trina inherited, she'd be easier to manipulate and control into a favorable settlement. And yet . . . "Means" was a big old question mark, as was "Opportunity." The woman *was* at the inn and was seen speaking to Mandy, but if Jaymie thought Mandy had been drugged for some time, weeks or even months, it didn't seem likely that Shannon would have long-term access to her victim.

Candy: Motive: a lifelong up-and-down, back-and-forth relationship. *Means:* unknown. Did she have access to medication or drugs? Hard to say. *Opportunity:* of anyone, she surely had the easiest opportunity to get at the shake bottle on numerous occasions. For opportunity she shared the number-one spot with Ti.

Randall: Motive: Killing Mandy may have been his only choice if she was going to expose him as a cheat. If she was prepared to settle with Shannon — she only had that woman's word for it — maybe she expected Randall Kallis would be drummed out of Manor Homes. That would be ample motive. *Means:* unknown. *Opportunity:* same as Candy in some ways. He was in the office every day, and Jaymie had seen how Mandy left her shake bottle around, as well as packets of the drink powder. Almost too easy.

Connor Ward: Motive: He was angry that his house was in such bad shape and that they couldn't reach an agreement. It still seemed he was better off if Mandy was alive, though, especially if they were coming close to an agreement, as had been suggested. But angry people don't always act rationally, and he was *furious. Means:* question mark. There was one sticking point she kept coming up against: without knowing what substance was being fed to Mandy — or, in all honesty, *if* she was being drugged — she could not know how it was obtained. *Opportunity:* another problem. He was certainly close enough Sunday evening to have slipped something in her drink, but not if she had been drugged over the long term. He would not, in all probability, have the ability to do that.

She struck Connor Ward off the list. She didn't believe he was the killer.

There had to be one piece of information that would make it all click into place, something she was overlooking. But what was it? It could be anything that would clarify motive, means or opportunity.

She stuck the notebook back in her purse and continued shopping.

Ah, the snack aisle, the bane of her existence. Cookies, chips, nuts? Nope. Keep it simple. She tossed all the makings for s'mores in the cart. They'd have a fire in either the backyard or, if it was too cold, the fireplace and make the delicious treat. She finished shopping, packed it in cloth bags, stowed them in the back of the SUV and got in, then headed into Queensville. She called Mrs. Stubbs and was enthusiastically invited to a late lunch.

Trying to make amends to the needy Edith, Mrs. Stubbs had invited her to dine with them in her room. Delighted, the woman provided a sumptuous feast from the inn kitchen: roasted cauliflower soup, cheese croissants stuffed with salmon, and for dessert a pastry sampler. Conversation flowed, Edith was thrilled, but Jaymie could not wait until she had Mrs. Stubbs to herself so she could ask questions relating to her investigation.

They finished with tea, then Edith and Jaymie did the dishes. While they did that, Mrs. Stubbs had laid out the print edition of the week's *Wolverhampton Weekly Howler*. With a strong light over her table, and powerful reading glasses on her nose, she read carefully from back to front.

Edith, with a cheery wave, returned to her duties at the reservation desk.

Jaymie sat down with her friend, and Mrs. Stubbs folded the paper, setting it aside. "I'll read the rest later. Got to keep abreast of all the latest. I see they're covering Mandy de Boer's death with great care but are pointedly saying the police are not being forthcoming about the cause of death."

"I know. I wish —" Her phone chirped. It was Val. Jaymie cast a glance to Mrs. Stubbs, who nodded. She invited her friend to have tea with them. "Come to the patio door," she said. It was the easiest way and saved Val from having to march through the inn proper.

Jaymie made more tea and they all settled

at the little table by the patio doors, looking out onto the chill but beautiful late October day — brilliant blue sky, sun sparkling, leaves shimmering gold in the breeze. Val, bored and restless, seemed out of sorts. She needed a resolution, and so did Mandy's family.

Jaymie told them everything she had learned, all she suspected and all she feared. She then turned to Val. "I'm going to preface this by saying I don't exactly know what to think. Maybe you can help." She told Val what she had discussed with Greg Vasiliev, and about seeing his initials in Mandy's calendar. "He seemed suspicious of me and wouldn't tell me if he saw Mandy at all on Sunday."

Val blinked, owl-like, at Jaymie, and shoved her glasses up on her nose. There was something on her mind, something she was loath to say. Mrs. Stubbs watched the two, her gaze slewing back and forth.

"Val, you can say anything to me, you must know that."

She shook her head, got out her phone, and tapped in a text. Looking up, she said, "Give me a minute." She stepped out through the patio doors and made a phone call, pacing as she spoke, her breath coming in wispy puffs.

"I wonder what that's all about?" Jaymie said, frowning and staring out the door.

"Everyone has a private life, Jaymie. There are parts of Valetta's world she doesn't share even with you, her closest friend."

Jaymie swiveled her gaze to Mrs. Stubbs in dismay. "Am I a nosy parker? Do I act like I need to know everything?"

"Sometimes."

Val was her best pal, her confidante, her rock, always there when she needed her. She hoped she was the same in return, but realized she had taken it for granted that Val's whole life was her family, her friends, and her work, which left no personal life. "I've been selfish," she whispered, her throat closing.

"Nonsense," Mrs. Stubbs said. "Valetta Nibley is an intensely private woman and that invites an assumption that there is nothing more to know. She'll tell you what she wants you to know. Until then, carry on as before."

"She's talking to Greg Vasiliev," Jaymie said.

This was confirmed a moment later when Val reentered with a smile that she quickly hid. "Greg says he met with Mandy late Sunday afternoon at the Manor Homes office."

"He couldn't say that to me?"

"He doesn't know you or your motives. He knows how it looks, a secret meeting with her right before she died. I told him you won't jump to any conclusions. I won't let you. She wanted to pick his brain about the fixes she needed to order for the houses that were having problems. Also, she asked him to put together a list of reputable contractors, people he could vouch for and had worked with. They'd met a couple of times and he said he felt like he was sneaking around, keeping it a secret from everyone. He was so relieved to tell me! Mandy knew she could trust him, that's all." She paused, then said, "I told him I knew about my brother's involvement with Manor Homes. He hadn't wanted to mention it before to me because of Brock."

That was what he had told Jaymie, too. "Did Mandy seem okay to him on Sunday?"

"She was clear-ish, but angry about something."

"That aligns with what her father said." And yet later that night when she spoke to Val on the phone she was confused and seemed intoxicated. "What time was that?"

"They met at the office at about four, or closer to four thirty. He was there at four and had to wait a few minutes for her in the parking lot. She pulled in, and they went into the office to talk. It took longer than he thought it would because she wanted to show him stuff on her computer. She had begun to gather information. As the company bookkeeper for several years, she was familiar with their financial structure. She had to give that up after her husband died to focus on running the company. But lately she had been looking through the bookkeeper's files and found irregularities, things that didn't look right to her."

Interesting. That was another angle she hadn't considered, that keeping Mandy closely tied to the business benefited Randall. She was no longer doing the books and keeping such a close eye on the finances. It may have given him more opportunity to cheat Manor Homes. "How long were they inside?"

"An hour, maybe an hour and a half."

"He's not sure?"

"Not everyone watches the time, especially on a Sunday," Val retorted.

Mandy *had* to be in Queensville by five thirty-ish, because she had careened into Bonnie's car, and that woman had waited a half hour for the police. Bonnie got to the inn minutes after Mandy, though, according to Taylor. Maybe Mandy pulled over some-

344

where to straighten herself out after nicking Bonnie's car.

"How did Mandy seem to him?"

"He was worried about her appearance. She was always super neat in the past, he said, but she seemed haggard and . . . what did he call it? Rumpled. Her hair was crazy and her clothes were wrinkled."

"So to be clear, Mandy was looking for outside contractors, which means she was planning to cut Win Pham out of the business." With Ti, Helen and Pham's tangled relationship with Mandy, that could lead to hurt feelings or worse. Had it led to her death? "Did she mention anything about Randall Kallis?"

"Yup. Listen to this: she told Greg in confidence that she was convinced Randall was taking kickbacks from subcontractors. As soon as she had definitive proof, Randall would be out on his ear for breach of trust. She was going to talk to her lawyers on Monday."

Mandy hadn't made it to Monday, when she was planning to see her lawyers and settle things with Shannon Manor-Billings, perhaps offering her a bigger cut of the company. That bigger cut would have come once Kallis had been ousted from Manor Homes for his illegal activities. Jaymie recalled how patiently Kallis had sat, answering her questions. Maybe he was trying to allay her suspicions, or digging to see how much she knew. Win Pham and Randall Kallis had zoomed up her list of suspects, competing for the top spot. Kallis had seemed a cold and calculating man, and she'd never forget the spurt of fear she experienced when she saw the anger in his eyes. What would he do to protect himself?

Val didn't have a lot more to say and Jaymie fell quiet, not sure how to think of her friend now, with her new perspective. Val kept darting her glances, but Jaymie wasn't ready to talk, yet. She had never even considered her best friend as more than her friend, but Val was a woman, with a life that comprised more than what she could do for others. Why had her view of Val not evolved over the years? She had been selfish in this relationship, and it hurt her heart. How could she make up to Valetta for the years of taking her for granted?

"I have to go," Val finally said. "I'm supposed to pick up Will and Eva from school today and we're going over to Heartbreak Island to the tart shop. Brock has several showings this weekend so tomorrow is going to be a Saturday of eating junk food and playing video games for us. I know you have the girls' sleepover tonight," she said to Jaymie. "Call me tomorrow, okay, and tell me how it went?"

Distracted, Jaymie sat in silence for a while, long enough so that Mrs. Stubbs took up the newspaper again and began where she left off, reading the back of one page with travel ads. "Oh, how I'd love a monthlong cruise on the Rhine," she murmured.

Wistfully, Jaymie watched her friend, who would never be able to take that monthlong cruise. "Is that where you'd go, if you could?"

Mrs. Stubbs smiled. "Oh, I don't know. If I *could* I'd be Agatha Christie, cruising along the Nile, stopping only for an archaeological expedition or two. Maybe in my next life. Instead, I'm rereading *Murder on the Nile,*" she said, waving to a large-print book from the Wolverhampton library.

"Not Mexico, then?" Jaymie asked with a laugh, tapping the ad that showed an all-expenses-paid trip to Cancun.

"Good Lord, no. Edith is going down with a girlfriend who swears it is to get her husband his ED medication on the cheap. I guess you can buy all sorts of drugs down there." She snorted. "Edith thinks I don't know why she's really going, which is to get an eyelift done in Tijuana. They have a

347

name for it! It's called a medical vacation."

"It's too bad she doesn't feel able to tell you the truth. Maybe she worries she'll be judged for it?"

Mrs. Stubbs nodded, a thoughtful expression on her face. "That is something for me to ponder, my dear. As always, our chat has been illuminating."

"To both of us, it seems," Jaymie said, thinking of her new insight to her friendship with Val. "I have to go, unfortunately." Jaymie stood and hefted her purse. "I promised Becca I'd meet her at the Queensville house," she said, of the yellow brick Queen Anne they had been given by their parents, who had moved to Boca Raton a few years before. "She has been 'clearing the clutter,' " she said, sketching air quotes. "Which means getting rid of my vintage stuff. She has more boxes she wants me to go through." Jaymie rolled her eyes. The battle between her and Becca over Jaymie's "junk" was ongoing, and maybe getting worse now that Becca and Kevin had Queensville Fine Antiques and spent so much more time in the Queensville house. "But first, I think I'll go pick up my little girl and take her to see her aunt."

"That'll distract Rebecca."

"That's my plan."

348

Twenty-Four

Jocie didn't even make it into the Queens-ville house. The moment they got out of Jay-mie's SUV — parked at the curb, not the parking lane behind the house, since Jaymie didn't intend to be there long — the girl headed down the street with a breezy shout that she was going to visit Peyton, one of her best friends, who lived one block over. Out of the corner of her eye Jaymie saw a maroon SUV and for a second thought of Mandy. She shook her head at the stupid thought. There must be a dozen like Mandy's in and around Queensville.

Jaymie had pictured a pitched battle over the vintage kitchen stuff she had decorated with, but Becca was in the front hall, frantic, pacing and yelling into her cell phone. "What do you mean my car won't be ready until tomorrow?" She paused, then grum-bled, "I guess there's nothing I can do about it now." She hung up and stared disconsolately at the pile of boxes by the door ready to deliver to a customer in Wolverhampton.

"What's up? What's wrong with your car?"

"It's in the shop in Wolverhampton. What am I going to do? My customer needs the Royal Imari stat!"

"A dinnerware emergency?"

Becca gave her a cold look. "She has family coming in from New York this weekend and she's already bragged to her snooty sister-in-law about the furniture and china. I had my guys deliver that dining room suite, but I don't trust them to take this," she said, waving a hand at the boxes. "I promised her!"

"I can drop it off," Jaymie said, undoing her coatigan.

Becca stared at her, wordless.

"Ah, okay, I get it. You don't trust anyone to take it but you."

Reluctantly, Becca admitted it. "It's taken me almost three years to sell these dishes. If she doesn't have them for this weekend, she has threatened to pull out of the sale. With Kevin away at an antique show until late tonight, and my car in the shop, I'll have to rent a car, and to do that, I'll have to go to Wolverhampton. That's stupid! I only need a vehicle to take this stuff to my client, and besides . . . it would be crazy to rent a car for twelve hours." She paused, eyeing her sister, then said, "I have a thought! My mechanic is going to have my car ready tomorrow afternoon. Jakob can pick up you and Jocie here. Leave your SUV with me. He can drive you home and bring you back tomorrow to get your SUV. Easy peasy."

Jaymie stared at her older sister with exasperation. "Hold your horses! Not easy peasy. I promised *all* the girls a sleepover tonight. And they're going to Gemma's piano recital in the morning, so I *need* my SUV. Jakob's truck isn't suitable for five kids."

With a crafty look, Becca said, "They can have the sleepover here."

Jaymie eyed her with surprise. Five excited ten-year-old girls at once? She was almost tempted to go along with it. But no, it would be too much for her fifty-something sister, who had never had children and had no clue what she was letting herself in for. "It wouldn't work," she said regretfully.

"Why not? Her friends live right here in Queensville, it would be super easy."

"Gemma, Peyton and Noor do, but Kim was going to drop Mia off at the cabin."

"She wouldn't mind dropping her off here in Queensville, I'm sure. Text her. It will give me a chance to chat with her if she comes in to drop off Mia."

Jaymie texted Jakob and he said he didn't mind if she didn't. Jocie — who kept a couple of changes of clothes and sleepwear at the Queensville house for times when they stayed in town — could ride with Becca into Wolverhampton to deliver the china before the sleepover happened. Jaymie texted the other moms. They all knew Becca and the Queensville house and were fine with it, as was Kim Hansen, Mia's grandmother. Gemma's mom added that she'd be picking her own girl up early the next morning and could give Becca the itinerary for the recital then.

"It looks like it's a go," Jaymie said, clicking off her phone. Jocie, back from Peyton's house, was ecstatic. Jaymie handed over the SUV keys to Becca. "I'll get the rest of my groceries out and take them home with Jakob, but there's a box in the back of s'mores supplies, snack food, and some Lego I borrowed from Noor's parents. If you have any questions —"

"I know, I know," Becca said shortly. "If it has to do with Jocie, I'll text you. If I have a question about one of the other kids, I will text or call their parents. Jaymie, I've been babysitting my whole life. I have handled multiple children many times."

Jaymie took a deep breath. She needed to start being more mindful of her tendency to overexplain and micromanage everything. "Being a mom is relatively new to me, Becca. I don't mean to patronize or condescend. I'm good to go," she said as Jakob pulled up to the curb in his truck. They transferred the groceries to the pickup, and said goodbye to Jocie.

As they drove out of town toward home, Jakob noticed Jaymie checking the rearview mirror. "What's up?"

"I can't shake this feeling lately, like I'm being followed."

"Followed? Who by?"

"I don't know. It's just a feeling or . . ."

He stayed silent, letting her arrange her thoughts.

"The other afternoon when I was going to see Henry de Boer, a white sedan zoomed past me. Scared the heck out of me. Another day I was at the Queensville Inn talking to Taylor Bellwood. She was telling me everything that had happened the Sunday night Mandy died. A similar car cruised through the parking lot without stopping and then went back out to the street. I know I've seen that car before. I feel like I'm missing something. Oh, I'm all in a jumble. There is something nagging at me, and I can't for the life of me think what it is. I know it has to do with Mandy's death and something else I've heard lately. But I don't know what it is."

"You need to stop thinking about it all for a little while. It'll pop up clear as day when it's worked its way through your subconscious."

"Maybe. I feel stupid. I'm sure I've seen something or noticed something."

"To do with the car?"

"Maybe. Maybe not."

She expected him to brush it all off, to make some joke, to dismiss it. Instead, he knit his brow. "Did you get a plate number of the car? Or at least a type of vehicle? Maybe you could get Vestry to look into it."

"No plate, but in two cases it was a white four-door sedan . . . like a Sunfire, probably early twenty-tens."

"And the third case?"

"That was just a while ago, when I took Jocie into Queensville. I got out of the car at the curb and walked toward the door. Jocie was heading off to Peyton's house. I stopped and looked over my shoulder. I don't know why, but I had a sensation of being watched, you know, that feeling at the back of your neck, or between your shoulder blades? And then . . . Jakob, I'd have sworn it was Mandy's maroon SUV. But it couldn't be, so I dismissed it."

"Couldn't be?"

"Okay, nothing is impossible. I did see it parked at Mandy's house. Trina says it's drivable. But there must be many maroon SUVs in Queensville, right?"

"Sure. Did the one you saw have front-end damage?"

"I don't know. It was past before I thought to look."

"If you see the car again, take down the plate number. As far as Mandy's SUV goes, Trina could be driving it, right?"

"Maybe, if she found the key fob." As they got out of the truck at the cabin, a chill wind scudded down the road. Jaymie shivered, hugging the coatigan around her. "Darn it, I left my scarf and hat in the SUV. I knew I forgot something!"

"We can go back into town and get them," Jakob said, putting his arm around her shoulders.

"No, it's okay. I've got others. I can do without them for one day." She smiled up at him, shrugging off her uneasiness. "We have the whole night to ourselves."

"I know," he said, kissing the top of her head as they walked toward the cabin, stopping on the threshold. "Trust me, I know."

Jaymie put her arms around Jakob's neck. "It feels like forever since we've been alone," she said against his beard.

He chuckled and kissed her. "Let's go in and get comfortable on the sofa."

It was a wonderful evening followed by a wonderful night. Jakob brought her coffee in bed the next morning as the wind whipped up, cold rain occasionally pattering on the roof. Jaymie sipped her coffee and chuckled as she read out loud a text from Becca in which she described how she "enjoyed" having five ten-year-old girls hopped up on hot chocolate and marshmallows bedded down on the parlor floor for the night. "Hah! She had no clue what she was in for! Bet she's exhausted."

"How can you get that from a text?" Jakob said as he dropped down beside her.

"Whoa, be careful there! Almost wore the coffee," she said, setting the mug aside on the bedside table. "I can tell. Trust me. Gemma's mom has already picked her up to get her ready for the recital. Becca is going to take the girls to the recital, then take Mia home, then drop Jocie off here. I'll drive Becca back into town and do a few errands."

"Don't forget, Jocie is supposed to spend

the night with my mom and dad."

"Good heavens, two nights in a row alone with you? What *will* I do?" Jaymie giggled and rolled into his arms.

Some time later they got up, showered, dressed and drank their second coffees of the day while eating. "Good heavens, it is one in the afternoon! Where has the time gone?" Jaymie said, checking her phone.

He looked up from his phone and frowned. "I thought Becca would have Jocie back here by now."

"Me too. Maybe they lingered over lunch." She texted Becca and received a quick reply. Her sister had, on her own initiative (and maybe after some begging from Jocie), taken all the girls out after the recital — while they were still dressed up — to a "fancy" brunch at the Queensville Inn, with Mrs. Stubbs in attendance. She was loading them in the SUV that moment to return them to their parents.

"Thank goodness," Jaymie said and sighed. The formless worry that had begun to nag at her dissipated. "Becca says they're on their way home."

"Good. I know Jocie's cousins have some kind of plan for later today. We'll let her play with Lilibet and take Hoppy for a walk, then I'll bundle her off to Oma and Opa's."

There was cleaning to do. She and Jakob decided to divide and conquer. She tackled the downstairs bathroom and the kitchen, he did some laundry and cleaned their en suite bathroom, then picked up Jocie's room. She was normally in charge of that herself, but her weekend was so busy he volunteered to spruce it up for her.

More than an hour had passed. They met back in the kitchen as Jaymie was hanging up the damp dishtowel on the rack. She had been checking her phone for the last few minutes and was starting to worry. "Where are they?" she fretted to Jakob.

His phone rang and he answered. Jaymie watched as his face bleached of color and followed him as he grabbed his keys and jacket even as he listened. "We'll be right there!" he yelped into the phone.

"What is it? What's wrong?" Jaymie bleated, clutching at his sleeve, her vision swimming, fear clenching her stomach.

"There's been an accident. Becca and Jocie are in the hospital. We have to go. *Now!*"

The next minutes were a nightmare of fear and horror. They roared into Wolverhampton, then navigated the ER of Wolverhampton General, finding first Jocie, who was bruised and crying and moaning. She wanted Jakob and no one but Jakob. He took his child in his arms as best he could past a tangle of monitors and cords. The doctor wanted to speak with him, but he indicated that Jaymie should talk to her. Comforting Jocie was his priority. The doctor, a new trauma physician Jaymie was not familiar with, ushered her out to the hall, clipboard in hand.

"What happened, Doctor? Is she okay? She looks terrible!" Jaymie cried, her voice quivering, tears choking her throat.

The doctor, a young Black woman with kind eyes and a neutral expression, held up one hand. "Ms. Müller, I take it? Jocie's mom?"

"I am," Jaymie said, taking a deep, shuddering breath.

"I know it looks scary, but we've done preliminary scans and there is minimal damage, no broken bones, and as far as we can tell no brain trauma." Jocie had been protected by the seat and harness they used for her small frame and stature. "You've done everything right to protect her and it worked."

She explained more, and Jaymie took it in, calming as she listened. "What about my sister, Becca? She was driving. What do you know about her?"

"I'm not her physician." She checked her

clipboard. "She's in room C-110, if you want to go now. Her husband is here. I do know she's considered stable."

"Okay." Jaymie's heart thudded at the thought of Becca injured. Her beloved sister. "What happened? Do you know?"

She shook her head. "I'm sorry, I don't. But the police are speaking with your sister right now."

"The police?" she exclaimed. The woman shrugged.

Jaymie checked back in with Jakob and whispered what the doctor had told her. More tests were needed to be sure there was no brain bleed from the traumatic jolt. She would have to stay overnight, but given that Jocie didn't have a headache or blurred vision, the medical staff was cautiously optimistic. Jakob urged Jaymie to go talk to Becca, in part to discover what happened. She made her way from pediatrics ER to the adult section. Kevin was in the sitting room, slumped in a chair, head in hands.

"Kevin, is she okay?" He looked up, and her heart lurched at the tears streaming down his face. She sank down beside him. "Kevin, tell me . . . is she . . ."

He grabbed her hands and squeezed. "No, no, luv, she's okay. I was praying. I haven't done that in donkey's years. The best thing you can do is tell me, how is Jocie?"

"She's going to be okay. She's scared, and bruised, and they'll be doing *more* tests, but she's okay."

He exhaled a great gust of air and dropped his head, whispering a thank-you. Then he looked up again and his eyes were pooled with water. "Thank God. We have to tell Becca. She's mad with worry."

"Why aren't you in there with her?"

"The police are still talking to her."

"The police? It was an accident, right?"

He shook his head. "It was no accident. She was run off the road."

Even as she recounted to Jakob — outside of Jocie's hearing — the conversation she had with an almost hysterical Becca, fury lashed through Jaymie. "Becca noticed a vehicle following her, but didn't think anything of it until she got onto the country road where Mia's house is. She was dropping Mia off there."

"And she's sure of the description and what happened?"

Jaymie nodded. "A maroon SUV with front-end damage had been following her for some time, pulled off as she let Mia off, then continued following them. It forced her off the road about a quarter mile along."

"A maroon SUV. Mandy de Boer's vehicle."

"The police aren't sure. They don't have a plate number. They'll trace where it is right now and see if there is more damage. It's too much of a coincidence. It must be Mandy's SUV."

His voice guttural with anger, he said, "Whoever was driving Mandy de Boer's maroon SUV was trying to kill our child."

Jaymie sobbed and shook her head. "No, Jakob, they weren't trying to kill Jocie, but they didn't care if she died!" She wept, but through it, almost incoherent with rage and fear, she said, "Whoever it was, was trying to kill *me.*"

"Why do you say that?"

"It was *my* vehicle Becca was driving. The weather's frigid today with that wicked wind that's come up, so she was wearing *my* red hat and scarf, the ones your mother made for me. Whoever did that despicable thing thought I was driving. They didn't care if they killed Jocie, as long as they killed me." She sobbed and wept. "Jakob, it's all my fault. They almost killed Jocie and it's all my fault!"

Twenty-Five

Both patients would stay in the hospital overnight. Kevin refused to go home so a reclining chair was set up for him in Becca's room. He joked that his bad back would love it better than his expensive adjustable bed at home. Jakob likewise insisted on staying with Jocie, and said he'd feel happier if Jaymie went home to look after the animals and get some sleep. Reluctantly, she agreed.

Val had arrived at the hospital full of anxiety until she saw both patients were recovering. Back in Jocie's room after visiting Becca and Kevin, she said, "I'll take Jaymie home, Jakob, and stay with her." A determined light glowed in her eyes as she shoved her glasses up on her nose. She then headed down to the gift shop at Jocie's request to see if they had the latest trading cards she and her friends were collecting. "I'll be back up in fifteen minutes," she promised.

Jaymie followed her friend into the hall. Val eyed her soberly. "You look awful. Worse than Becca."

"Val! I'm scared."

"Do you think it has anything to do with . . ." She paused, pushed her glasses up, and shook her head, unable to continue.

Jaymie nodded. "I'm afraid," she admitted, her voice choked with tears. "And angry! Did Becca tell you what happened? Someone used Mandy's SUV as a weapon, trying to kill me, and instead they almost killed my sister and my little girl."

"You don't know for sure."

"But I do," she said, and explained about the scarlet scarf and hat, and how it concealed Becca's identity from the killer. Val was silent, unwilling to accede to the logic, and yet unable to assail it. "Go to the gift shop. I'll be okay. Let me think." Jaymie paced outside Jocie's room, unwilling to burden Jakob with her suspicions. He had enough to worry about.

Val came back with a full bag: puzzle books, pens, comics, toothpaste and toothbrush, slippers for Jakob, and treats. She had two packs of the excitingly varied trading cards. She shooed Jaymie and Jakob away for a few moments together while she regaled Jocie with stories of her niece and nephew's adventures and promised to take them all for a jaunt to Legoland in Ohio next summer, before Will was out of the Lego phase.

Jaymie and Jakob held each other in the hall, supporting each other, melding into one unit, rocking comfort into each other in a heartbeat rhythm. She stared up into his brown eyes, red-rimmed with his fear. "It'll be okay," she whispered, hoping it would be. He nodded, leaning his head into her palm as she scruffed his beard.

"I love you," he said.

They kissed and said their temporary goodbyes. Jaymie reentered the room to say a cheery farewell to Jocie. The little girl, beginning to feel better, chattered nonstop about the sleepover, the recital, and her brave Aunt Becca. She gave instructions for kisses to Lilibet and Hoppy. "Play with them, Mama, and let Lilibet sleep with you and Hoppy so she won't be lonely." Her round face set in a serious expression. "And tell them I'll be home tomorrow."

"I will do all that and more, my little chickadee," Jaymie said, hugging her and breathing in her ineffable scent, mingled now with hospital smells.

Jakob's phone rang, but it was a call for Jocie from Mia, who had heard about the accident and wanted to talk to her new best friend.

It seemed like the day had lasted a lifetime, but when Val and Jaymie emerged from the hospital into the brilliant hard coldness of a chilly snap, it was just dinnertime, the sun setting low over the hospital, coloring the sky with orange and reds though it was only five thirty. Jaymie shivered and leaned against the brick wall of the hospital, hot tears trailing down her cold cheeks. It had taken everything in her to smile and hold herself up and be normal with Jakob and Jocie and even Becca.

Val touched her shoulder. "You okay, kiddo?"

Jaymie turned a bleak examining gaze on her friend, her lifeline, her port in any storm. "No, and I won't be until whoever almost killed my baby is in jail."

"What can we do to make it happen?"

That was the answer she needed. "I'll tell you on the way home. I have two theories, and a way to find out which is correct."

They went back to the cabin. Jaymie entered, feeling strangely as if she was seeing it for the first time in months. She half expected dust and cobwebs, but it was clean, as they had left it mere hours ago. Nothing felt right and would never again, until she discovered who was after her, and why.

In the pit of her stomach she knew — had always known — who killed Mandy de Boer, even when looking directly into the killer's eyes. And yet every fiber of her being had resisted the truth. This was evil: malicious, deadly, rotten-to-the-core evil, a person so lacking in scruples that they would risk the life of a child in the pursuit of their goal.

Val made a pot of tea, tiptoeing around Jaymie's weepy emotionalism. Even the animals were wary. Seeing Hoppy watch her, his black button eyes holding worry, she got angry, this time, at herself.

"Enough. We are going to fix this. I've done it before, and I'll do it again," Jaymie said. As Val sat down beside her, she hugged her friend. "*We'll* do it. I will not let this beat me. It's time to corner a killer." She then related to Val her conversation with Mel Heath about how the murder could have occurred with few signs of violence. "I missed clues. I thought the bruising around her mouth was from the accidents she was in, that the blood from the injuries had sunk, like that from a black eye does. But now I think it was from the murder and I'd bet the medical examiner has told the police exactly that."

Val nodded. "I should have thought of what Melody said myself. I was intent on proving that I and my pharmacy had no part in the death and shied away from any pharmaceutical explanation. But we do know that Mandy was on blood pressure medication. Too much and it would, indeed, depress her breathing, making it shallow and slow."

"I do think other drugs were given to Mandy, maybe even roofies," she said, using the common street name for benzodiaz-epine, a drug used to incapacitate victims of assault. "She was given a chemical cocktail."

"You never mentioned *that* notion before."

Jaymie explained to a startled Val why she had hit on benzodiazepine and how — and who — could have used it. "The idea came to me when Mel and I were discussing the murder. There had to be some explanation for why Mandy was so loopy lately. That drug given to her at intervals would make her forgetful, wonky, unlike herself, more so when she had been drugged, and less so as it wore off. Then the combination of benzo-diazepine and an overdose of blood pres-sure meds would have been enough to render her unconscious the evening she died. It would slow her breathing."

"But it must have been given to her at the inn."

"Exactly."

"She'd function for a while and then pass out, making it a relatively simple matter to smother her," Val said.

Jaymie nodded. "With very little bruising and only a little petechiae, explainable by other causes. It may have been passed off as a natural death, and if it didn't, planting Mandy there, on the back doorstep of the pharmacy, pointed to you."

"So, someone —"

"Someone who was at the Queensville Inn that night —"

"— overheard her say she'd meet me there. But why *did* Mandy want to meet me? I don't understand."

"Because you're a pharmacist. She couldn't ask Helen because of the connection to Ti. She still wasn't sure of her theories, and worried that Ti's loyalties would be divided. Val, when it comes down to it, after thinking things over in a more rational state of mind, Mandy decided that she trusted you. That held, I believe, even as more drugs coursed through her system, making her wonky and, eventually, sleepy."

Val nodded, speechless for the moment, tears welling. Trust was vital to her. It touched her to know Mandy had, at the end, trusted her to tell her the truth. "I think that's what I heard in her voice, fear, doubt, suspicion."

"Suspicion of someone close to her."

"She thought I'd at least be an impartial ear," Val said sadly. "Maybe she would have told me that she thought she was being poisoned or drugged. I wish I had let her come to see me."

"She would never have made it. If I'm right, she didn't die on the back stoop. The killer knew there was a chance you'd go to meet her and it was important that Mandy not be rescued. She was killed elsewhere and dropped on the back porch, arranged for you to find in the morning."

"That was the car screeching that Taylor heard, the killer taking off."

Jaymie nodded, then explained everything else.

Val, in shocked silence, listened and nodded. "Call Vestry and tell her."

"Uh-uh. I'll tell you what I'm going to do instead." Jaymie told Val her plan, which her friend vehemently rejected.

"You can't expose yourself that way. I won't let you. Becca would never forgive me. *Jakob* would never forgive me. I would never forgive *myself.*" Her normally calm tone held a note of panic at the thought of what Jaymie proposed doing.

"You can't stop me," Jaymie said. "As much as I value your advice and opinion, Val, I have to do this." She looked at her wise friend and pondered what she was about to say next. There was nothing for it but to ask. "Val, we've been friends my whole life. I trust you more than any single person I know. You're uniquely qualified to help me with this plan, but I would never put the slightest pressure on you to help." She paused, thought, then shook her head. "No. Look, if you stay here and look after the animals and man the phone — put Jakob off if he asks where I am and why I'm not answering my cell phone or the landline — it will be all the help I need."

"This is insane!" Val said, leaping to her feet and pacing. "You can't do this."

"Jocie is in the hospital and safe right now, but she'll be out tomorrow." Urgency coursed through Jaymie, pounding her heart, throbbing in her veins. "If I don't do this now, the killer will still be out there tomorrow. This is the only chance I might have to end this before anyone else gets hurt." She paused and quirked a smile. "What are you going to do, tie me down?"

Val glared down at her. "If you think for

one moment I'm going to let you do this alone, you're crazy."

"I won't be alone," Jaymie said, her smile dying in the face of her friend's fury. "You may think I'm crazy, but I'm not. I fully intend to tell Detective Vestry what I'm up to."

Mollified, Val said, "Vestry won't let you do it."

"I'm not going to *ask* her, I'm going to *tell* her what I'm about to do. Short of detaining me, she's got no choice, and I won't be waiting around for her to try it." Jaymie moved restlessly on the sofa. She didn't feel like herself. She was nervous and angry and ready to jump out of her skin. "I could tell Vestry all of this and it might help. But it would leave the killer out there free for who knows how long. I prefer my short-cut. The police may be on this path already. I've given Vestry every bit of information I've received all along the way — except for this last bit that I've just figured out. And she's a smart woman with more resources than I have. But they don't have *proof.*"

Jaymie leaned forward as Val plunked down to sit on the coffee table in front of her. "I can get them the proof," she said urgently. "There's no point to this if she doesn't catch the culprit. I'm not about to make a citizen's arrest or anything foolish like that. This is a tough determined murderer and I'm no idiot."

"Okay, point taken." Val shoved her glasses up on her nose and said, "I'm in this all the way. It started with me, and it'll end with me. I'll make the call. You know it'll be more convincing coming from me."

Jaymie nodded. "That was my first thought. You can sell it. I mean, I could stumble through it, but you're far more likely to sound credible. This *is* something you would have figured out."

"Except I didn't."

"I had unique information that came to me at the right moment," she said, thinking of the newspaper Mrs. Stubbs had been reading, and how it reminded her of the torn *Howler* piece in Mandy's dead hand. Sometimes you need to turn things over and read the small print.

Val made the call, bluntly stated their hypothesis, and said she was willing to be talked out of her theory. She then asked the salient question. The killer agreed to meet, stating that Val had it all wrong. *I'll answer all your questions,* the murderer said. They needed neutral ground. Val suggested they meet in one hour by the silo in the Vintage Manor Estates development.

Val hung up and nodded, pushing her glasses up on her nose. "It's a yes."

"Now to call Vestry."

"How did she sound?" Val asked of the detective as they sat in her car idling by the tall silo in the vacant development.

"Angry. *Furious,* as a matter of fact. She threatened to arrest me for obstruction of justice, which is why I didn't tell her until I was out the door and on the way here."

"You don't think that was a bit manipulative?"

"It was a *lot* manipulative, but I can't be sorry about that right now. I'll be sorry later." Jaymie sighed. "I can't explain it, Val, but I am all kinds of angry and scared and determined. I'm going to jump out of my skin if I don't do something. Seeing my poor little Jocie, hooked up to machines and with bruises . . . she's endured so much in her life." Being a little person wasn't always easy, but she faced every obstacle with intelligence and determination helped by the best dad any child could have. "Someone tried to kill her. I'll face the consequences of Vestry's anger *after* we catch this jerk. There are some things worth that kind of trouble."

"Did she threaten legal consequences?"

Jaymie frowned. "No. She sounded understanding. Sympathetic, even. She's worried for my safety and told me that if I gave her the information, she'd face the killer here instead of me. Vestry doesn't say a lot, and I never know what she's thinking, but I know she'd do her darnedest to bring in the killer. However, that animal almost killed my sister and my daughter and cannot go unpunished a moment longer."

Her voice sounded cold even to herself, and she recognized in that moment how motherhood had changed her, shifting both her priorities and her goals, strengthening her backbone, making her more certain of right and wrong and her place in the equation. Jocie's safety was all she cared about.

"I wasn't absolutely positive of your reasoning — it all hung together and I could imagine why it worked and I thought you were right, but I wasn't sure — until the phone conversation," Val said. "*Now* I'm sure. The more I think about it the more I'm glad you talked me into this."

"I didn't talk you into this. Oh, Val, please don't say that!" Jaymie turned to her friend in the darkness of the car interior.

"Jaymie, it's okay, I misspoke. You didn't talk me into it. I'm happy you felt safe enough to tell me what you were going to do, and that you invited my help. I'm happy I'm here with you." She paused, then said, "How do you think Jakob will react when he hears about it?"

Jaymie's stomach turned over. She had been fretting over that. "I hope he'll understand. I know he'd do the same thing."

"There is a time for thinking and a time for action," Val murmured. She ducked her head and squinted out into the darkness. "Do you have this all planned out?"

"You get out first and —"

The flash of headlights approached slowly, pointing up and then down as the car moved over ruts and bumps.

"It's showtime," Jaymie murmured, bringing up an app on her phone while Val dialed a number on her own phone, then palmed it, pulling her jacket sleeve down to cover it in her hand. "You get out first and I'll follow," Jaymie said. She ducked down in the seat and waited until the car had pulled to a stop and the driver had emerged into the shadows by the old silo. "Don't close your door all the way," Jaymie hissed. "I don't want the interior lights going off, then coming on when I exit."

Val got out, leaving her door ajar. Jaymie slid out her door and duck-walked along the car, staying concealed, until she was close enough to hear the conversation.

". . . but I knew that I had done nothing wrong and I wondered all along who changed the dispensing of Mandy's anti-anxiety prescription," Val said. "That was my first clue. Why was the prescription sent to *my* pharmacy? It didn't make sense. The ruse was meant to cause confusion and upset Mandy." No response. "Then I put together traits she was exhibiting: paranoia, confusion, clumsiness, disorientation. At first, I thought of a head injury, but I ruled that out. And then Jaymie came to me with some information."

At Jaymie's name the killer made a rude noise, but Val ignored that. "You didn't count on Jaymie being with me the morning I found Mandy's body, did you? And you didn't notice that Mandy had a newspaper clipping clutched in her hand. Death grip, I guess. You were in too much of a hurry, weren't you, when you smothered her and then when you dumped her body on the pharmacy back step? Yes, I *know* you smothered her. It was so easy. Her breathing was already depressed because of the drugs."

Silence.

"How did you know, I wonder, that an excess of blood pressure pills would make her breathing shallow, and make her easier to smother? I suspect the police would find searches buried on your phone or computer somewhere." Val paused, waiting for a response. The point was to prod or startle the killer into a hasty admission. There was nothing, so she went on.

"The newspaper piece had something about local developers being accused of bribery on one side," Val continued, plowing ahead with their agreed-upon script while Jaymie listened, hearing the faint suggestion of a quiver, a sound she had heard in her own voice at times when facing a killer. "But ultimately the real clue, the whole reason Mandy was coming to me, a pharmacist, was a column on pharmaceutical travel. I know plenty of people who take their prescriptions abroad with them to countries where meds are cheaper, but that's not exactly the case here, is it? You went to Mexico specifically for a certain drug not available here, because Mandy had to die. When Jaymie asked me a pointed question, I could tell her, yes, there are many drugs available virtually OTC in Mexico that you can't get here."

"So what? I went to Mexico. That doesn't prove anything," the killer finally said.

They weren't getting what they needed.

Maybe a shock would help. Jaymie rose and viewed the scene, Mandy's murderer standing illuminated by the car headlights, Val in the shadows. "It may not *prove* anything, but it was the final clue we needed," she said loudly. Candy whirled and peered through the gathering gloom at Jaymie. "At the auction Mandy mentioned you being in Mexico, though you tried to say you were skiing in Colorado," Jaymie continued. "I remember thinking, skiing in October? Not unheard of, but unlikely. You can get drugs legally in Mexico that aren't available here." She paused and said, with great emphasis, "Even what's called roofies, the assault drug. It incapacitates the victim and causes amnesia."

"What is this, some kind of ambush?" Candy said, her tone harsh. "You think you've found somebody to blame?"

"Face it, you did it and we can *prove* you did it." Jaymie held her cell phone, recording the encounter. At the same time Val's phone was transmitting the conversation to Vestry. *If* Candy was speaking loudly enough. "You repeatedly roofied your sister, making her seem wonky and crazy and paranoid," Jaymie said, to elicit a denial or a confession. "She was forgetful. Clumsy. And the car accidents!"

"Helen and Win were in Mexico last spring."

"But nothing fits with them."

"Randall went to Mexico, too, you know," Candy said. Her expression in the dim illumination of car lights was panicked.

Candy's lifetime of wild living, sudden decisions, and risky behavior had led to this, a sense of invulnerability now being tested. Anger at her sister over too many slights and fights to count, combined with a financial incentive of becoming the sole beneficiary of their father's estate and insurance — dear old Dad would have been dear old *dead* soon, no doubt — added up to murder that was more clever than it seemed, on the surface. Roofied keto shake powder in Mandy's shakes, with an additional jolt of blood pressure medication that last evening, was all it took to render Mandy clumsy, dizzy, amnesiac at times, paranoid and finally vulnerable to murder at the hands of her sister.

Jaymie didn't care about explanations or motives, not when Candy threatened her sister's and daughter's lives. "A case *could* be made against Randall," Jaymie admitted, watching Candy's eyes. "He had access to the shake container, and he's not burdened by high morals or ethics. Randall's got his own legal problems coming. But Mandy's death probably hurt him more than helped him. As long as she was alive, he could keep collecting his bribes, and if things got too hot, he'd abscond. He didn't know she was secretly planning his ouster from the company. Nope, it's *you,* Candy. You killed your own sister," Jaymie said, disgust lacing her voice. "And you planned it months ahead of time."

"I didn't."

"Was the last straw the fact that Mandy went to Greg for help in her business troubles?"

Candy made a choked exclamation.

"Aha, that was it!" Jaymie said triumphantly. "Your ex-husband, that must have stung," she goaded. "But he did date her first, after all, back in high school. She *dumped* him." She hardened her heart to steel and said, "And then he dumped *you* after two years of marriage." Greg hadn't said as much, but Candy didn't know that.

Candy's expression was a furious grimace, but she stayed silent, showing more discipline than Jaymie had expected of a woman described by many as impulsive. They had to break her, but how? The night was still and frigid. Jaymie shivered. All she could hear was the sound of her own blood pounding in her ears.

"Greg never loved Candy," Val said to Jaymie, twisting the knife. "He *always* had a thing for Mandy. Marrying Candy made it possible to stay close to Mandy."

The woman grunted and opened her mouth to speak but closed it again.

How to push the already teetering Candy over the edge? Time for a guess. Knowing Randall Kallis's character, she made a stab at it. To Val she observed, "It must have been humiliating when Mandy's husband died, and she stole Randall Kallis away from Candy."

Candy's face reddened to an alarming maroon and her fists clenched at her sides. "I never wanted that jerk."

"But you did date him. And then he dumped you and took up with her," Jaymie said. "It kept happening, didn't it?"

"Mandy had to have *everyone*!" Candy shrieked, flinging her arms up to the sky. "Like you, Val, back in high school, such good buddies! She had a million friends, but just had to steal you from me too, when you and I were lab partners, study buddies. Well, I broke *that* up. I told her you called her fat behind her back." She shrieked with a hysterical bubble of laughter.

"So that's what happened, why she

stopped speaking to me," Val muttered.

"And she had to have *all* the boys. In high school I made the mistake of telling her that I liked Greg, and what does she do but waltz in and take him."

"Candy, he always had a crush on her," Val argued. "I knew it even then."

"Who cares now? She's dead, and I'm not." Candy stared at Val. "But I've heard that you've been seen at Ambrosia with him. With Greg. That won't do."

Jaymie experienced a jolt of fear at the cold calculation in Candy's steady stare at Val. They needed to get her back on track. "It seems like you were always jealous of your little sister."

She snorted in disgust. "Did you ever see her yearbook entry? Best everything, including Best *Hair.*" She dug in her coat pocket, pulled out a red wig and shook it. "Anyone can buy great hair."

"Wait, that was *you* in the maroon SUV when it hit Bonnie Smith!" Jaymie exclaimed. "You did it on purpose and drove away so it would be another thing blamed on Mandy."

She smiled. "That was fun. Little Miss Head of Cheer Squad. Best Smile. Best Legs. Most Likely to Succeed. Huh! Most likely to screw her sister over and then marry rich is more like it."

The venom in her voice was toxic. They were getting close to a confession, but she hadn't said it yet. There must be a way to get her to admit her crime. The woman reminded Jaymie of an animal Jocie had been studying, the spitting cobra, which could launch its deadly spittle almost seven feet when it felt threatened.

When it felt threatened . . .

Twenty-Six

"Mandy was on to you, wasn't she?" Jaymie funneled all her anger and disgust into a malicious tone. "She'd finally figured out what you were doing, that you were drugging her diet shake mix. You kept pushing her to drink it, you kept her off-kilter and confused and forgetful . . . and clumsy." Her eyes widened.

Mandy had been right about one thing. It was Candy who had been in her house, poisoning her shake container, moving things around, rifling through drawers. Maybe she had even rigged up a wire or some device so Mandy would trip and fall down the basement stairs. Jaymie turned to Val. "She was trying to kill her more than a month ago. That fall down the basement stairs, I'll bet she set it up! But Mandy didn't die. Candy had to find another way to kill her own sister."

Candy, pushed past endurance, threw the

red wig down on the ground and stomped it into the mud. "She never gave a damn about me. It was sweet to see her finally looking like a ragged-ass sad sack. At first I wasn't going to kill her. I wanted to see her fail. Daddy was going to get sick, and she was going to have to spend more and more time with him, leaving that thief, Randall, to loot the company. I wanted her health to fail. She'd become a pathetic wretch!" She burst into laughter that echoed like a thunderclap in the cold clear darkness. "You're right about Bonnie Smith, you know. It was *hilarious* watching Bonnie light into poor befuddled Mandy when it was *me* behind the wheel of her car smashing into that old woman's Caddy!"

"You *were* driving her SUV that night?"

"Sure. But Mandy never did figure *that* out," she boasted. The floodgates were open, all inhibitions thrown to the wind. "I've had her extra key fob this whole time," she gloated at her own cleverness. "I took the car when she was at Manor Homes talking to Greg Sunday evening, before the food bank meeting. She was at it again, luring him in with her neediness. I was so *mad*! I had it all planned out. Greg and I were both single, and he's been so nice to me." She gave Val a squinty-eyed glare, but then dismissed her as competition. "We could get back together, but no, she was drawing him in!"

"He wasn't interested in her like that. Not now," Val said.

"What were you thinking, running into Bonnie's car?" Jaymie asked, trying to keep Candy on topic. They almost had enough, she hoped. "It doesn't make any sense. Weren't you taking a chance Mandy would come out of the Manor Homes office and find her car gone?"

She laughed, the mirthless sound lifting and carrying as gusts of wind swept across the property. "I had time and I knew it. She told me she'd be there going through the books with kind, wonderful Greg. I followed her there, took the car and rocketed into Queensville. There had to be someone's car to hit there, some way to push Mandy even closer to the edge. She knew she was forgetting stuff, so she took the blame!

"Maybe it pushed her too far. She was getting suspicious. That last conversation, Sunday night at the inn . . ." Her voice became distant, and she gazed off into the dark distance. "I saw it in her eyes. She was afraid of me. Me, her own sister! She stopped drinking the shake and pushed it away. Asked if I'd messed with her shake packets. No more fooling around, it had to be that night."

"*What* had to be?" Val asked, but Candy shook her head, not willing to say it out loud.

"Did you hear her asking Connor Ward to meet her in the inn parking lot?" Jaymie said.

"Yeah. Why was that?"

"She was going to make the Wards an offer, or at least a tentative offer. After meeting with Greg, she was back in control and attempting to do an end run around Randall. She thought she could work to fix the problems with her company."

Poor woman. Despite all her sister had thrown at her, she finally had an action plan to sort out her life. She was going to talk to Val about her suspicions that her sister was drugging her, but she never made it.

There was still the problem of how to prove it.

Candy was talking again to Val. "And then I caught her talking to you on the phone. Texting, and then yakking . . . suddenly besties. It was disgusting. She had to die, and on the back steps of the pharmacy waiting for you was perfect."

Jaymie held her breath, afraid to say anything. This was it, the full admission they needed, but this moment was Val's.

"I understand all of that," Val said. "But why did Mandy turn against me after all these years? Why accuse me of tampering with the medication? Why say I was stalking her?"

Jaymie watched Candy. Would the woman answer?

Candy had an odd lopsided smile when she was pleased with herself. "That was pure fun for me, the fake social media account, the switched prescription. Spinster Valetta, so smart, so perfect. Greg thinks you're the best. I was *sick* of hearing about you! You being a pharmacist made it easy. But I miscalculated," she said, grimacing. "You always worked Tuesdays but you weren't there that day! That was a sticking point, Mandy kept coming back to it. How could you tamper with her meds when you weren't even working? I'd gone to so much trouble, taking her phone, switching the prescription, being so puzzled about how it could happen unless *you* did it. And then Helen got mixed up in it, Ti's sister-in-law!"

"You've always been a screwup," Val said, "even in school. That science project we did together, or rather, I did. You messed it up so bad we would have gotten a C if I hadn't worked it all out. It doesn't surprise me that you made such a mess of murder."

Candy kept her mouth shut and glared.

"You fed a pack of lies to Greg, didn't you?" Jaymie said, suddenly realizing how much of what she heard had come indirectly from Candy. "You had him convinced Randall was the killer. You told him that Kallis had been blackmailing Mandy over dirty photos, and that's how he became a partner. It's crap, though, meant to sully your sister in his eyes. The truth is a whole lot simpler. Mandy made Randall Kallis a partner because she couldn't run Manor Homes without him. He backed her into a corner. Heck, he bragged about that to me."

"I loved the guy, but where women were concerned Greg was an idiot," she said with a sneer.

"You killed Mandy. How? After the drugging, I mean." Val had the right tone, careful, curious, calm.

Candy started to move. "I suppose there's no harm in telling you."

Jaymie's heart pounded. Maybe Val didn't get it, but the only reason it didn't matter if Candy told them how she killed her sister was because she intended to kill *them.*

"It was tricky, let me tell you."

As Jaymie made sure her cell phone was clear of her pocket, recording the conversation, she recalled something Taylor said, that Mandy sat with Candy when *she came back in.* Back in from where? "You were in and out of the inn restaurant that evening. Busy setting things up to kill Mandy?"

She snorted as she kept moving, her gaze darting into the dark, her footsteps careful on the rutted earth. "I was a busy little bee, you're right. I had to get the stuff out of my car once I realized that was going to be my best shot at taking care of business. That last drink was a fun cocktail of pharmaceuticals. I got lucky. She was all over the place yakking at people so I had the time I needed to dump the ground-up tablets into the shake." She walked into shadows and out of them again. "Val, you say I'm a screwup? I say I'm *brilliant.* She drank enough before something . . ." She paused and sighed. "I dunno. She got suspicious, like she was working things out. I'd run out of time, and I had to make sure she didn't tell anyone what she suspected."

Jaymie, trembling, darted a glance at Val, who was wide-eyed and staring into the gloom as Candy moved back into the shadows. This was the payoff. This was the confession they needed.

"Thankfully, I knew where she was going from listening in on her conversation with you, Val," she said. "She was driving over to the pharmacy. She was gonna talk to you, then come back to the inn parking lot to meet that schlub Connor Ward." Her voice came from the shadowy darkness.

"But she never made it. Even if I'd been at the pharmacy, I couldn't have saved her," Val said hollowly.

"She pulled over before getting there, nearly passed out. I followed her and got lucky! Queensville streets are quiet at that hour."

"That's when you killed her," Jaymie said, not hiding the horror.

"Mandy was alive, wasn't she, even though she'd passed out?" Val said. "You could have gotten her help. She didn't have to die."

Candy stepped into the beam of her headlights, her blonde hair almost white, standing out in tufts. She ran her fingers through her mane, then looked down at her hands, clenching and unclenching her fists.

Jaymie pushed harder. "You had the best gift a girl could have in her life," she cried, thinking of Becca, her beloved sister, and Val, her sister by choice. "You had a *sister,* and you killed her!"

"She knew too much. Even if I wanted to . . ." She shook her head and again looked down at her hands. "It was easy," she whispered. "It shouldn't be so easy. When someone is drugged like that you pinch the nose and hold your hand over the mouth and slowly, slowly . . . barely any struggle, just sleep." Her face was wet, tears glittering in the headlights.

It was easy physically because Mandy was drugged. It was easy emotionally because Candy was evil. Jaymie was about to speak, but Val held up her hand. The woman had gone somewhere else, someplace away, or inside her mind, retreating to the pain of that moment when she took her sister's life.

"What happened then?" Val said softly.

"We sat for a while, sisters, like it was at first."

A sister who could be appreciated again because she was dead? Jaymie recoiled at the thought.

"We were close once. Two little kiddies, with a mommy who loved us, and who dressed us up the same, and took us out walking. Two little kiddies." She sank down onto the ground and stared down at her hands, splayed them out, grabbed a clod of damp dirt and threw it away, into the dark. "I thought I'd be glad she was dead. I didn't know that once she was gone she'd take all my memories of childhood. I can't remember one good moment now. Nothing." She

393

sobbed, rocking on her haunches. "She took it all with her!"

Val softly said, "And then? How did you get her to the pharmacy? *When* did you get her to the pharmacy?"

"I almost slipped up there. Ooops!" She giggled and hiccupped, then sobbed.

"What do you mean?" Val asked.

"I drove Mandy's car. If you were there I would have waited for you to leave, but you weren't. That waitress drove into the parking area behind the Emporium as I pulled around the corner. I had to stop. Finally the lights went out, and I hauled Mandy to the back step." She sobbed again. "Dragged her. Then I made her comfortable before I took off."

Slamming the car door and then gunning it, which is what Taylor heard. "And you left Mandy's car elsewhere," Jaymie said.

"I didn't know what else to do." She rocked back and forth, covering her face with her dirt-crusted hands and sobbing into them. "I didn't think I'd miss her! She's the only one who knew . . . the only one who understood how our mother played favorites. Mandy was 'baby,' the good little sweetie, and I was the jealous brat. Daddy was a mean old s-o-b. Needy. All the time, taking taking *taking* and never giving back.

Mandy remembered. I didn't have anyone who loved me. I suppose she tried to make up for it when we got older." She looked up, tears streaming down her face, bare trails through the smears of dirt. "Mandy's gone, and so are my memories."

"You killed her and now you're sorry. But why did you try to kill me and my daughter?" Jaymie burst out, fury in her voice.

"You wouldn't leave it all alone!" she shrieked, staggering back up to her feet. She balled her fists and shook them at Jaymie. "Why didn't you leave it alone? You kept talking to people, and asking questions and —"

"Because you set Val up to take the blame!" Jaymie yelled back.

Candy made a rude noise, dusting her hands off on her jeans. "Gimme a break. She would've gotten off. No one was going to convict precious perfect Valetta Nibley, pride of the MichiGirls."

"You didn't know that!" Val barked.

"Ti called me asking what I made of you investigating," Candy said to Jaymie, ignoring Val's outburst. "You were talking to Taylor, who saw me with Mandy that night at the inn. She was too close when Mandy said some things. I didn't figure she'd understand, but *you* might. You talked to Greg.

395

You talked to Trina and that witch, Shannon. *Auntie Shan!*" she said, with a snarl and mincing tone. "Auntie Shan, Trina's favorite aunt. *I* should have been her favorite aunt."

"The one who killed her mother? Seriously?" Jaymie said, glaring at Candy through the gloom.

Candy took a deep breath and shook herself, shedding every bit of the emotion that had wrought her into a wreck. "You had to go," she continued, still talking to Jaymie, her tone conversational and eminently reasonable. "It's your own fault. I'm sorry your daughter was in the car but I had to take the opportunity. I saw that red scarf and hat and *knew* it was you. I'm sorry that you weren't at the wheel and that it was that stupid whiny putz Becca instead."

Jaymie shuddered with anger, hands balled at her sides. Hysteria built in her, tears stinging her eyes. "You almost killed my daughter and my sister," she said, her voice choked with anger. "I'm not going to let that slide, you hear me? I'm going to —"

Val's warm hand on her arm stopped Jaymie from saying or doing something drastic.

"Seriously? Threats?" Candy said harshly. "And not even threats . . . *half* threats. What *are* we going to do about this? I hope you

396

don't think I'm going to go along to the police station with you and hand myself in." She held her hands out in front of her, wrists together. "I've been a naughty girl, killed my sister! *Bad* Candy!" She snorted with laughter, then relaxed her hands at her sides. "I can't take the chance the cops will believe you. This is the end. And some things are considerably more easy to get than drugs."

Jaymie and Val exchanged a look. Was she hinting that she had a gun? She was right about one thing, they needed to end this. It was fortunate Candy had a blind spot that didn't allow her to see she wasn't as smart as she thought herself, that others saw her for what she was and prepared accordingly.

"We wouldn't think you'd ever do anything like take responsibility for killing your sister and trying to kill my daughter and sister," Jaymie said. She saw movement in the dark. Bernie was approaching silently, gun raised, after Candy's vague threat transmitted to the police by the cell phone Val held.

Vestry stepped out of the shadows beside the silo, gun in hand. At the slightest tilt of her head five other officers burst forward with lights shone directly in the killer's eyes. Candy held up her hands in front of her face and made an inarticulate exclamation of surprise. "Candy Vasiliev, you're under arrest for the murder of Mandy de Boer," the detective said.

Candy whirled and bolted, running, gasping, panting and staggering across the rutted plots of land. Jaymie, shocked but still furious, bolted after her, but Bernie, more fleet of foot, tore after her too. She tackled the fleeing killer from behind and put her in a headlock before handcuffing her and reading her her rights. As she was frog-marched past Val and Jaymie, she glared at them, but then slumped and had to be half dragged and then shoved, whining about her wrists and her bad back, into a car.

It was all over in moments and Jaymie was left breathless at the sudden turn of events.

"She had a gun," Bernie grunted to the detective as she slammed the car door. "She pulled it out but dropped it back there when I tackled her."

"We'll get it. Secure the perimeter," Vestry barked to the other officers. "We'll get lights and search."

It was over. All of it. Jaymie dropped to her knees and wept.

Days passed. The chill deepened. Jocie clung to her parents with perhaps a bit more ferocity, but recovery was deepening into her heart as Jaymie and Jakob kept the lines of communication open. She went trick-or-treating with her friends in Queensville, then had a sleepover at the cabin, with spooky ghost stories around a campfire in the chill Michigan twilight.

The calendar flipped to a new month.

"I can't believe it's November," Jaymie said, wrapping her shawl around her shoulders as she sat in her favorite spot, the bench outside the cabin. Jakob sat down beside her and put his arm around her shoulders. She stared across the road in the fading light. The ditch work was complete, a culvert in place, and a gravel path over the top of it, leading to the handsome new gate Bram and Luuk had installed.

Bram had completely groomed the path already. It led from the road in front of Jaymie and Jakob's cabin through the woods to Alicia's home, where Mia now lived with her grandmother Kim and step-grandpa. Jaymie and Jocie had walked the path that morning to visit and take a housewarming gift, a basket of muffins proudly baked by Jocie.

"Lots to do this month. Are you ready for the rush?" Jakob asked, indicating with a nod to the left the Christmas tree fields. He had hired seasonal staff and training was about to begin.

She leaned on him, head on his shoulder. This was her favorite time of year. The forest across the road was exceptionally beautiful, the gold, russet and sage of the leaves and dying weeds a melancholy splash of fading beauty. Through bare spots gleamed a golden sunset. *"The woods are lovely, dark and deep,"* Jaymie murmured, quoting Robert Frost. Soon enough they would be snow-filled.

She roused herself to answer her husband's question. "I look forward to it. Next week we're doing a class tour at the historic house. My unit on kitchen utensils will be interesting, I hope. Bill Waterman helped me rig a hanging pot rack for all the sieves." She had been to see Trina and Shannon, who were going through Mandy's house in the beginning stages of settling the estate. Jaymie offered to buy the sieves Mandy had bought at auction, but Trina insisted Jaymie take them as a gift.

Everything else was working out gradually. Greg Vasiliev and Win Pham, working together, had figured out the problems at Manor Homes that led to the damage in the newest houses built by the company. Randall Kallis, who had been hours away from fleeing the country, had been arrested on several charges, including but not limited to fraud. Officials in the township zoning and planning departments might face charges too. Manor Homes was going through a rough patch, but Shannon, a force of nature with an iron will and the intelligence to understand that she didn't know everything, would help Trina get the family company back on track. To that end they hired Greg Vasiliev as a consultant.

Greg and Val were still "just friends."

"I'm grateful for everyone and everything," Jaymie said softly, a whispered puff of air in the chilly evening. "Mom and Dad will be here for Thanksgiving. Grandma Leighton will come over to spend time with Mrs. Stubbs. And we've got the first trail through the woods."

"I overheard Mia and Jocie making plans for next summer already," Jakob said. "They want to camp in the woods one night." He chuckled, a lovely deep sound in his chest.

Jaymie smiled. "Those girls are going to be lifelong friends." Jocie had many friends, and loved them all, but between her and Mia there was a special bond. The two girls were growing closer every day.

Friends for life.

"Mrs. Stubbs had fun with the girls at

Noor's Queensville Inn birthday tea party."

A few more minutes of desultory conversation about everyday things — the delight of everyday things was precious to Jaymie in ways she had never realized before — and they fell silent. It was dark and cold, time to go inside and warm up. She stood and held out her hand, looking down at Jakob's handsome face in the twilight. "It's Friday. Jocie is at Mia's for a movie night and we, my darling, are alone. Are you up for some popcorn and Hallmark holiday movies?"

He took her hand and brought it up to his mouth, kissing her palm. "Sounds like a plan."

VINTAGE EATS

BY JAYMIE LEIGHTON MÜLLER

CRAN-APPLE CRISP

Fall, my favorite season. For me it's all about the hot cup of tea I sip while staring at the falling leaves, the hand-knit sweater I cozy myself into, the nip in the air, and . . . the food! (Of course, the food. I'm a food columnist!) Once the calendar flips to November, I'm in holiday mode, and that means apples: apple pie, apple cinnamon tea, apples crisp and ripe as a delicious fresh treat. But we must not overlook that other seasonal fruit, cranberries! From the color I wear to the sauce I ladle onto my plate next to the turkey I love, cranberries are everywhere this time of year.

However, this delicious, beautiful fruit deserves to shine in places other than sauce.

As I rustled around in my Grandma Leighton's recipe book I came across an old recipe for apple crisp. I remember so well standing on a stepstool by the counter while she sliced apples, mixed the fragrant spices and concocted the "crisp" topping with healthy oats and sweet brown sugar. I thought, why not add in the lovely jewel-colored fruit of the cranberry bush to make this a fallish delight? And while I was at it, I realized that as busy people, we often don't eat dessert together, or at all sometimes. Individual crisps was the way to go. These sweet treats can be cooked, relished, and the extras put in the fridge or even frozen to be enjoyed later.

You'll need four eight-fluid-ounce oven-safe ramekins for this dessert. You can easily double this recipe to eight ramekins, or cook the larger amount in a nine-by-thirteen baking dish, if you prefer.

Individual Cran-Apple Crisp

Serves 4

Apple Filling

6 Honeycrisp apples (6 if they are small,
  4 if they are medium to large)
3/4 cup whole cranberries
1/4 cup white sugar
1/4 cup golden brown sugar
1/2 teaspoon cinnamon
1/8 teaspoon nutmeg
1/8 teaspoon salt
2 teaspoons lemon juice
1 tablespoon butter, unsalted (if using
  salted, omit salt from recipe!)

Crisp Topping

1/2 cup all-purpose flour
1/2 cup old-fashioned rolled oats
1/4 cup golden brown sugar
1/2 teaspoon cinnamon
pinch nutmeg
6 tablespoons butter, cold!

Preheat oven to 375, with a rack in the center of the oven.

Prep apples: peel, core and cut apples into

thumbnail-size chunks. You can slice them instead, but with small ramekins I think chunks are better.

Blend sugar and spice ingredients — except for the butter! — then toss the apple chunks and whole cranberries into the blended ingredients.

Melt butter in a medium frying pan, then toss in the apple-cranberry mixture and sauté on low until tender but not mushy! Do *not* brown this on too high a heat. The cranberries should "pop" while this is going on. That's a good thing. About 10–15 minutes.

Spoon equal amounts of the apple mixture into each of the four lightly buttered ramekins.

Blend dry topping ingredients, then add the cold butter. Using your hands is best for this, and quickly, so the butter doesn't melt. Cube the butter then rub it into the dry topping ingredients, but *don't overdo it*! You want the mixture to be *coarse,* the texture of pea gravel.

Sprinkle the topping over the filling in the

ramekins — don't pat it down! — and pop them into the oven. If you like (I did this and I think it made the crisp nicer) add a few dots of extra butter over the topping in each ramekin. Bake for 30–35 minutes, or until the topping is golden brown.

Serve warm with ice cream or whip cream, and enjoy the fall flavor explosion! As a lovely bonus, your house will smell marvelous when you bake these little beauties.

*These can be covered and frozen, but in that case, do *not* reheat in an oven until they are thawed. Never put an ice-cold container in a hot oven.

ABOUT THE AUTHOR

Victoria Hamilton is the pseudonym of nationally bestselling romance author Donna Lea Simpson. Victoria is the bestselling author of three mystery series, the Lady Anne Addison Mysteries, the Vintage Kitchen Mysteries, and the Merry Muffin Mysteries. Her latest adventure in writing is a Regency-set historical mystery series, starting with *A Gentlewoman's Guide to Murder.*

Victoria loves to read, especially mystery novels, and enjoys good tea and cheap wine, the company of friends, and has a newfound appreciation for opera. She enjoys crocheting and beading, but a good book can tempt her away from almost anything . . . except writing!

Visit Victoria at www.victoriahamiltonmysteries.com.